HOLLOWING SCREAMS

A PARANORMAL THRILLER

BARBARA WATKINS

BNW PUBLISHING

Published by
BNW Publishing

ISBN 13: 978-0692324462
ISBN 10: 0692324461

Visit the author at:
www.barbarawatkins.net
www.barbarawatkins.blogspot.com
www.facebook.com/Watkinsfanpage
www.twitter.com/paranormawriter
www.imdb.com/name/nm3634934/

Purchase other books by Barbara Watkins in
print, eBook, or audio by scanning the QR code.

PRAISE FOR *HOLLOWING SCREAMS*

...very creepy with so many twists and turns that it kept me enthralled till the final page. It's a book that would make a terrific movie and a book a director would have a field day with. Characters are well drawn and immediately engaging. It's one of the few times that back story is so compelling that the reader is committed to see the outcome....and the outcome delivers big time. Well told and makes for a great read.

Armand Mastroianni
Shore Road Entertainment, Producer and Director

This is one outstanding novel whose characters teach you the true meaning of treachery, fear, deception, lies, and betrayal. An author so creative that she weaves a plot so intricate with incidents that not only blindside some of the characters, but the reader too, this is one novel that is anything but hollow: filled with substance, plot, and keeping you on the edge of your seat from start to finish.

Fran Lewis
Amazon Reviewer/Internet Talk Show Host

I found the story so interesting; I actually read it in a matter of a few hours. Ms. Watkins wrote one heck of a story and she's given me inspiration to try again.

Bobby Harwell
Television/Movie Actor/Producer, and Author of *Flawed*

...a wonderful paranormal thriller. You'll be wondering who's doing what to whom as the ghostly insanity goes on in the sleepy little town of Patton, Missouri.

Michelle Anne Cox-lomas
The Review Maven

ALSO BY BARBARA WATKINS

Novels
Thorns of an Innocent Soul

Short Stories
Mortal Abomination
Awaken Spirit

Short Story Collections with Betty Dravis
Six-Pack of Blood
Six-Pack of Fear

Articles
A Testament to Poets
Cold Coffee Magazine

Film
BlindSide
2010 Movie Short
Zodiac Entertainment
Voice-over Monologue

ACKNOWLEDGEMENTS

To my publicist, Christy Bradshaw:

Without your constant praise, loyalty, and dedication to promote my work, I would have never come this far. Thank you, baby girl!

To Kay, Steve, and Mary:

We have a never-ending bond of love, devotion, and respect. It is because of you that I thrive to be the best I can be, as a human being, and as a writer. I love you all!

To Stephen King, Anne Rice, Clive Barker and to all the great writers who through blood, sweat, and tears dedicate their lives to entertain us with their awe-inspiring imaginations:

I give my sincere gratitude.

To Zodiac Entertainment/Dimi Nakov:

Your sincere belief in me and my work have been proven time and time again. Exciting times lay ahead! Thank you for giving me a glorious dream that I can look forward to becoming a reality!

DEDICATION

I would like to dedicate this book to my husband and my children for their love, patience, and support.

In particular, Betty Hornback's love, guidance and her undying belief that her daughter, from the time of birth, was destined to achieve success beyond her wildest imagination. I love you, mom.

I would also like to dedicate this book to all my readers whom without their loyalty and faithful following, I could not have achieved the level of success that I have so far.

Last but certainly not least, I dedicate *Hollowing Screams* to an extraordinary woman whom I was fortunate to have the opportunity to be introduced to many years ago. She had been blessed with a unique ability—what many would call a paranormal ability to foretell the future. She opened up my mind to accepting the reality that not all of our experiences in this life lay inside the range of normal, and that a scientific explanation of proof is not needed for those who encounter and witness what is referred to as paranormal phenomena. She was "the" inspiration for my book, and although she passed away many years ago, she found her way back to me through *Hollowing Screams*.

CHAPTER
1

IN 1941, Howard White received an honorable discharge from the Navy because of an injury he sustained while serving his country. As luck would have it, he survived the devastating attack on Pearl Harbor. Unfortunately, many of his comrades did not.

Opening his eyes, he slowly turned his head from side to side, squinting repeatedly. He tried desperately to focus on something, anything.

"There, there," the nurse said, gently rubbing his forehead with a wet cloth. "I'm not the enemy, and you're not captive. You're in the naval base hospital, and I'm your nurse, Lia. You're going to be just fine."

His mouth was dry; his vision still blurry. "What about my men, my infantry?"

She did not answer him in the form of a sentence. The deadening silence signified his worse fear. Lying in his hospital bed, surrounded by the stench of death, deafened by the suffering screams of the injured, he yearned for the safety of home: Missouri. Home, where the sight of tugboats gently maneuvering barges down the Mississippi replaced battleships, a place with rich farmland far beyond the bloody battlefields he had become accustomed to. Home, where he would find the love of his life, or so he hoped.

In 1942, shortly after arriving back in his homeland of Missouri, he met and fell in love with Katrina Rosenberg, only child of Charles and Elizabeth Rosenberg. After a brief courtship, the couple wed. Tragedy soon struck when Elizabeth Rosenberg, afflicted for years with excruciating headaches, died in her sleep from an overdose of laudanum.

Two weeks later, tragedy struck again. A farmhand found Katrina's father hanging from a noose in the barn, not far from the main house. Katrina was devastated by the tragic loss of both her parents and sank deeply into depression. Howard fought to protect their assets and to manage the land they consequently inherited.

"I don't want it anymore, Howard," Katrina said.

"Don't want what anymore?"

"All this. The land, the house."

"Look out there, Katrina." Howard shook his head in disbelief, pointing out across the land. "You want to sell this land, this house, and everything your father and mother worked for and left to you? And do what?"

"It's cursed, Howard."

"What are you talking about?"

"I never said anything, but do you remember two weeks after Mother's death, the morning you found me asleep in her room?"

"Yeah, you were distraught and had a nightmare. You were sleepwalking."

"It wasn't a nightmare. It was real. She was here, just as we are now. She spoke to me, Howard."

Howard leaned back against the porch railing. "Honey, you know that's impossible."

Stepping down off the porch, she leaned over, picked up a handful of dirt, and shook her fist. "I'm telling you, she warned me this land was cursed, and if we stay we'll end up dead just like they did!"

She stomped off, slamming the door behind her with such force that it wrenched the hinges from the wooden frame.

Howard spent the next few hours sitting outside on the porch, contemplating his life in general. He questioned the existence of God. If God did exist, for what reason had he spared his life that fateful day in Pearl Harbor?

Placing his hand underneath the sleeve of his flannel shirt, he ran his fingers over the eight-inch scar on his arm where shrapnel still lay lodged from a grenade. He searched his memory to find what he had seen in Katrina that had captivated him so, and then he smiled when he remembered. But how could a relationship full of love and passion turn into such turmoil so quickly? His mind began to wander back to the first day he had set eyes on her.

He worked for Carl Dean, who owned the only body shop in Patton. To say Carl ran a tight ship would be putting it mildly. So, when he gave his men an early night off, they didn't ask why.

That day Carl said, "Howard, I'm going to close up shop early today, going to take the little woman over to Sedgewickville to the fair. Now I'll grant ya it ain't my cup of tea, but I figure it only comes around once a year."

After Howard lost both of his parents to tuberculosis when he was a teenager, Carl was the first to pitch in by offering him work and a place to stay. Times were tough and jobs were scarce. Howard was thankful he had something familiar to come home to upon returning home from war.

"Can't say no to an early night off, Carl, but what about old man Rosenberg's farm truck, wasn't he needing it delivered today?"

"Got her fixed and ready to go," Carl said with a hint of mischief in his voice. "I told the old man you'd deliver it if he could bring you back to town. Who knows, if you're lucky, maybe you can hitch a ride back with his daughter, Katrina."

Howard rolled his eyes to the side and shook his head. "Ah, Carl, she don't want nothing to do with me. She could have her pick of any guy in this town."

Carl patted him on the shoulder. "Now I saw the way you two looked at each other when she came with old man Rosenberg to drop the truck off. Ya don't see sparks flying around like that every-day. That is unless it involves working on a piece of machinery."

Indeed Carl was right. Howard had been mesmerized with Katrina the moment he first saw her. The moment she stepped out of her father's old farm truck, he knew she was the one. With a lustrous fiery red head of hair that draped her shoulders and a flawless fair complexion, she could and had turned the heads of many young available men. However, Katrina was not the first lovely woman that Howard had ever laid eyes on, but she was the first woman that he had felt an instant connection with. It was something in her eyes that spoke to him, a glimpse of vulnerability mixed with an intense need for passion and adventure, everything he had wanted in a woman and had dreamed about.

As fate would have it, Katrina gave him a ride back to his truck that night, and many a moonlight drive ensued as their passion for one another ignited.

Never opening up to anyone about the atrocities that he had endured in the war, he found himself pouring his heart out to Katrina. He proposed marriage after a few short months which might have seemed hasty to some, but Howard could not wait to spend the rest of his life with who he believed was his soul mate.

As he leaned his head back on the top rung of the rocking chair, he wondered if the tragic deaths of her parents were the cause of her recent behavior—saying strange things and forgetting she said them. Or could it be something more sinister?

Reaching into his back pocket, he pulled out a flask filled with whiskey and put it to his lips, a new habit he had recently acquired.

Early the next morning, Howard awoke to find Katrina's side of the bed empty. He rolled out of bed, grabbed his slippers and headed downstairs. Bacon sizzling and a hint of maple wafting in the air caught his attention as he rounded the bottom of the stairs.

"Something sure does smell good," he said with a smile.

Katrina turned and smiled. "Nothing like fresh eggs from the farm, sweet blueberry pancakes, and maple syrup of course, with bacon crispy just the way you like it."

Howard sat down at the table and looked up at her. "I'm glad to see you're in better spirits today. I hope this means no more talk about selling the place."

Katrina raised a quizzical brow as she set his plate in front of him and sat down to eat. "Selling the place? What on earth are you talking about, Howard?"

Howard choked down a piece of bacon. "You just said last night you thought it was haunted, couldn't wait to get rid of it and move on."

"Howard, why on earth would you make up such nonsense? Have you been drinking again?"

"Stop eating for a minute and listen to me, Katrina," he said. "Living with you is like living with two different people. From day to day I never know which one's going to show up. Maybe it's time you saw someone. You know, someone who can help you put things into perspective."

She took a bite of her pancake, wiped her mouth with a linen napkin, and then folded it neatly on her plate. "Maybe you need to slow down on your drinking. You think I don't know what's really in that thermos of yours? Maybe you're the one hallucinating."

The table shook and moved three inches as Howard rose from his chair. "Yeah. I'm sad to say I've found more comfort in a bottle of whiskey than I have with you for some time now."

Katrina flashed a malevolent smile as she stood. "What was it that you promised me standing before God? Oh, yeah. I remember. To honor me in sickness and in health, or till death do we part."

His eyes never left her as she calmly walked past him and out of the room. If questioned later, would she remember what had just taken place? He thought with certainty that she would not. If he honored his commitment to her, would he eventually succumb to her madness? He thought in all probability that he would.

Nevertheless, Howard White made what he believed to be a noble decision that day to stay and fight for his marriage.

CHAPTER
2

THE BRISK wind scooped up a dormant pile of leaves lying next to the old oak tree. They appeared to come to life, twisting, whirling, and dancing about.

As soon as Howard stepped outside, he began to shiver, tugging his overcoat tighter around his body. If he hurried, he just might make it to town before the feed store closed.

The man at the counter greeted him with a smile. "Hey there, Howard. What can I do you for today?"

"Glad I caught you before you closed, Pete," he replied, unbuttoning his overcoat. "I'm running low on chicken feed and I need to stock up on some bales of hay."

"No problem. Hey, I've been meaning to ask you, is everything okay with Katrina?"

Howard nodded. "Yeah, she's fine."

"That's good. I saw her walking out of Doc Miller's office yesterday. It looked like she'd been crying."

A ball of tension radiated up between Howard's shoulder blades. "Say ya saw her leaving the doc's office yesterday, huh?"

"I didn't mean to upset you, Howard. I'm sure it's nothing serious or she would have told ya. You know how women are; they cry at the slightest thing."

Howard shrugged. "Yeah, well, I better get my things and get back to the farm. There's a lot of work to be done."

He could not load his truck fast enough. Putting pressure to the pedal, he rushed home to find out what Katrina had been hiding from him.

As he drove up the gravel road leading to the house, he spotted her sitting on the porch. In haste, he scarcely managed to get the truck parked before getting out.

"You want to tell me what the hell is going on, Katrina!"

"What's a matter with your face, honey? Why's it so red?"

"I don't know, maybe cause my head is about to explode!"

"I don't know what you're talking about, Howard."

"You can begin by telling me why you were at Doc Miller's office yesterday. Pete said he saw you leave from there, crying."

A moment of exhausting silence shared with the chill in the air made Howard shiver uncontrollably.

"Pete needs to mind his own business."

"Yeah well, the way you're acting it must be something serious. I know you're not pregnant. That'd be damn near impossible since we seldom share the same bed."

Puckering her lips, she raised an eyebrow.

"That's it, isn't it?" he shouted. "You're pregnant!"

She looked at him, her face contorted in an all-consuming anger. "I don't see anything to be excited about."

His mood changed to a gentleness as he knelt in front of his wife. "Honey, think of this as our chance to start over. A baby, Katrina, our baby. If it's a boy, we can name him after my father, and if it's a girl—"

Waving her hands in front of his face, she motioned him to stop. "Howard, listen to yourself. What kind of life would it have? Our marriage is hanging by a thread."

"This could be the miracle we've been looking for," Howard exclaimed, reaching out for her hand.

Pushing him back, she turned away. "Don't, Howard. Don't make this out to be something it isn't. The fact is you're a drunk."

"I'll get sober, I swear."

His eyes followed her as she walked into the house without saying a word. Her sudden silence left him feeling apprehensive. He dreaded what she might be planning next.

As it turned out, after several unsuccessful attempts to terminate the pregnancy, one of which nearly resulted in her own death, Katrina gave birth to a healthy six-pound baby girl.

For some time Howard had wished for a miracle, one that would destroy his wife's inner demons, praying that miracle would be their first-born child.

However, shortly after the birth of their daughter, Katrina's behavior worsened to the point of bizarre.

Hoping to lift Katrina's spirits, one afternoon Howard stopped by the local flower shop and purchased a dozen red roses. Upon entering the house with a bouquet of roses hidden behind his back, he hurried up the stairs, skipping every other step. Rounding the top of the stairs, he hesitated before going any further. What sounded like a muffled cry led him straight toward his infant daughter's room. His pulse beat rapidly as he approached the baby's crib.

Wrapped like a mummy from the tip of her head to the bottom of her feet, she lay gasping for air. He lifted her tiny head in his hands and swiftly removed the blanket that lay covering her face like a veil of death.

"There, there, my precious baby girl. Daddy's here now." His hands trembled as he cuddled her in his arms. Her loud cries comforted his heart and he breathed a sigh of relief. As she snuggled close to his chest, he rocked her back and forth in his arms. When she was fast asleep, he placed her back into the crib, tenderly kissing her forehead.

Within seconds, his nurturing instincts turned to rage toward Katrina. He would hold her accountable for the near tragedy.

An aroma of sweet vanilla filled the air as he approached their master bathroom. Inside, Katrina lay relaxing in a steaming bath. Howard stood silently in the doorway, looking on in disbelief. With the cunning moves of a lion meticulously sizing up his prey, moving in for the kill, he clenched both hands around her neck and pushed her downward under the water. With every thrash of her body, water sloshed over the sides of the tub, spilling onto the linoleum floor. Just at the point of no return, Howard loosened his grip, as if suddenly waking from a deep trance.

"That's attempted murder, you drunken bastard!" She yelled, climbing out of the tub and grabbing a towel. "I'll have you arrested for this!"

Howard gazed down at the deep claw marks on his hands and arms, questioning himself as to why he had stopped. Yanking the towel from her hands and revealing her naked body, he turned her toward the mirror.

"Take a good, long look at yourself!" He stroked the side of her face, running his fingertips down the side of her bruised neck. "Oh, there's no question; you're beautiful."

She squirmed, trying to jerk free as he tightened his grip and continued. "Enjoy this beautiful body of life you have, because if you ever again put our child's life in danger, I'll kill you dead!"

Never again would she put their child's life in jeopardy as to risk her own. However, psychological abuse was far less detectable and easier to assert.

CHAPTER
3

SHANNON STOOD gawking out the window, nose pressed against the freezing glass, anxiously waiting for her father to return. It was her seventh birthday and this year he had promised to bring her something special.

"Shannon, what are you doing staring out that window?" her mother asked. "Tell me you're not waiting for that worthless father of yours to show up."

Shannon spun around to face her. "Mama, don't call him that!"

"Oh, I'm sorry, baby. I meant that no-good, drunken, worthless father of yours."

"Daddy promised to bring me a surprise for my birthday and I just know he will."

"Promised you?" her mother sneered. "Yeah, your father is good at making promises he can't keep. Now pull yourself away from that window and keep the wood burning in that fireplace until I get back. I have a few errands to run."

Convinced her mother might be right, Shannon wiped away her tears and headed back upstairs to her room. Just as she set foot on the top stairs, her father stumbled in through the front door. Falling forward, he dropped her gift, almost crushing it beneath him.

Startled by the commotion, Shannon ran down the stairs to her father lying facedown on the living room floor, passed out cold. She let go a giggle when her birthday surprise hiked its leg over her father's backside and relieved itself. This time not even her father's lewd behavior could stifle her excitement.

A few days later, Shannon bought her puppy a shiny new tag with the name 'Star' engraved on the front. She bought it with the money she had snuck out of her mother's coin purse.

Katrina, not happy with the new addition to their family, took a dislike to the puppy immediately.

"Shannon, don't feed that damn mutt at this table!" her mother yelled. "Take his ass out and put him on the chain."

"Can't we have one peaceful night at the dinner table?" Howard slammed his beer can down. "Why do you always have to make a big deal out of the smallest thing?"

Katrina pushed herself up from the chair and grabbed the puppy by his collar. "Maybe I'm trying to teach her some manners. Something you know nothing about."

"Mama, don't!" Shannon pleaded, her hands folded like in prayer. She dropped to her knees. "You're hurting him!"

Howard stood up. "Katrina, you hurt that dog and I swear I'll hurt—"

"You're not going to do anything except go get drunk like you do every night." Katrina cut him off.

With tears trickling down her cheeks, Shannon looked over at her father and caught him glaring at her mother with such rage in his eyes that, for a moment she thought for sure he could kill her, and for a moment she wished he would.

After dinner, Shannon sat on the windowsill in her room, gazing out at Star chained to the fence. She thought again about the threats her father had made toward her mother. She had never seen him lay a hand on her, but now she was thinking he might. She blamed her mother for her father's excessive drinking, and despised the way she treated him. Above all, Shannon longed for the day she could escape her mother's wrath and take her father with her.

Later that night, after drifting off to sleep, a loud noise from downstairs awakened her. She crouched down behind the bedroom door. Peeking around the door, she watched for movement down the hall.

"Shannon! Wake your ass up and get down here! I need your help right now!"

"Mama, what's wrong?" Shannon called out from behind the door.

"Get your ass down here right this minute, or I'll come and drag you down those stairs!"

Shannon's knees buckled with each step as she crept down the long, dark staircase. Every sound she heard was amplified: the creaking of the door as she opened it, the squeaking boards beneath her feet, and the beating of her own heart.

When she reached the bottom of the stairs, she pried her fingers loose from the banister. Walking toward the kitchen, she could see her mother's silhouette in the dim light. She nervously wrapped the drawstring of her housecoat around her index finger and peeked around the corner into the kitchen.

Dishes lay broken, pieces scattered about across the kitchen floor. Blood dripped from her mother's arms into the sink, down the cabinet, and onto the floor as she turned around.

"Did you not hear me screaming for you?" Her mother held her arms out in front of her. "Get me a towel! What took you so damn long?"

She raced to the cabinet where her mother kept the towels. Her small hands trembled as she laid the towels over her mother's arms. Urine trickled down Shannon's legs, forming a puddle between her feet.

Her mother calmly flashed a sinister grin. "Clean up this mess."

Shannon looked on in disbelief as her mother walked out of the kitchen and up the stairs, as if nothing had happened. Fearing what might occur if she did not do as her mother instructed, she began gathering up bloody towels, placing them in the sink.

It took her eyes several minutes to focus on what she saw. In the sink lay a blood-stained knife, several bloody towels, and a tiny metal tag. The room began to spin as she read the name on the tag. She fell to her knees and curled up in a fetal position.

Some time later, she awoke to find her father standing over her in a drunken stupor.

"Shannon, I don't know what you've done here, but you better clean this mess up before your mother sees it."

"No, Daddy, you don't understand!" she cried out. "I think mama killed Star and she—"

"You ain't making no sense, little girl, and Daddy don't feel like listening to such nonsense."

"Daddy, you have to believe me!"

Ignoring her cries, he stumbled to keep his footing as he walked away.

When he sobered up the next morning, Howard faintly remembered Shannon's bizarre story. It was enough to question Katrina's involvement.

"Katrina, wake up. We need to talk."

"Leave me alone." she pulled the covers over her head. "I'm tired. I didn't get much sleep last night."

"What's this crazy story Shannon is telling me? Something about you killing her dog."

Throwing back the covers, she sat straight up in bed. "What the hell are you talking about?"

"As I recall, I seem to remember coming in last night to find her crying, curled up on the kitchen floor, smeared in what appeared to be ketchup of all things."

Katrina rolled her eyes. "That's what your drinking will do for you, Howard."

"Don't patronize me! Something is going on here. Something terrified that girl last night and I think you know what it is."

"Well, as a matter of fact, it wasn't ketchup. It was blood," Katrina said, hopping out of bed and reaching for her robe. "She woke me in the middle of the night, screaming and carrying on in the kitchen, God knows doing what. By the time I got downstairs, she had blood smeared everywhere and was holding a knife. Hell, at first I thought she had cut herself, and then come to find out she hadn't. Furthermore, she couldn't explain where the blood came from. Maybe she's the one you should be interrogating instead of me."

Surviving the attack on Pearl Harbor, Howard had witnessed atrocities no human being should ever have endured. He knew what he must do to survive what life he had left.

As he packed the last item in his suitcase, Katrina could no longer stay silent.

"You're not taking our daughter. You know that, right?"

He moved toward her, shaking his fist. "You can believe this: whenever I get myself together, I'll be back to get her, and I pray you don't try to stop me."

"Don't go, Daddy!" Shannon cried from nearby, startling him.

Howard stared at her in surprise. "Baby, how long have you been standing there?" He reached out, gathering her up into his arms.

She wrapped her arms around his neck and laid her head on his shoulder. She whispered, "If you love me, Daddy, you'll take me with you."

A stabbing pain of guilt pierced his heart, leaving him weak in the knees and breathless. Trying to regain some sort of composure, he traded his tears for a smile. "You know Daddy loves you but I can't take you with me just yet. I promise I'll be back soon to get you."

Katrina wasted no time stepping in, pulling Shannon from his arms. "And we know how Daddy likes to keep his promises, don't we?"

CHAPTER
4

THE NEW school year had started out relatively quiet, but things were about to change. Making the transition from elementary to junior high could often be stressful for a young student, especially if her name happened to be Shannon White.

"Okay class," the teacher spoke up, "let's settle down and open our books to page thirty-one where we left off yesterday."

"Looks like Shannon don't have her book again today, Mrs. Walters," said one of the students. "Maybe her mother thought it was a sandwich and ate it!"

Shannon lowered her head in embarrassment as the kids roared with laughter.

"Okay, Jefery Taylor, that will be enough!" Mrs. Walters scolded. "Shannon, did you forget your book again today?"

Shannon barely spoke over a whisper. "Yes ma'am."

"Can you call your mother and have her bring it to you?"

"We don't have a phone anymore."

"That's 'cause she don't have a dad and her crazy mother can't work!" Jeffrey sneered.

"That's enough! You can just march yourself right on down to Principal Knight's office!" Mrs. Walters turned to Shannon. "I'm sorry, Shannon, but if you don't have your book tomorrow, I'll have to give you a detention."

For the next hour, Shannon sat with her eyes glued to the front of the classroom. She did not dare look around the room for fear she would see fingers pointing in her direction. When the bell rang, she made a dash for the exit and did not stop until she made it home.

"Hey, where are you running to in such a hurry?" her mother demanded when she burst through the front door. "I know you better get back outside and take those shoes off at the door. And where are your manners? Say hello to Mr. Morgan."

Mr. Morgan had become a frequent visitor. Katrina had hired him to help with the yard work and to do some minor repairs around the house. Shannon, as young as she was, knew they could not afford to hire such help, but had a good idea how her mother repaid him for his services.

The man looked her up and down. "My, my, little girl, you sure are starting to blossom out. Bet you drive those little boys wild over yonder at that school of yours."

Self-conscious, Shannon folded her arms over her breasts. Katrina firmly took Mr. Morgan by the hand and marched him out onto the front porch.

"I think you should finish your work outside today, Mr. Morgan, and when you're done I'll have a proper meal waiting for you inside."

"I'm looking forward to it," he said, swatting her on the butt as she turned.

Humiliated, Shannon ran up the stairs to her room and locked herself in. She watched out her window as Mr. Morgan started up the lawnmower and proceeded to cut the lawn. She fantasized that he would somehow trip and be mauled by the spinning blades of the mower. She cackled as she pictured her mother witnessing the entire episode. She took great pleasure in her dark fantasy.

"Shannon, what are you doing up there?" Her mother yelled from downstairs. What's so funny?"

"Uh, I was thinking of a joke I heard at school today," Shannon yelled back.

"Well, it's time you come down here and help me fix some dinner. It's getting late."

Dinner would be much like every other night, mundane and scarce. They couldn't afford luxuries such as desserts or snacks. To have fruit and vegetables available more than twice a week was a treat. Money had been scarce since Howard had left. Katrina had ended up having to sell most of the land except for the house and the ground it sat upon.

Shannon entered the kitchen and frowned. "Beans and cornbread again?"

"Yes, beans and cornbread again. You could be doing without any dinner, and if I hadn't finished that sewing job for Mrs. Butler down the street, you would be. As a matter of fact, she was so pleased with my work that she hired me on to do her ironing and whatever other odd jobs she needs doing."

"Mr. Morgan isn't eating dinner with us again tonight, is he?"

"Yes he is, smart mouth, and I expect you to be gracious. He's doing a lot of work around here for practically nothing. Now take his bowl and finish filling it while I get the cornbread out of the oven."

They were setting the table when Mr. Morgan entered the room.

"Wow, I tell ya, I worked up an appetite out there. Sure smells good."

"Here you go, Mr. Morgan." Shannon handed him a bowl of beans and a side of cornbread. "Hope you enjoy."

"No need to be so proper, little girl. I think we know each other well enough now to go by our first names. Just call me Ray."

"Whatever you say, Ray, but my name isn't 'little girl.' It's Shannon."

"You'll have to excuse her, Ray." Katrina cut her eyes toward Shannon. "She hasn't had a good ass-whipping lately. Now if everybody's ready, let's eat."

Mr. Morgan took a bite of his beans and frowned. "Um, Katrina?"

"Yes?"

"Did you add something different to the beans this time?"

"No, I made them the same way I always have. Is something wrong?"

"No, no, just taste a little different this time. Could be my taste buds are out of whack."

Shannon pushed her bowl away and stood up. "I'm not much hungry tonight, so can I be excused?"

"No you may not! What's your problem tonight anyway?"

"The kids are teasing me at school and I've got to find my history book by tomorrow or Mrs. Walters is going to give me a detention."

"Teasing you? What about?"

Shannon shook her head. "It doesn't matter. He's just a stupid boy that likes to say hurtful things."

Katrina's eyes lit up. "Well, I had a little extra money today and bought some brownie mix. I was going to make it for dessert tonight, but now I think I'll make them for your class tomorrow. No better way to make friends than to give them a treat, am I right?"

Shannon knew when to leave well enough alone. Katrina had many disturbing traits to her personality, but this one she could live with.

"Ray, are you feeling alright? You don't look so good," Shannon said, dipping a piece of cornbread into her bowl of beans.

Pushing his dinner plate away, he wiped the sweat from his forehead. "I must be getting the stomach flu or something like it. Think I better head on home early tonight."

Shannon forced away a smile. "Mother's beans making you sick?"

Katrina again cut her eyes toward Shannon. "If you're not going to eat, then get up and look for that damn book of yours."

Shannon was more than happy to be excused from the dinner table, but finding her lost book was not on her mind. Taking pleasure in Ray's sudden illness was. She thought about the time her father had come home drunk and how she had witnessed her mother take revenge by adding a few drops of eyewash to his beer. He did not come out of the bathroom for two days.

Closing the bedroom door behind her, she flipped the lock, pulled the half-empty bottle of eyewash out of her pocket, wrapped it in toilet paper, and threw it away. She changed into her pajamas, reached under the bed for her slippers, and smiled when she saw her school book lying open on the floor. She thought it wasn't such a bad day after all.

The next day at school went without a hitch. Katrina's brownies were a hit with the class and little Jeffery Taylor was the first in line to grab one.

"I want this one!" he yelled. "It's the biggest and has more icing than the others."

"That's funny, that's the one my mother said you would pick."

"Okay class, wash your hands, and let's get down to work. Shannon, do we have our book today?" the teacher asked.

"Yes, Mrs. Walters."

"Mrs. Walters?"

"Yes Jeffery, what is it?"

"I don't feel so good."

"Why, I'm not surprised the way you were choking that brownie down. You probably just ate too fast."

Jeffrey leaned over his desk, clutching his stomach. "I—I think I'm going to be sick, Mrs. Walters."

"Okay, come with me and I'll take you down to Nurse Judy's office. Shannon, I'm leaving you in charge as class monitor while

I'm gone and, class, you better be on your best behavior. Come along, Jeffery."

All eyes were on Shannon as Mrs. Walters left the room.

But why? Why had Mrs. Walters chosen her to be in charge of the group, the kid they so often taunted and harassed? It made no sense. Was Mrs. Walters trying to help Shannon gain some respect from her classmates by leaving her in charge, or was there really no motive behind her decision? Whatever the reason, Shannon decided to take advantage of her newfound authority.

"Why don't we just sit and read our books quietly until Mrs. Walters gets back," she suggested.

"You don't really think we're going to listen to you, do ya?" Asked one of her classmates.

This would be a defining moment for Shannon.

"Yeah, I do. Unless you want me to report you to the teacher, Bradley Allen, and I don't think you want that."

The thought of having control over their actions was exhilarating. Her eyes skimmed over each and every one in the class. Setting her sights directly on her adversary she said, "Just you try me, Bradley, and you'll see what happens."

In those few crucial moments she had shown some strength in her character, an ability to stand up for herself, and her classmates took notice. It would not mark an end to being subjected occasionally to mockery, especially when it pertained to her dysfunctional family life, but Mrs. Walters' decision to leave Shannon in charge that day brought about a drastic change in her personality. No longer the introvert, she would soon become quite the opposite. Although some would say that, at times, she could take her assertiveness too far.

Katrina was sitting in the rocker on the front porch sipping on a cold glass of lemonade when Shannon stepped off the bus.

"Where's Ray?" Shannon asked her mother as she sat her book bag on the step and leaned against the porch railing. "He's not still sick, is he?"

"It's Mr. Morgan to you, and yes, smart ass, he is. I went over to check on him today and he looked quite ill. Says he's not coming back, thinks one of us put something in his food, tried to poison him."

Shannon almost giggled. "That's just crazy."

"Oh well, it's not like he was that productive around here, anyway. By the way, how did your brownies go over with the class today? Did that kid that was giving you trouble in class pick the biggest one like I said he would?"

"Yeah," Shannon laughed, "he pushed his way in line just to get at it. Funny thing is, he got sick right after eating it, and Mrs. Walters had to take him down to the nurse. She left me in charge of the class. The other kids were so jealous."

"Liked having the upper hand over those kids, didn't ya? Ah, I always knew we were a lot alike, you and I."

Shannon stared down at the porch, running her fingers through her hair. "We're far from being alike."

"Would you be a dear and pour me some more lemonade? It's mighty hot out today."

Shannon grabbed her book bag, stood up, and snatched the empty glass out of her mother's hand, mumbling obscenities under her breath all the way into the kitchen. Reaching for the pitcher of lemonade, she glanced over and saw the empty eyewash bottle that she had thrown away the day before, unwrapped and in plain view, sitting on the counter.

"Oh Shannon, while you're in the kitchen would you mind bringing me that new bottle of eyewash?" Katrina called from the porch. "I only used a few drops out of it. It's sitting next to the empty brownie box I forgot to throw away. This hot sun does wreak havoc on one's eyes."

The prior events were never spoken of again, both knowing what the other had done. No matter how much Shannon did not want to admit it, they shared many of the same character flaws. Flaws she would forever struggle to overcome.

CHAPTER
5

IN 1971, fresh out of college with a Ph.D. in psychology, Shannon opened up a practice in her hometown of Patton, Missouri. The intense years of studying, together with the long hours she put in her practice, began to overwhelm her. The lack of a good night's sleep added years to her young features. Her glowing, delicate ivory skin appeared dull; tiny lines had formed around her eyes and the sparkle in them now appeared jaded. Her fiery red hair lacked its luster; tiny strands of gray mingled in her braid. The slump of her posture took away the beauty from her once tall, slender body.

Finishing the last session of the day with a client, she opted to dictate her notes at home. After the long day at the office, all she wanted to do was go home and relax.

As she walked up the steps to her front porch, she hesitated for a moment when she heard profanities blaring from inside of the house.

"Son of a bitch! Can't you stupid-ass Cardinals get your shit together and win a game?" James threw his ball cap on the floor and stomped on it. "Shannon, can you believe this shit? The Cardinals lost again."

"I really don't care, James. All I want is a little peace and quiet right now." She threw her notebooks onto the coffee table and flopped down on the couch. "So can you keep it down a little?"

Not long ago, she and James had enjoyed watching ballgames together, but lately she had lost interest.

James had a feeling that the ballgame was not the only thing in which she had lost interest. "Hey, don't take it out on me because you're exhausted. I told you months ago you were taking on too many patients, but did you listen? Hell no!"

Shannon snapped back. "Tell you what, why don't you go down to Larry's Bar and you and your boys can have an in-depth conversation about how baseball is the answer to all of life's problems."

Had he believed he could win the argument, he might have stuck around and stood his ground. But he knew the best thing to do when Shannon was in one of her moods was to give her some space.

Larry's Bar had become James's second home lately, and in a small town where there aren't many choices of recreation, Larry's Bar was the place to congregate to play darts, checkers, a game of pool, and knock back a few.

The owner, Larry Jacobs, had previously worked at the local grain mill for thirty years before purchasing the bar. Then, short of his retirement, a freak accident happened. While sorting grain, his left arm got caught in the conveyer belt. Crushed badly, it had to be amputated. Larry, not the kind of man to wallow in self-pity, learned to adjust quickly.

Larry's wife, Edith, helped with the finances and often handled the books; that is to say, as long as it did not interfere with her church functions. She embodied the characteristics of one's favorite granny. Kind and joyful, she stood with a slight slump in her shoulders. She wore a pair of wire-frame bifocals that always seemed to creep toward the end of her nose. Under no circumstances would you ever see her without her silver hair in a tidy, tight bun. She took great pride in caring for her husband and her home. They never had any children to spoil, so they spoiled each other.

Larry was setting up the checker board for a couple of his regulars when James came plowing through the door.

"Give me a shot of Jack and leave the bottle," he grumbled, laying his money on the bar. "Shannon's in another one of those moods again and I'm apt to be here awhile."

Larry flashed a grin as he reached for the bottle of Jack. "You're becoming a regular fixture around here lately, James. If you don't watch out, I'm gonna have to put you to work."

"Yeah, be funny, why don't ya. This is getting serious, Larry. I don't know how much more of her attitude I can take. Lately everything I do is wrong."

"You know this ain't the answer." Larry poured James a drink, took his money, and pointed to the bottle. "You told me once before that when you both got serious, it wasn't gonna be easy. Anyway, that job of hers has got to be stressful."

"Well, I'll tell you what, although I knew it wasn't going to be easy, now it's getting damn near impossible." James downed his drink and pointed to his empty glass. "I'm beginning to think if getting married and having to spend the rest of my life means accommodating to her every mood—well, I'm not so sure I can do it or even want to do it."

Larry put the cap back on the whiskey bottle and placed it on the shelf. "Go home, James. Forget about all this crap and think about how lonely you'd be without her. And on your way home stop at Maggie's store and buy Shannon one of those roses they always have at the checkout counter. Women love flowers."

James put the rest of his money back into his wallet, got off the bar stool, and stood straight as a soldier at attention. With a big smile, he saluted Larry. "Yes, Sir!"

Maggie had the key in the lock when James jumped out of his truck. "No, no! Wait, Maggie! Wait!"

Maggie flinched and spun around. "James King, you scared the crap out of me!"

"Sorry. I didn't mean to scare you. I need to buy a rose for Shannon."

Inside the shop Maggie started pacing nervously back and forth in front of the store window.

"Is something wrong?" James asked.

"I'm not sure," she shrugged. "Early this morning on my way to open the store, I passed an old woman walking on the road out by Larry's Bar. When I turned around to see if she needed a ride, she'd disappeared. Then right before you pulled up I saw her again. Just now, while I was shutting the blinds, I saw her across the street. She was sitting on the bench in front of Clair's Boutique. Now she's gone again."

"Why does she make you nervous?"

"I don't know why. It's just that something don't feel right."

"You want me to take a look out front?" James offered.

Maggie smiled. "Could you?"

He went outside.

She locked the door behind him and watched through the window as he crossed the street.

James stood six feet tall and weighed two hundred and fifty pounds, pretty much all muscle from working in construction. He had been in a few brawls and always held his own, and he was not going to be frightened by some old woman.

Halfway down the alley he stopped, looked over his shoulder, then back up the alley. Seeing what he thought to be a shadow, he stood still, watching for any sign of movement. When realizing what he had seen had been his own shadow, he shook his head and thought how silly it was to be looking for some old woman down a dark alleyway.

He turned back toward the store and caught a glimpse of Maggie peeping out through the blinds. Once again, she unlocked the door and let him in.

"Well, did you see anything? Did you find her?"

James shook his head. "Nope, didn't see a thing. What'd she look like, anyway?"

"She was dressed like an old gypsy and had one of those bandanas wrapped around her head. Her dress looked like it was made out of long, tattered scarves."

"Well, maybe she's just passing through on her way to catch up with the circus." James chuckled.

Maggie was not amused. It wasn't like a stranger passed through their little town every day looking as if they walked out of an episode of The Twilight Zone.

"I'd be happy to follow you home," James offered.

"Are you sure? I know Shannon is waiting for you."

"It's no trouble at all. Shannon will understand if I'm a few minutes late," he said, hoping she believed him.

At one time, he and Maggie had been madly in love, or so he'd thought. However, Maggie's insecurities and bouts with depression proved to be more than he could handle. He often blamed himself for the breakup. The guilt of not being able to help her only added more stress to their strained relationship. Still, Maggie had been his first love, and he would always be protective of her.

CHAPTER

6

SHANNON WATCHED the minute hand on the clock, waiting for James to come home. Curling up next to his pillow, she thought back on her earlier years in life. She thought about her only childhood friend, Maggie Simmons. When the other kids teased her, saying cruel things about her family, Maggie always stepped in to defend her. The first time they met, they immediately formed a bond. Both girls' lives were often in turmoil, for Maggie's father was an acute alcoholic as well. Both girls carried the scars and trauma that often accompany such a disease.

She recalled her first encounter with James. When she returned home after college, Maggie had been the first person she contacted. She needed to find the perfect place to open up her new practice, and with very little money and no clientele, she needed something affordable. Maggie found the perfect place: a vacant building with a spacious layout needing only minor repairs.

"Well, what do you think, Shannon?" Maggie asked.

"It's plenty spacious enough, that's for sure, but it's in dire need of repairs, repairs I don't think I can afford."

"Well, you're in luck. The guy I told you I'd been seeing for some time now just happens to be a carpenter, and a pretty damn good one at that. I'm pretty sure he'll cut you a deal, as a favor to me."

Shannon looked at the plaster peeling away from the walls, bent down and picked up a rotted board that lay in her path and said, "I hope it's a hell of a good deal, because it's going to take a lot of work."

"Oh, speaking of James, here he is now."

"Sorry I'm late, Maggie," James said, stepping out of his truck and grabbing his tool belt. "I can't seem to get my ass in gear today for some reason."

"Uh, honey, this is Shannon, my friend I was telling you about earlier."

Flustered by her beauty and trying his best not to be too obvious, he straightened the tool belt around his waist and fixed his eyes on Maggie, waiting to be introduced.

"Shannon, this is James, the best damn carpenter in all of Patton." Maggie wrapped her arm around his and placed a kiss on his lips. "And, I might add, the love of my life. For now, anyway."

If their two-minute handshake had not been enough to spark Maggie's attention, the long silence as Shannon and James stood gazing into each other's eyes should have been enough to provoke concern.

Thinking back now, she knew Maggie had to have known at that very moment what was taking place.

Shannon emptied the thoughts from her head and lit a cigarette. While rewriting her notes from the day's sessions, she looked up and saw James coming through the front door.

He stood in the hallway, smiling, hiding a long-stem rose behind his back. "Hey baby, what you still doing awake?"

"James, I want to apologize. I know I've not been easy to live with lately." Putting her cigarette out in the ashtray, she went to him and planted a kiss on his lips. "And I promise I'm going to make an effort to change."

"You're working too damn hard, Shannon. Maybe what you need is a vacation. We could take that trip we've talked about for some time. Relax for a couple of weeks. What do you say, sound good?"

Leaning in, he handed her the rose and gave her another kiss.

"Ah, you brought me a rose?" She smiled and thought for a moment. "Where on earth did you get a rose this late at night? You didn't pick it out of Mrs. Harris's garden from next door, did you?"

"No, I stopped by Maggie's store. She was closing but kind enough to let me grab one before she locked up."

She turned abruptly, stuck the rose in an empty coffee mug on her desk, and reached for her lighter to light another cigarette.

"So what do you think about what I said, baby? Vacation sound good?"

"I've got paperwork up to my ears and I'm behind on my notes. I can't leave my practice for two weeks to go anywhere."

"Tell you what, hon; why don't you just go ahead and finish what you're doing. And another thing, I'll just sleep in the guestroom tonight again and when you find out what it'll take to make you happy without jeopardizing your precious career, come and let me know, okay?"

"Don't hold your breath," Shannon murmured.

SATURDAY HAPPENED to be one of the busiest days at Clair's Boutique. The twice-a-year fifty-percent discount sale always brought in a crowd. Clair Sims and her husband Buddy once owned a large percent of the farmland that stretched across Patton.

One hot July morning, just before sunrise, Buddy hopped into the seat of his tractor and took off into the field. When he did not return for lunch, Clair went to investigate and found her husband's lifeless body. Part of his clothing had become entangled in the unguarded shaft of the tractor. Not reacting in time for whatever reason, his body had been yanked unmercifully into the turning blades.

Clair and their two sons were immediately thrust into the responsibility of running the family farm. Fifty years old at the time of his death, both boys grown, Clair made a decision to try something new. She divided the land equally between her boys and opened a women's clothing store in town. She hired her closest friend, Nadine Castle, to help her run the store.

Nadine had a knack for conversation. She stood barely five feet tall and weighed less than a hundred pounds, but her personality was explosive. She had recently lost her husband to cancer and had never remarried. They had always wanted children of their own, but the time had never come.

Nadine loved to gossip about everything, from Reverend Thompson running off with his young assistant, to how she thought pop music was the work of the devil.

"Clair, you're not going to believe what I heard through the grapevine!"

"Slow down, Nadine." Clair replied, reaching out to put both hands on Nadine's shoulders. "You're hyperventilating."

"Will you just listen," she said, still breathing heavily. "I went to that new furniture store over in Sedgewickville yesterday looking for a new mattress. Remember, I told you the one I have is killing my back? Well, anyway, I stopped at the little café. You know, the one we always have lunch at."

"Could you just get to the point of your story? We have to open up here shortly."

"Okay, but listen to me now. I overheard a couple of women talking about this old fortune teller. They were discussing how some of the town people had got together and ran her out of town. I heard them say they thought she was possessed. Now get this, they said the last they'd heard, she was headed for Patton."

Clair threw her head back and laughed. "I don't think we have anything to worry about. So, what if she does come here? Are you going to be scared of some old fortune-teller woman? You don't possibly believe in all that crap, do you?"

Shrugging, Nadine's face turned three shades of red, as she appeared to be in deep thought.

Clair dreaded having to hear the same story again each time one of their friends came in, but was certain she would.

Maggie placed the 'out for lunch' sign on the front door, locked up and headed across the street to check out Clair's sale. She barely made it in the door when Nadine approached her with the story.

Clair overheard their conversation and joined in. "Maggie, did I hear you say that you've seen the old woman Nadine's been rambling on about?"

"I think maybe I did. Last night, right before I locked up at the store, I glanced across the street, and I could've swore I saw her sitting on the bench in front of your store. When I turned away, and looked back again, she had disappeared. James pulled up about that time. And, being a sweetheart, he offered to check things out."

Clair leaned in and whispered. "Are you and James seeing each other again?"

"No, we're not. He just stopped by the store to get something. As a matter of fact, it was a rose for Shannon."

Nadine decided to put in her two cents. "Well, the way I hear it, James has been spending more time at Larry's Bar than he has with Shannon. Word gets around, you know. Maybe you ought to—"

"Nadine!" Clair interrupted. "Maybe we should get back on the subject of the old woman. I think we all need to calm down and not read so much into all this. She may have just been passing through. Then again, she could turn out to be one of our new neighbors."

Clair knew if the conversation continued, they would never make a sale. Taking Maggie by the arm, she walked her over to one of the sale racks, pulling out some of her best bargains.

JAMES HAD made reservations for dinner and plans for a movie weeks earlier. However, Shannon had a feeling that, after the way things had been going, the odds were against it happening. He had abruptly left, giving no indication of where he was going or if he was even coming back. She had a good idea where he might be, though.

The phone only rang a couple of times before Larry answered. "Larry's Bar. Can I help ya?"

"Yeah Larry, would James happen to be there?"

"No, Shannon, I haven't seen him today. If he comes in, I'll be sure to let him know you're looking for him. By the way, how have you been?"

"Thanks for asking. I've been okay. And you?"

"Oh, I'm okay, but from what James has been saying, you've been working yourself too hard. You know that all work and no play ain't good for ya."

Shannon chuckled. "Don't worry. I'm going to slow down soon. Please tell James to call me if you see him, okay?"

"Will do. Now you and James stop by the house and I'll have Edith whip you up some of her famous dumplings. You take care."

Trying to get her mind off James, Shannon looked around the house for something to do. It had been a while since she had done any major cleaning, so she decided now would be a good time.

She started in the den by picking up a stack of novels sitting on the end table, only a few of which she had actually read. At the bottom of the stack laid a book titled "The Prodromal Period" by Dr. Henry Pelzer. This one she had read often. It told of individuals who were at high risk for developing psychotic illnesses, and how to recognize the signs. She had underlined several passages pertaining to her mother. Dealing with the human mind and the emotional process of one's journey had become her life's study.

She sank back into the couch, lit a cigarette, and sighed. She jumped straight up when a loud thump from the basement startled her. She thought it had to be a mouse. Inside a kitchen drawer, she found the flashlight and cursed upon finding the battery compartment empty. She grabbed a broom and headed to the basement.

Shannon propped the door open behind her and flicked the switch on her cigarette lighter, praying it would not run out. Halfway down the steps, a foul odor smacked her in the face. She wrinkled her nose and covered her mouth while trying not to breathe in too deeply.

The cigarette lighter slipped through her fingers as she missed a step and stumbled forward when the basement door above her slammed shut with such force that it shook the entire house. Shannon tried desperately to keep her balance, grasping for anything to hold on to. Profanity flew from her lips as her knuckles scraped along the concrete steps, tearing away flesh from her fingers.

Her mind raced with panic and fear as she searched for her lighter in the dark. She exhaled a sigh of relief when she saw a faint trace of light coming in through the tiny basement window. On her hands and knees, she inched her way across the cold concrete floor, feeling for her lighter.

Quickly she pushed forward when she heard what sounded like a heavy chain clanking against the concrete floor, followed by a muffled cry in the darkness coming from somewhere behind her. Panicking, her lungs fighting against her body, she struggled to take a breath as the room closed in on her. Numb with fright, she listened in horror as the muffle turned to screams of desperation.

Again, her lungs gasped for air. She prayed aloud, "God, please let this be a nightmare!"

"Shannon, it's me, James," came a voice from the darkness. "I'm here, baby. Are you okay? Open your eyes."

Relaxing her body to the sound of James's voice, she opened her eyes.

"I don't think I've ever heard you scream in your sleep like that. Must have been one hell of a nightmare!"

The smell of cigarette smoke still lingered in the air as her burnt cigarette lay smoldering in the ashtray in front of her. James reached over and took the copy of the Pelzer book that lay open in her lap and placed it on the table.

"There's something down there," Shannon whispered as she attempted to get to her feet. "Something in that basement. We have to get out of here, now!"

"Listen to me," James said, taking her hand in his. "You must have dozed off and had a bad dream."

She leaned on James's arm for support and staggered to her feet.

James knew the best thing he could do was to prove to her that nothing was as it seemed. He led her toward the basement, opened the door, and flipped the light switch.

"See baby, there's nothing. It was all just a bad dream."

"I have to go back down there. Shannon insisted. I have to see."

Her hand wrapped tightly around his, she made it to the first step, to the second step, and then to the third before turning around. "I don't need to go any further."

They returned to the kitchen.

"I'm going to say it again…you've been working way too much lately. Too much negative stress affects not only your health but your mind as well. Isn't that what you preach to your patients?"

"I don't preach to my patients, James, but yes, I'm well aware of what stress can do to a person's overall health."

"I'll run you a hot bath to soak in, but not too long. Remember, we have reservations," James said, pointing his finger at her and grinning. "And I can only think of one good reason to be late. I think you know what that is."

Alone in the kitchen, Shannon stared at the basement door, wanting to open it again, but her feet would not budge. She ran her fingers across one another, looking and feeling for some sign of wounds from the fall, but there were none. She searched her mind for an image of her mother, the way she looked, the sound of her voice, but nothing came. It had been a nightmare, one in all probability brought on by feelings of guilt in an unconscious effort to drudge up the past, a past memory she would just as soon keep locked away.

With the disturbing events of the day behind her, Shannon looked forward to a relaxing night out in Sedgewickville. As they passed the last turnoff before exiting Patton, she glanced over at an unfamiliar road sign with an arrow pointing toward an abandoned farmhouse.

"You know, I heard that some old woman moved into the old Parker farmhouse," James said. One of my workers said his wife heard she could tell fortunes or some crazy shit like that. He said they'd heard she'd been run out of Sedgewickville. Supposedly, the town sheriff's wife went for one of those readings and the old woman told her that her husband had been cheating on her, even told her who the woman was. Crazy thing is they said she was right. Guess the sheriff didn't appreciate that much."

Not wanting to appear too enthused by his silly story, she reached for her purse, pulled out her makeup compact and shook her head. "Sounds like a lot of crap to me. There has to be more to it than that. You can't run somebody out of town for something they said. Surely you're not as gullible as to believe in such nonsense."

Nevertheless, Shannon couldn't help but be somewhat intrigued by it. She closed her compact and slid next to him in the seat. "Okay, you have my full attention. Is there more to the story?"

"The night I stopped by Maggie's store, she mentioned seeing an old woman on the road outside of Larry's bar. She said a short time later she saw her again across the street in front of Clair's Boutique, but every time she tried to get a better look, the old woman disappeared. Hell, she was so shook up about it she asked me to look around outside. Wonder if it could be the same old woman."

"You know what, come to think of it; when I stopped by Maggie's store to get your rose that night she mentioned seeing this old gypsy-looking woman on the road.

"So that's why you were so late coming home," Shannon mumbled, putting distance between them again. "You were busy being Maggie's big, strong protector, out looking for her disappearing ghost."

James pulled up to the restaurant, parked, and leaning in close, kissed her gently on the hand. "We're here now, my lady, so let's just have a nice dinner, see a movie, and forget all about fortune tellers and ghosts."

Larry could not recall a night when the bar had been so full of customers. On this particular night, he happened to notice a man sitting alone at the back of the bar. He thought it strange that while everyone else was drinking and mingling, the stranger kept eerily to himself.

He found himself staring at the man's left arm that revealed a tattoo of a devil holding a pitchfork. He looked on with disgust as the stranger ran his fingers through his stringy, shoulder-length hair that hung out from under the cap he wore backwards.

Curious, Larry moved in closer to get a better look at his face. "Looks like you could use another beer there, fella. Can I get ya one?"

Looking down, Larry noticed a black suitcase propped up against the stranger's chair.

The stranger took a long drag off his cigarette, exhaling slowly. "Don't think so, old-timer. I've had all the warm beer I can stand."

Larry puffed out his chest and cocked his head to the side. "I don't recall ever serving warm beer in my bar, fella. By the way, see ya got a suitcase there. Just passing through our little town, I guess?"

The stranger pointed toward the bar. "It looks like your barmaid is trying to get your attention."

Larry looked back over his shoulder. "What ya need now, Carla?" he yelled.

"The beer is running low up here," Carla answered. "Should I go to the back and get some more?"

He averted his attention away from the stranger long enough to head to the backroom for more beer.

He had just entered the back of the bar when Frank Phillips rushed in behind him, out of breath.

"Slow down, Frank. Did ya run all the way here from your hardware store?"

"Did you hear the news about that new family that just moved into town?" Frank asked, bent over and out of breath.

"You talking about the young couple, the ones with the two little kids that moved into Old Man Jenkins's place?"

Frank nodded. "That's them. Found them all dead earlier today. People are saying it looks like a robbery gone bad. They found the folks tied up and shot in the head, and the kids appeared to have been strangled. What kind of monster would do that, Larry?"

Larry shook his head solemnly. "I can't imagine. That poor family. It doesn't make any sense. What else did the news say?"

"Neighbors said they heard gunshots, couldn't tell for sure where they came from. Then they saw the family's white Lincoln peeling out of the driveway. The killers are probably long gone by now though, don't you think?"

The stranger entered Larry's mind. Running to the front, he looked over at the empty table where he had been sitting.

"Carla, where did that stranger go I was talking to a few minutes ago?"

"He paid his tab and left right after you went to the back. Guess it was about the time Frank came running in."

"What's going on?" Frank asked. "Who are you looking for?"

"This stranger came in the bar tonight," Larry explained. "I know you shouldn't judge a book by its cover, but something wasn't right with this guy. He had tattoos all over him, a regular smartass. I've never seen him around these parts before, that's for sure."

Frank gasped. "You don't think—Oh, Larry! What if he was the killer?"

Pulling his friend aside, Larry whispered, "Keep it down, will ya? Ain't no need to cause a panic. Hand me the phone and I'll call the sheriff."

"What are ya going to tell 'im?"

"I'll just describe the fellow and tell 'im how he'd been acting, so nervous an' all."

"Wouldn't that be something? I mean, if you find out you had the killer right here in your bar and didn't even know it!"

"Yeah, that'd be something, alright." Larry replied.

CHAPTER
7

NADINE HELD the title as chairperson of the town council. Upon hearing of the tragic murders that had taken place, she immediately called for an emergency meeting. Among the close-knit community to show up for the meeting were Shannon and James. They had heard the terrible news while listening to the radio on their way back from Sedgewickville the night before. The town sheriff also showed up to give what little information he could about the case.

"For anyone here who doesn't know me, I'm Nadine Castle, chairperson of the town council."

"We all know who you are!" shouted a voice from the crowd.

Nadine ignored the heckler in the back of the room and continued. "Anyway, I've called this meeting asking Sheriff Bill Chesterton if he would graciously update us on our town's recent tragedy, and tell us what steps we need to take as a community to keep our people safe. Now in saying that, I hand the floor over to the sheriff."

The sheriff stood and walked to the podium. "First, I'd like to begin by saying we are going to do everything in our power to apprehend the person or persons responsible for these vicious crimes committed in our community. However, as you may know, I'm not at liberty to give out specifics of the ongoing investigation, but we have accumulated many leads and we're following up on all of them. We have no reason to believe the suspect or suspects are still in this area. In the meantime, there are many things you can do as a community pulling together that will make you feel safe."

Larry listened closely to what the sheriff had to say. He could not dismiss the feeling he might have already encountered the killer and had let him slip through his fingers.

Finally, he stood up. "Bill, speaking for myself and Edith, I'm sure you're doing everything you can. I'm wondering, though, is your department big enough to handle something like this? I mean, well, what I'm trying to say is, it couldn't hurt to get some help from the department in Sedgewickville or one of the other bigger towns, could it?"

The sheriff stood a little taller, bit his bottom lip, and loosened his tie. I appreciate your concern, but Sedgewickville has already sent a team down here. We're working together to solve this case as quickly as possible."

Maggie joined in the conversation. "If I may make a suggestion…as neighbors, we could volunteer to periodically drive by and check on one another, especially people who live in the isolated areas of town."

James nodded. "I think Maggie's idea is a good one. I don't think anybody should be going home to an empty house alone, especially late at night. We need someone to make sure everything is safe and secure for them. I don't mind volunteering."

Frank rocked back and forth in his chair, itching to get a word in. "Sheriff, you know yourself I've said many times, that if someone tries to break into my home or threaten my family, I'd have no problem shooting them dead. I think y'all should think about purchasing a firearm to protect your own homes."

"Now that's exactly what we don't need," Sheriff Chesterton said, shaking his finger at Frank. "We don't need a lot of panicked trigger-happy people running out to buy guns. What everybody needs to do is to look out for each other, and to report anything suspicious. Most importantly, you don't need to panic. I've got men out there patrolling all over town."

Clair stood up. "Bill's right, Frank. There's no need to have a bunch of people out there toting guns around. Somebody innocent is apt to get hurt."

Frank sat back down and slammed his fist on his knee. "I'll do what I have to do to keep safe. If some son of a bitch tries to come into my home uninvited, I'll blow his fool head off."

Nadine was about to adjourn the meeting when a stranger from the back of the room spoke in a whispery voice.

"Come forward, please," Nadine replied. "We can't hear you from way back there."

"This horror that's happened in your town has caused you to fear a stranger. Those who were killed were pawns in a game meant to distract you. His vicious act was random. I'm here to tell you to fear that stranger no more; the evil spirit that possessed him has devoured his soul. Your little town has been blessed for many years, but now evil will emerge. This evil will work with calculation. It is not a stranger you should fear. It is one of your own. My spirits tell me another tragedy is destined to strike. One of you is closely attached to this evil entity and you will be given several warning signs. If you ignore the signs, the evil one will consume you."

The old woman slowly began to move, making her way toward the exit. Everyone stood silent in disbelief, shocked by what she had said.

Before she could get out the door, the sheriff called out to her. "Just one minute, ma'am. Would you mind telling us who you are and where you come from? Why should we believe your nonsense?"

The old woman stopped, turned, and looked directly at the sheriff. "My name is Lola Chicome. My home is here for now. What I speak to you is the truth. Make no mistake; my spirits have brought me here to warn you. I see that you doubt what I say to be true, so I will tell you that this evil stranger that you seek, who took those innocent lives, is in an abandoned mine not far from here. He lies dead from the very thing in his life he could not live without. Your proof will be there."

She turned her eyes from Sheriff Chesterton to Larry. "This feeling you have, you will find out in time, is much more than that. You are a good man, and you have many good spirits that walk with you. You should learn to listen to them."

Larry's jaw dropped. He looked over at Edith and squeezed her hand. "Is she referring to me?" he whispered.

Not wanting a panic to break out, Sheriff Chesterton quickly took control. "All right, everyone, it's clear to me that what we just witnessed is the ramblings of one disturbed old woman. I can promise you I will get to the bottom of this nonsense."

Most everyone left the meeting shaking their heads while talking amongst themselves, believing the old woman to be crazy and deranged.

Frank cackled. "Hey Shannon, I think that nutcase could use some of your expert advice."

"Yeah, Frank, and maybe you could come with her. We could discuss your obsession with firearms."

Larry couldn't help jumping in. "Hey Frank, don't you need to go and clean your guns?"

"Yeah, y'all are very funny." Frank grumbled.

"Shannon, what do you make of all this?"

"I'm not sure, Clair. I'd like to be able to talk to her one-on-one, find out why she believes she has supernatural powers."

"I don't know," Larry added. "The same night of the murders I had an outsider in my bar. He gave me a real uneasy feeling.

Right after that, Frank came in and told me about the murders. Next thing you know the stranger was gone. That same uneasy feeling told me he might have been the killer. I wish I hadn't let him get away."

Shannon placed her hand on Larry's shoulder. "You said it yourself that the person was a stranger. He looked different, that's all. Of course you're going to feel apprehensive. Most anyone would. I can assure you those feelings you were having were not some old supernatural spirit trying to give you a clue. There's no way you could have known he was the killer, if in fact he was."

"Yeah, I guess you're right. I'm putting too much into it." Larry said.

"Maggie, you're being awfully quiet." Nadine nudged her on the arm.

"I was just thinking. Remember when you were telling the story about the fortune teller being run out of Sedgewickville?"

"Yeah."

"Remember I'd said I seen some old woman sitting on Clair's bench the night before?"

Nadine nodded. "Yeah, I remember that."

"Do you think it's possible she's the same old woman?"

"Could be."

"I'm not sure, though. Maggie shook her head. "I didn't get a good enough look at her that night, but it sure sounds like too much of a coincidence."

"I don't know about you guys," James said, leaning back in his chair, "as for me and Shannon, we had a late night last night and all this excitement is wearing thin."

Clair nodded and grabbed her purse. "James is right. We all need to go home and relax. It's Sunday, after all. We'll all have plenty of time to ponder on this subject."

CHAPTER

8

THE NEXT morning turned out to be hectic for Shannon and James.

Shannon, still groggy, rolled over and reached for the alarm clock. Rubbing her eyes, she tried to focus on the numbers. She sat up quickly. "James, wake up! I forgot to set the alarm. We're going to be late!"

Applying the last coat of lipstick, she blotted her lips. "Is something on your mind, hon?"

James tapped his razor on the edge of the sink, then wiped away the shaving cream from his chin. "You know, I've been thinking. Remember me telling you the story my buddy told me, the one about the old fortune teller woman being run out of Sedgewickville?"

"Yeah, so exactly where is this leading to?"

"Well, it only makes sense that it has to be the same old woman from the town meeting. Probably the same woman Maggie saw that night walking on the highway in front of Larry's Bar, then again across the street. What doesn't make sense to me is how she could've disappeared so fast. The old woman we saw could barely walk."

Shannon thought about it. "I'm sure there's a logical explanation behind the disappearing act. I have to admit; she is intriguing, to say the least. I'd love to evaluate her. I think it'd be interesting and challenging to have her as a patient."

James chuckled. "Hey, I know. You could invite her over for dinner one night; ask her to read your palm. Who knows, she might end up evaluating you instead."

Shannon dabbed him on the cheek with shaving cream. "Now there's a good idea! Why didn't I think of that?"

SEVENTY-FIVE MILES away, in the city of Thebes, Doctor Matt Delacruz and his assistant Dr. Mary Delaney were celebrating. Having administered Thorazine as treatment to a psychotic mental patient who was under their care and who was making remarkable improvements. Diagnosed as having paranoid schizophrenia, it was later determined that their patient suffered from undifferentiated schizophrenia. When first institutionalized, the patient showed evidence of suicidal tendencies as well. Extensive psychoanalysis, along with the Thorazine, made it quite possible that the patient could live a somewhat normal life.

Through more extensive evaluations over time from several highly respected colleagues, it had been determined that Dr. Delacruz's patient could now be released. Although certain strict conditions had to be met, Dr. Delacruz felt confident about her release.

Rounding the third corridor on the fourth floor, he stopped and picked a rose from a vase that sat on the nurse's counter. The security guard unlocked the door leading to the fifth wing of the hospital and they entered.

Dr. Delacruz passed by several rooms before reaching his patient. Each room had a three-inch-thick steel door with triple-pane glass windows. Double foam padding covered the walls and floor. The only accessories were a toilet in the corner and a cot that was bolted down. The Eight-by-nine-foot rooms were home to the patients. This wing held the most violent and mentally disturbed. The other wings in the hospital were not as sparse or heavily guarded. He hoped soon his patient would no longer have to endure such isolation.

The guard unbolted the thick steel door and Dr. Delacruz entered. Kissing his patient's cheek softly, he handed her the rose. For a few seconds they looked at each other in silence.

"It's unanimous, Katrina. The state medical board agreed. You are well enough to leave here. However, there is a stipulation. You must stay in therapy indefinitely. Since your daughter is the only family you have, she must agree to take guardianship over you and your future affairs. Do you think your daughter will agree with our request?"

"She must," she whispered. "It's my only hope."

"I'll get in touch with her immediately. I'm sure she'll be excited, but do understand that she may be skeptical of our decision."

"You just get her here, Doc. We'll prove to her I'm well enough to work on building a new life for myself."

CHAPTER
9

AS LOW, black clouds moved in, the thunder shook the earth beneath the little town of Patton. Animals, large and small, sought shelter as jagged laser-streaks of light struck at random, bringing with them drenching periods of rainfall. The much-needed rain came as a blessing for the farmers tending their crops, but as far as Larry was concerned, it could not have come at a worse time.

"Edith, I'd better get myself down to the bar and check on that leaky roof. There's not much telling what kinda mess I'll find."

"I thought you were going to hire someone to fix that roof months ago. Don't get down there and exhaust yourself."

"Yeah, yeah, you worry too much."

Grabbing his raincoat and some extra buckets from underneath the counter, Larry headed out the door. But before he could get the key in the ignition, Sheriff Chesterton pulled into the driveway behind him.

"You got a minute, Larry? I'd really like to talk to you."

Larry rolled down his window to answer him. "I'm headed to the bar right now, Sheriff. Have to check on my roof, but you can follow me if you want. We can talk there."

"Sounds good. I'll meet you there."

LARRY WAS right about his roof. Water seeped through the ceiling onto the bar, soaking the carpets.

He looked curiously at the sheriff, "So what's going on? Must be something important to follow me all the way out here."

"Larry, we've known each other for a long time, and I've always thought of you as a friend." Removing his hat the Sheriff took a deep breath. "And as my friend, I need you to help me make sense of something that's happened."

"Sure, Bill. Tell me what's got you so upset."

"After the town meeting, the old woman got just out of my sight when I began to follow her. I rounded the curve where I saw her last and then nothing. I thought maybe someone stopped to give her a ride, but there were no vehicles in sight, coming or going. I remembered her saying we'd find the suspect in an old abandoned mine. Well, I thought about the old mine down by Birches Corner. You know, the one they shut down a couple of years ago. I thought it couldn't hurt to check it out.

"I parked my patrol car a few yards away from the mineshaft and got out. I can't explain it, but something told me to look down in that deep gully, the one across from the mine. I noticed quite a few of the big trees had been twisted, broken, and turned over. Then something caught my eye; something white and shiny, barely visible through the debris.

"So I crawled into the gully to get a better look, and realized that it was a wrecked car turned on its side with the passenger-side door facing me. The tags were bent, but I could still read the number, so I called it in on my radio, told my deputy to put a trace on it. It was a stolen vehicle, Larry, the one from the crime scene, the white Lincoln."

Larry's eyes widened. "Oh my God, Bill, you've go to be kidding! What'd you do next?"

"Well, it gets crazier." The sheriff pulled a handkerchief from his pocket and wiped his brow. "I kept hearing the old woman's voice in my head, telling me to look in the mine, so I called for backup. I know the procedure is to wait for backup. But, I didn't. I hadn't got but a couple of feet inside when a foul smell hit me. There lay a body, decayed and covered with maggots. There were hypodermic needles laying all around the body and what appeared to be drugs. Later we found the murder weapon in the vehicle. There's no doubt, Larry, this was our killer."

"I know you're on duty Bill, but this calls for a double shot of whiskey."

Larry filled his glass, took a swig, and handed the bottle to the sheriff. "I wish I knew the answer, Bill. Do you remember when the gypsy woman pointed me out at the meeting, telling me I needed to listen to my spirits for guidance? Well, I had a talk with Shannon afterwards. She thinks it was a bunch of mumbo-jumbo. But this is proof that that old woman has some kinda voodoo powers going on. How else could she have known those things?"

"It only gets better," Bill grinned. "I did some checking on our mystery woman. It appears her identity is as much of a mystery as she is. I did find out that she apparently makes one-of-a-kind handmade quilts. Supposedly, that's how she makes her living. She's also known to dabble in telling peoples' fortunes from time to time. Poking around, I found out that the sheriff in Sedgewickville could vouch for that. A source told me the sheriff's wife saw the old woman for a reading. The old woman gave her details on her husband's womanizing ways. When I questioned him about it, he said it was all nonsense. He said the old woman didn't have a license to sell her services. He gave her a choice, either get one or move on."

Goose bumps rose on Larry's arms. "You know, come to think of it, I thought I'd seen a sign right outside of town pointing toward the old Parker's farm that said—"

"Yep, 'Hand-stitched Embroidered Quilts.' I saw it, too. After I did some more investigating, come to find out, who do you think is running this operation?"

Larry hesitated before gulping his shot of whiskey. "Wait, don't tell me, could it be our little old mystery woman?"

"You got it." Bill said.

"I think this calls for another." Larry twisted off the cap on a new bottle of whiskey. "Sheriff, I hope your shift is about over, 'cause neither one of us may be able to walk out of this bar."

The rain started again as the sun went down, filling every bucket to the brim. Nevertheless, the conversation between Larry and Bill concerning the old woman never wavered. Both men tried to make sense of what they were going through. Neither one believed in ghosts nor spiritual folklore, each certain there had to be a logical explanation. Neither Bill nor Larry could have known they were in for a rude awakening.

CHAPTER
10

MAGGIE HAD her hands full doing inventory while wait-ing on customers. Her mind, still occupied by the events that had taken place at the town meeting, made it difficult for her to concen-trate on anything. She did not want to believe in such nonsense, but it frightened her all the same.

The thought of living alone scared her. She envied what Shan-non and James had together. Lonely for so long, Maggie was sure true love would never come. Her heart ached for James and she often fantasized about him. She had tried the dating scene for a while, but her heart wasn't in it. She hated herself for giving up on their relationship, blaming her own insecurities for their breakup. Some people would say Shannon's deceitful actions regarding their friendship were unforgivable. However, Maggie had no choice but to forgive Shannon. Anything less would have meant sure death for one of them. Still, letting go and forgetting were impossible.

Unable to focus on her work, Maggie decided to close the store an hour early. Before she could put the key in the lock, Nadine walked in. Grabbing the 'closed' sign while looking at Nadine, she shook her head.

"I'm not feeling well today," Maggie told her. "You'll have to come back tomorrow."

"Oh, I'm sorry to hear that. Is it the stomach flu? It's been going around, you know."

"Yeah," Maggie sighed. "That's probably it."

"Well, I won't keep you but a minute. Have you been listening to the news?"

Maggie bit her bottom lip. "No. I've been trying to get some work done. Has there been another murder in our sleepy little town?"

Nadine arched a brow. "My, we're a little testy today, aren't we?"

"I'm sorry. So, what happened?"

"They found the man that killed those poor people. Guess where they found him!"

Maggie sighed tiredly. "I don't know, Nadine. Tell me."

"Right where the old woman said he'd be. News says Sheriff Chesterton on a hunch took it upon himself to do his own investigating. Found him and the stolen car at some old, abandoned mine just like the old woman said. You and I both know, like many others by now, it wasn't just a hunch. I tell you, there's something freaky going on."

"Now Nadine, I'm sure there's a logical explanation. There's no way that old woman could've known that. They'll probably find out she had something to do with the murders, probably investigating her right now."

Nadine shrugged. "I hope she did have something to do with it. At least that'd make more sense."

SHANNON FINISHED her last session of the day, and none too soon. She looked forward to her appointment at the beauty salon; recently deciding it might be just what she needed to lift her spirits.

She thought a lot about the young family that had been brutally murdered. The tragedy helped to remind her how sudden a life could be cut short. She thought by taking steps to improve her appearance, it might help in her love life as well. It also bothered her to think of Maggie being the same age, yet looking much younger. In high school, she had wanted to look like Maggie: five-foot-five, blond hair and petite, instead of tall and lanky with bright red hair. Truth was, she envied her as much now as she did then.

Late for her appointment, one foot out the door, she hesitated when the phone rang. At the thought that it might be an emergency, she answered.

"Dr. Delacruz? What's wrong? Is it my mother?"

"Relax, Shannon. Your mother is all right. In fact, she's better than all right. That's the reason I'm calling. I know it's been awhile since you've seen her. I'm aware she wasn't doing so great the last time you visited. Since then, we have made great progress working towards your mother's recovery. However, I would rather talk to you in person about this matter, if that were possible."

"When should I come?"

"I have some of your mother's paperwork to finish going through. If you could come first thing tomorrow, I'll fill you in on all the details."

Caught off guard by the telephone call, Shannon completely forgot about her beauty appointment and drove straight home.

As a doctor of psychology herself, she understood the medical aspect of her mother's mental illness and silently questioned her progress.

CLAIR COULD hardly wait to close up shop. She had done most of the work while Nadine spent all her time gossiping with every customer that came in. She wished her friend hadn't convinced her to put a television behind the counter. Every time the news came on reporting something new about the murders, Nadine stopped to listen.

Marking the last item of the day, she noticed Nadine glued to the set yet again. Clair crept up behind her and slammed the 'closed' sign on the counter.

"If you think it's not too much trouble—and you can pry yourself away from that television set for five seconds, I'd like some help finishing up so we can close. What do think? Can you do that for me?" she demanded, clearly exasperated.

Nadine clutched her heart. "Damn it, Clair! You ought not to sneak up on an old woman like that! You could've given me a heart attack. I about pissed my pants!"

Clair grumbled. "You're going to give yourself a heart attack letting yourself get all riled up over something that's over and done. They found the person responsible, so we can all go back to our peaceful, normal lives. Well, peaceful, anyway." She snickered.

Nadine flashed a sheepish grin. "Now Clair, you can't tell me you're not just a little curious how that old woman knew those things. I was talking to Maggie and she said in her opinion—"

"Now you listen to me, and listen close. A couple of years before Buddy died, God rest his soul, he took me to see a magic show over in Hot Springs and did I ever tell you they have one of the finest wax museums?"

"What's this got to do with anything?" Nadine smirked.

"Okay, okay. I'll get to the point. They had this magician there. I think his name was…well, I can't remember, but supposedly he could read people's minds. I'd seen it on TV a million times. I knew it had to be a trick but never could figure it out. It just so happened that, after the show, Buddy told him I was dying. I know, don't say it. He told him it had always been a wish of mine to know the trick. Do you know how they do it, Nadine?"

"No. So are you going to tell me sometime today?"

"I'm trying to tell you, if you'll listen. They have what is called a 'plant' in the audience. People working with him are put in the audience to find out information. They send it back to each other in codes. That's what's going on. We're going to find out this old woman is working with someone, trying, for whatever reason, to scare us. So yeah, I'm curious as to how she knew those things, but I know there's a logical explanation."

Nadine placed her hands on her hips. "Well, that was a fine story. That explains it all. We have a surefire magician in our town. Do ya think she planted the body there, too? Or maybe he told her in some sort of code what he was going to do before he blew his head off."

Clair clenched her fists. "How about I send you a code right now. Can you read my mind?"

Nadine moved closer, pointing her finger in Clair's face. "I'll finish up while you close out the cash drawer. You might want to loosen up them fists. You're liable to bust a vein."

FRANK WAS busy moving stock around on the shelves when Maggie came through the door. He had not expected her in for another two weeks, but it was a nice surprise.

As a young man in high school, he had carried a crush for Maggie, but after asking her out on more than one occasion, and being turned down, he had finally given up.

Divorced for two years, he shared custody of his thirteen-year-old son Joe, whom he adored. Very private about his personal life, he never spoke much about his troubled marriage. His ex-wife Lisa, on the other hand, had mentioned to friends on several occasions that she feared his obsession with guns.

Frank was an old-school kind of guy, thought the husband should be the breadwinner, while the wife's duty was to take care of the home. His old-fashioned ways put a damper on his dating scene. He spent most of his free time at gun shows and Larry's Bar on the weekends. Truth was, he'd never gotten over his schoolboy crush on Maggie, and thought of her as the one that got away.

With a broad smile, he straightened his tie and jumped over the counter as she walked in the door.

"How are we doing today, Maggie?"

"I'm okay, Frank, just a little tired. I was on my way home from work, thought I'd check on that ceiling fan I ordered. Has it come in yet?"

"I'm sorry, that particular one is on back order, but it should be in any day. I promise, the minute it arrives I'll call you. Speaking of calling," he muttered, nervously tapping his fingers on the counter, "I worry about you living alone way out there."

He reached under the counter and pulled out a handgun. He offered it to Maggie. "I know how you feel about guns, but you'll probably never have to use it. Just put it in your drawer and it'll be there if you need it."

Maggie shook her head. "I don't know the first thing about using a weapon. I'm not sure it would make me feel safer."

"Well, I disagree. I don't know about you, but I don't want to depend on our tiny little police force to protect us. I'll come by soon and show you how to use it. There's nothing to it. Just aim and pull the trigger."

While thinking about it, she slid the gun into her purse, thinking why not?

Frank smiled. "I'm going to call you soon and we'll get together."

"Feel free to try," Maggie whispered, glad to be out of the store.

CHAPTER
11

SHOWERS GAVE way to a magnificent rainbow, arching from one end of Patton to the other. Brilliant colors were magnified by the rolling hills that sat high above the valley below.

"Shannon, baby," James whispered, "look outside at how beautiful it is."

Glancing outside, Shannon quickly looked back. "Yeah, sweetie, that's nice. Guess what happened today? You're never going to guess!"

"Did Ed McMahan call? Did we win a million dollars?"

Shannon playfully poked him in the chest. "Stop playing around and listen."

"Okay, I give. What happened?"

"Dr. Delacruz called today from the institution over in Thebes. It appears my mother has taken a turn for the better. He wants me to meet him at the hospital in the morning so he can go over her progress."

James smiled. "That's great news, honey. Do you think she may be released?"

Shannon lit a cigarette and exhaled. "You know what, maybe we shouldn't make this out to be more than it is. I'm sure she still has a long way to go in her recovery before they would make such a decision."

James sensed her tension. "Why don't I get us a couple of beers? We can relax on the porch and watch the sunset."

Shannon relaxed her head on James's shoulder and gazed up at the sky. "The sunset is spectacular."

Stroking her cheek, he gazed directly into her eyes. "Yeah, almost as beautiful as you."

"James."

"What, sweetie?"

"I know I can be a bit much sometimes, but I don't know what I'd do if I didn't have you in my life."

"I feel the same way, babe."

They sat in silence, holding each other. All the craziness in their lives seemed to disappear, if only for a short while.

Across town, Maggie stood and gazed at the same sunset, but found it difficult to find any beauty in it.

Placing her hair in a ponytail, she slid into her pajamas and tried to relax. She poured a glass of wine and flipped through the channels, but nothing caught her attention. Her mind began to wander.

A dark, repressed secret resurfaced. She closed her eyes and slumped back into the recliner. Her pulse began to race as panic overtook her. The dead silence surrounded the anguish of what lie ahead. In the dim light, she saw his shadow as he crept toward her. She would not make a sound. She could not. She felt the calluses on his hand as he clasped her mouth. The touch of the cold floor on her back did not lessen the painful burning inside. With each thrust, she could feel her soul being ripped away. Clutching her teddy bear, she prayed this time would be the last.

Maggie had never revealed her dark secret to anyone except Shannon. Her father took their secret to his grave. Maggie knew that when her mother died, she had not been aware of his illicit acts, as she had been a victim of his violence and deceitfulness as well.

CHAPTER

12

LARRY AWOKE at five a.m. as usual to the aroma of fresh coffee and Edith's homemade biscuits. He had not slept but a few hours as he and the sheriff had overindulged themselves the night before with shots of their favorite whiskey.

Pouring Larry a fresh cup of coffee and buttering him a biscuit, Edith sat down across from him. "Okay mister, you want to tell me what went on last night?"

"I'm sorry, honey." Larry patted her hand. "It won't happen again. We just got a little carried away, that's all."

"Uh-huh. You've got to do better than that," Edith replied, raising a brow.

"Well, remember the unsolved murder of that poor family? How they were looking for the people responsible? Bill found him."

Edith grinned. "That's great news!"

"Yeah, but there's more to the story." Larry's voice rose with excitement. "He found him exactly where the old woman said he would. The circumstances are odd, don't ya think?"

Edith leaned forward. "Old woman? I recall that old woman had a name. Lola, I believe it was, and whether she knew somehow by the grace of God, or be it just coincidence, people ought to be thankful that she was right."

"Yeah, but—"

"Enough of this." Edith pointed toward the sink, full of dirty dishes. "I've got a million things to do around here today. I have to bake cakes for the church, then—"

Frank stood up. "Okay, okay, I get it. I need to get a hold of James, anyway, to see if he can help me finish patching that leaky roof at the bar."

CHAPTER
13

JAMES RAN a comb through his hair as he stood looking out the window. "Looks like rain again. What time is the appointment with your mother's doctor?"

"This morning, "Shannon answered, "but I've got to run by the office and finish up some paperwork first. Then I guess I'll head over that way."

"I'm sure everything will be fine. Your mother is getting better, so that's exciting news in itself, isn't it?"

Shannon nodded in agreement, as she took her hair down and began redoing it for the fourth time.

James started to leave the room just as the phone rang. He stopped to answer it.

"That was Larry wanting me to come by the bar later and take a look at his roof. I might be a little late getting back," he said as he kissed her goodbye. "Okay, I'm off."

Shannon sat on the edge of the bed trying to collect her thoughts. She recalled the day they took her mother away; a memory she had suppressed for years.

Shannon had asked her mother that fateful day…"What do you think about going to the drive-in and catching a picture show? I heard they're having a double feature over in Delta tonight."

Then when they were on the way to the movie, Katrina fidgeted in the driver's seat, first looking in the rearview mirror and then to the side in a panic.

"You see that car behind us," Katrina murmured. "I think it's following us."

There's no one there." Shannon looked in her side mirror but saw no one. "They must've turned off."

Katrina's face was flushed, and tiny beads of sweat were forming on her upper lip. Her hands shook as she clenched the steering wheel. The look in her eyes was that of a frightened animal. She began to weave back and forth across the centerline.

Fearing a disaster, Shannon begged her mother to pull over and stop.

Reluctantly, her mother agreed.

"Mother, why don't you give me the keys? I'll drive the rest of the way home. You can sit back and relax. It's been a long day."

Katrina handed her the keys, calmly stepped out of the car and made her way around to the other side. She opened the passenger door, leaned in, and began waving her hands hysterically.

"You're not safe with me, baby. They're coming after me!"

Shannon rolled her eyes. "No one is coming after you. Just get in the car."

Katrina looked around wildly. "Do you hear that? I hear them coming. I told you they were following us!"

Looking in the rearview, Shannon could see a vehicle approaching. She made one last plea. "Mother, please get in the car so we can go home!"

Katrina backed slowly away from the car. "I will let them kill me, baby. That's what they want to do, anyway."

Shannon watched helplessly as her mother walked directly in front of the oncoming car. Before she could stop her, it was over. The tires screeched as the car slid sideways, scraping the side of her mother's body.

Amazingly, Katrina made a full recovery. This was just one of many death-defying stunts she had pulled. Nevertheless, her paranoia and schizophrenic behavior had now taken complete control over her life.

Gently rubbing her temples, Shannon laid back on the mattress. Terrorizing memories such as this made her head throb and her stomach queasy. She thought of her father often and missed him dearly. It did not matter to her that he had been a drunk and seldom ever there for her. She loved him just the same, or as much as one could, given the circumstances.

CHAPTER
14

IT WAS a slow start of the workweek and Clair could not get motivated. The steady thud of a bass drum beat in her ears brought about nausea with the slightest movement. As usual, the day she could have really used her help, Nadine was late again.

Grabbing a cola out of the cooler, Clair popped a couple of aspirins and prayed for relief.

In the middle of dressing one of the mannequins, she stopped for a moment, looking through the window and across the street. She saw the 'closed' sign still hanging in Maggie's window and her parking space empty. Maybe she's just running late, Clair thought as she finished dressing the mannequin.

Nadine came bouncing through the door, half out of breath. "Sorry I'm late. I chased Arnold around the yard for thirty minutes trying to get him into the house. I finally bribed him inside with a hotdog."

Arnold was Nadine's Chihuahua, her prized possession. She'd rescued him from the dog pound before they could put him to sleep. Feeling lonely after her husband had died and not having any children to fill the void, Arnold became her family. Small but fearless, he made her feel safe.

Clair tried to keep a straight face, which was nearly impossible. Visualizing Nadine chasing after Arnold and enticing him with a hotdog was highly entertaining.

"Here," Clair said, handing her a clipboard. "Go start the inventory. I'll dress the other mannequin."

Nadine directed Clair's attention across the street. "By the way, did you notice Maggie isn't at work yet?"

"Yeah, I hope nothing's wrong."

"Well, a little bird told me they overheard Maggie and Frank talking at the hardware store. It sounded as if they were making a date. Maybe they're both going to be late for work today."

Clair huffed an indignant breath. "Nadine!"

"What?"

"Do you believe everything you hear? Anyway, it's none of our business."

"Well, there's no way that'll work out." Nadine said, tapping her pencil against the clipboard. "You know Frank's light bulb ain't too bright as it is."

"Nadine, I swear!"

"What? You know I'm telling the truth. He's just a little too close to those guns of his. No, now that I think about it, no one has seen or heard from Frank's ex-wife since she left town. Maybe she never left town, maybe old Frank took one of his guns and—"

"Okay, that's enough," Clair cut her off. "We've got work to do."

Finishing the last touches on the mannequin in the window display, Clair glanced across the street again, only to wonder, with so many crazy things happening lately, what might happen next.

ON THE way to Larry's Bar, James made a last-minute decision and took a detour. He stopped the car a few feet from the turnoff leading to the old Parker's farm, and he sat for a moment staring at the sign that read 'Hand-stitched Embroidered Quilts.' He tapped his fingers on the steering wheel as he looked from side to side, glancing in the rearview mirror, then back straight ahead. Curious, he turned and drove up the gravel road about a mile before stopping at the edge of the driveway.

He noticed right away that two years of being vacant had taken its toll on what was once a beautiful two-story home. Now overgrown with shrubbery, a loose shutter torn away by the wind flapped back and forth; the white paint was yellowed and chipped from neglect. The branches of a weeping willow cradled a small, rusted swing not far from the house, a sad reminder of happier times.

Wanting to turn and get the hell out of there, while at the same time drawn to venture further, he decided to continue on. Before he could knock on the door, it opened.

"Welcome, my child. What took you so long?" Lola asked.

"Uh-huh. How do you do, ma'am? I was just passing by and thought I'd take a look at your quilts for sale," James answered nervously, adjusting his ball cap.

"Yes, I have many lovely quilts, but that's not what you came for," the old woman replied.

"Well, yes ma'am, it is. I read your sign. They are for sale, right?"

"Lola."

James blinked. "Excuse me?"

"Call me Lola," the old woman said. "Have you ever had a reading, my son?"

James shook his head. "I don't really believe in—"

"Oh, but you will, dear. Come in," she insisted. "Sit down and relax. I'll get us a cup of tea."

He thought it odd that the normal sounds of a teakettle whistling in the kitchen, and Lola's cane tapping the floor as she moved about in the other room, now came across as eerie.

On the coffee table in front of him sat a rather large black book outlined in gold trim with undecipherable writing on the front cover. Curious, he reached to open it, when unexpectedly something brushed up against the bottom of his pant leg.

Staring up at him with intense green eyes, tail swishing back and forth, was a cat as black as night. Yep, made sense. A witch usually owned a black cat.

Lola emerged from the kitchen, cane in one hand while trying to balance the tray.

James moved toward her. "Here, let me help you with that."

"Thank you dear. By the way, I see you've met Mila. Do you think that is a fitting name for a witch's cat?"

"Are you really a witch?"

"Are you?" Lola asked, looking him up and down.

"I'm not the one going around scaring people with outrageous stories, talking about disasters and dark omens that are supposedly going to take place. You are."

Lola's expression darkened. "What's your definition of a witch, James?"

"Well I really don't—"

"No, you don't. Let's just say I'd rather you refer to me as a spiritual guide. Make no mistake, James, evil is lurking closer than you think."

"If you know so much, why don't you tell us who or what this danger is, so we can stop it before it happens?"

She picked up the book that lay in front of him, and shoved it into his hands. "Until you believe, I cannot help you. Open it, James. Inside you will find some valuable information. It will reveal the dark side of the people you love. You will find out who is not as loyal as you think. I'm giving you a chance to see into the future."

Laying the book on the table, he backed away. "I don't want any part of this book, or you, for that matter. There's been nothing but chaos since you arrived here. Best thing you could do is to go back to where you came from. I don't even know why I stopped here."

Their eyes met for a moment before he shook his head in disbelief and headed out the door.

CHAPTER
15

SHANNON, NERVOUS about her impending visit with Dr. Delacruz, had used every excuse she could to stay at the office. Therefore, now to arrive on time she had no choice but to take the shortcut to the interstate, a drive she and many of the other townspeople often tried to avoid. The scenery along the way was somewhat unsettling.

Cutting across a twisted gravel road onto County Road 107, just a mile and a half from the interstate, high above the valley, she could see it: the old Hillcrest Asylum. Rusted wrought-iron gates outlined the front of the huge moss-covered concrete structure, looking like a place right out of an Alfred Hitchcock movie. It was said that when the wind blew just right, you could hear blood-curdling screams echoing below. Hillcrest was known to accommodate some of the most psychotic criminals in the state. Shannon made good time, and arrived in Thebes earlier than expected.

Dr. Mary Delaney met her at the front desk and introduced herself. "I'm Dr. Delaney, Dr. Delacruz's assistant, and you must be Shannon."

"Yes, I'm Katrina White's daughter and I have an appointment," Shannon said, shaking his hand.

"Please have a seat. Dr. Delacruz will be with you very shortly. May I get you a cup of coffee?"

"No, thank you. I've had enough caffeine for one day already."

Shannon looked around for something familiar. Everything appeared much different than she remembered. Patients now walked around freely, enjoying conversations with one another. Glancing out onto the gated landscape through an enormous glass window to her right, she observed patients mingling with one another. Previously, under no circumstances were patients allowed outside, and the frequent screams of the insane echoed from within the walls.

"Hello, Shannon. I'm sorry I kept you waiting." Dr. Delacruz reached for her hand. "I know you're anxious to see your mother. I have some paperwork we need to go over in my office first, and then we can proceed."

Shannon followed him and settled in a chair across from his desk.

"I know you're eager to know why I've scheduled this meeting, my dear. Your mother has made tremendous improvement, and in the past few months, my colleagues and I have extensively evaluated her. We agree that, with the combination of her medicines and psychotherapy, she will be able to cope in the outside world."

"I didn't expect this," Shannon said quietly.

"As you know, there have been several key innovations in the medical field since the time your mother arrived here. I feel that your knowledge in the field of psychology will be an advantage to you both. We can release your mother, but only if you agree to be her sole guardian. Katrina must meet with her therapist once a week and her medicine schedule should be strictly enforced. I know this is a huge responsibility, but you must make a decision, one way or another."

Shannon was silent for a long moment. "I must say this is somewhat of a shock," she said. "I never really thought this day would come."

The doctor smiled. "Why don't I take you to her room now, so you can witness your mother's improvement for yourself."

They walked the long corridor to the fifth wing, where they stopped in front of Katrina's small, isolated room. The guard unlocked the door and Shannon stepped in.

Katrina, looking fragile and pale, sat in the corner reading a book. Gone was the appearance of the strong, domineering woman that Shannon remembered.

Dropping her book, Katrina rushed to Shannon and wrapped her arms around her daughter. "Oh, my darling, you haven't forsaken me. My baby has come to take me home!"

Shannon's thoughts were grim, she knew her life was about to drastically change.

LARRY WAS getting worried. James should have been here by now. Just as he reached for the phone, James burst through the door, face flushed and covered in sweat.

"Hey buddy, you alright? You look like you just saw a ghost!"

"I think I just might have, at that. Is it too early for a drink?"

"Slow down, partner," Larry said.

James caught his breath. "On my way here I decided to stop off at that place right outside of town."

Larry lifted a brow. "You mean the old farmhouse on the Parkers' farm?"

"You heard about it?"

"Oh yeah," Larry confirmed, moving in closer. "The sheriff told me all about it. That Lola woman from the town meeting set up some sort of quilting store. Why on earth did you go there?"

"I don't know. Curiosity, I guess. I wish I hadn't."

"Well, what happened?"

"I'll tell ya what happened, she scared the crap out of me. She started acting like she could read my mind. She had this damn black cat. Without saying a word, I thought to myself, this makes sense. You know, a witch and a black cat. Then she called me on it. Asked me why I thought she was a witch."

Larry's eyes widened. "Hell, you say! So what'd ya say to that?"

"What could I say? Then she hands me this book, tells me to open it. Says the answers to everything she's warned us about are inside, tells me I just have to believe."

"Believe in what?

"Hell, I don't know. I guess believe in her bullshit."

"Well?"

"Well what, Larry?"

"Did ya look at the book?"

"Yeah, sure. It said you were going to grow a new arm and a full head of hair. Hell no, I didn't look at it! I threw it down and got the hell out of there."

Larry ran his hand over his bald head. "Just when I thought I was going to get my arm back."

"Oh hell, Larry. I'm sorry. I shouldn't have said that."

"Don't worry about it, son. You did the right thing. Getting the hell out of there, I mean. There's something too strange about that old dame. Come on, help me with this roof and I'll tell ya what the sheriff had to say."

"Don't tell anybody about this, especially Shannon, okay?" James begged.

"Hell no, son! My lips are sealed!"

CHAPTER
16

THE INVENTORY almost finished, Nadine took a break. She had just sat down to enjoy an ice-cold cola when Frank came plowing through the front door.

"My, to what do we owe this honor?" she asked. "Shouldn't you be over at your hardware store, cleaning a gun or something?"

Clair shot Nadine a sharp glare before turning to Frank. "You'll have to excuse Nadine. She's just pissy because she actually had to do some work around here. What can we do for you?"

Frank glanced down at his wristwatch. "Well, I thought I'd stop across the street and get a cup of coffee and visit with Maggie a minute before heading to work, but she wasn't there. Did she close the store today for some reason?"

Nadine smirked. "What did I tell you, Clair?" This earned her another glare from her friend.

Why don't you go in the back and price those new scarves that came in." Clair shook her head dismissively.

"To tell ya the truth Frank, I'm a little worried myself. I've never known Maggie to open up late. I hope she's not sick or something worse. Maybe one of us ought to drive out to her house.

Frank nodded. "You're right." He paced back and forth across the floor. "It's better to be safe than sorry, especially now that we know our little town isn't as safe as we thought it was. I'm going to take a drive out to her house, check on her."

"I'm sure everything is fine," Clair said, staring across the street. "We're probably making something out of nothing. She probably just overslept. But like you said, better to be safe than sorry."

MAGGIE ROLLED back and forth, fighting with the bed covers. Nightmares had kept her awake almost the entire night. She dragged herself out of bed, headed to the bathroom, and poured herself a glass of water from the faucet. Opening the store on time today was the furthest thing from her mind. Her head throbbed and her body ached all over. Scavenging through the medicine cabinet, she found an old prescription bottle half full of sedatives that Shannon had given her. Unscrewing the lid, she poured a couple of pills into her hand and swallowed them down with a gulp of water. She yanked the phone cord from the wall, sank back into bed, and pulled the covers over her head.

Dark thoughts twirled endlessly in her mind. Distorted images appeared, ravaging her body and soul. The more she tried to push them away, the more violent and forceful they became.

Maggie's dark thoughts were suddenly interrupted when she heard the front door open and slam shut. Her eyes fixed on the bedroom door, she watched in fright as the doorknob turned and the door began to slowly open.

She bolted straight up out of bed. Fearing for her life, she reached under the mattress, grabbed the handgun Frank had given her for protection. Jumping to her feet, without hesitation, she fired straight ahead. The cold steel in her hands numbed her fingers. With each release of the trigger, her ears rang. The deafening blasts echoed in the room. Her hands shook uncontrollably, causing her to drop the gun. What seemed like forever had been only seconds.

She opened her eyes and fell to her knees. Her bedroom door and wall were splattered with blood and shreds of human flesh. A trail of blood leading from the body trickled into the cracks of the hardwood floor. Just a few feet away a bullet-ridden body lie facedown.

Maggie reached for the phone. No dial tone. She thought the intruder must have cut the cord, forgetting that she had unplugged it herself. She crawled to the body, and, with all her strength, rolled him over.

Staring up at her, eyes glazed over, blood streaming out of his mouth, Frank gave one last breath, preceded by a gurgling sound, then there was silence.

Maggie, covered in Frank's blood, curled up in a fetal position not far from his body. "What have I done?" she cried repeatedly. Her mind could not grasp what had happened. Several moments passed before she finally realized what her foolish actions had caused.

She panicked. She felt no one would ever believe it was an accident. She'd have to make it all go away, like it never happened.

Wasting no time, she wrapped Frank's body in a blanket and dragged him to the back door. She raced to the bathroom, grabbed a bucket of bleach and a bundle of rags, only stopping long enough to vomit. Quick and calculating, she wiped away all traces of blood from the bedroom, taking caution to throw her nightgown, shell casings, and murder weapon into a plastic bag.

Out in the tool shed, she grabbed a shovel and began digging the hole that would become Frank's grave.

Finally, Maggie knelt down on trembling knees and, with every ounce of strength she had left, she rolled Frank's body into the hole, along with the plastic bag.

After she drove Frank's truck a couple of miles down the road, she hammered several nails into two of the tires, and then made sure to wipe away any traces of blood.

Furiously, she ran back to the house, jumped in the shower, and scrubbed her blood-stained skin until her flesh became raw. Her hands violently trembled as she fought to button her blouse. Pausing for a moment, she wandered through the house, looking for anything incriminating she might have missed.

Maggie's soul and mind no longer belonged to her; a cold and diabolical shell of a human being had replaced them.

CHAPTER
17

SHANNON GLANCED out her drivers' side window and then over toward her mother. "You know many things have changed in Patton, since you've been gone."

Katrina's eyes began to fill with tears. "I don't want to be a burden to you, Shannon. I know you've made your own way and I'm proud of you for that. I know you've always blamed me for your father leaving us, but it wasn't my fault. He was consumed by alcohol. That's what destroyed our lives and eventually his."

"That was a long time ago," Shannon said. "This is now. Let's take it one day at a time, shall we?"

"I don't remember much of my life back then," Katrina murmured, looking down at her hands folded in her lap.

Shannon never imagined that she would be sitting this close to her mother again; furthermore let alone conversing with her.

"You know what?" Shannon snapped, now agitated, "I've spent most of my life since that time trying to forget the past."

Katrina cleared her throat and smiled sadly at her daughter. "I've always loved you, Shannon."

Shannon tightened her grip on the steering wheel and slowly maneuvered the car onto the side of the road. "Loved me? Did I hear you say you've always loved me?"

"I've always loved—"

"No, no, let me tell you what I remember. I remember overhearing a conversation between you and my father in which you were cursing the day I was born, that's what I remember! Oh, and did you ever tell him about the numerous men you shared your bed with when he was away?"

"I've said and done many hurtful things," Katrina said, looking away. "I only wish I could take it all back."

Shannon sighed. "Let's just forget we had this conversation. Let's just try to concentrate on now." She proceeded to slowly navigate back onto the road.

Katrina suddenly yelled, "Stop the car! Stop the car! Did you see that?"

As quick as Shannon could stop the car, Katrina jumped out of the passenger side and pointed. "Over there, Shannon, you see? Is that the most beautiful sight you've ever seen?"

Up on the ridge overlooking them was a doe and her fawn, impervious to their presence.

Katrina smiled. "You know what? I would trade my soul in a minute to be wild and free like those creatures of God."

Shannon took away a somewhat different view and was quick to express it. "Be careful what you wish for, Katrina. In a few months those wild and free creatures of God will be hunted down and killed, heads taken as trophies."

LARRY AND James worked right through lunch laying the last few bundles of shingles when they discovered they were short of what was needed to finish the job.

Larry patted his belly. "What do you say we grab a burger?"

"Sounds good to me," James replied. "We can stop off at Frank's hardware afterwards and get some more shingles."

It seemed that everyone in town wanted to try out the new burger joint.

"Hey James, look. Isn't that Clair and Nadine sitting over there in that back booth?"

"Hey, how are you two beautiful ladies doing today?" James called out.

Nadine giggled. "Great, now that you handsome men are here to pick up our tab."

"On one condition," Larry said. "Only if you let us join you."

"By the way, where's Maggie?" James asked, looking around.

"That's a good question. Nadine said, moving her purse so he could sit down. "I think she and Frank probably had a late breakfast."

James looked surprised. "Since when did Maggie and Frank become an item?"

"Oh it's nothing like that. Clair quickly replied. "Frank just stopped by my boutique this morning and noticed Maggie hadn't opened the store. I asked him if he'd mind driving out to her place just to make certain everything was okay. She must have just over-slept or something, cause we saw her pull up as we were leaving. There's really nothing more to it."

Nadine butted in. "Well, Frank was pretty quick to volunteer his help. I think he'd use any excuse to go by her house. One of my friends overheard him asking her out the other day, and from what they said it sounded like she accepted."

James sipped on his cola as if unaware of Nadine's remarks. He knew that Nadine could exaggerate from time to time, so he changed the subject. "Well, I have some good news. Shannon is visiting her mother today. It appears the doctors think she's making major improvement."

"Oh James, that's great! Clair said. "That family has been through some tough times. I remember the day Katrina was hauled off to that sanitarium. It broke Shannon's heart. Is there a chance she may be released?"

"That's the way it looks."

"I think you and Shannon are a great little couple," I wish only the best for you both, and Katrina as well. Hey, this may be a new chapter in your life."

James smiled. "Can I ask you something?"

Clair nodded. "Sure."

"I know you've known Shannon and her family for years."

"Oh yes, since she was a little girl."

"Well, what I'm getting at is, she never has really opened up to me about her mother, told me it was a part of her life that she'd just as soon forget."

Nadine leaned across the table. "Oh, I could tell ya a few things!"

Larry patted her on the shoulder. "Why don't you come help me pick a song on the jukebox, Nadine, so James and Clair can have a minute alone."

Reluctantly she agreed.

Clair waited until Nadine and Larry were gone before continuing. "Now, where were we? Oh, yes. You were asking about Shannon's Mother. Well, as far back as I can remember, she had always been a sick woman."

"Exactly what do you mean by sick?" James asked.

Clair searched for the right words. "Feeble-minded. She had some mental issues."

"That I'm aware of, but did she ever abuse Shannon? I mean physically or mentally that you're aware of?"

Clair hesitated. "Well, it's really not my place to tell you this, but from what I remember after Howard left, things only got worse. Katrina could never hold a job for very long due to her nervous condition, and ended up having to take odd jobs as they came. Worse than that, she was well known around town as a loose woman, if you know what I mean."

James nodded. "I know it had to be difficult for Shannon, to see her mother with someone other than her father. She loved him so much."

"That wasn't the worst of it. Katrina would often have raging fits in public. Out of nowhere down at the A&P grocery store on Smith Street, she started stripping her clothes off and screaming obscenities at everyone around her. She spent more than a few nights in the psycho ward at the hospital."

"How old was Shannon at that time?" James asked.

"Oh, I'd say a very young teenager. I'll tell you the most disturbing thing during that time…many of their neighbors' pets came up missing, one by one. The kids in town tormented Shannon, said her crazy mother probably killed them and then buried them in their back yard."

James shook his head. "Kids can be cruel."

Everyone shook their heads in agreement.

James paused a moment, then replied, "Bet they didn't apologize when their pets came wandering back, did they?"

A few seconds passed as Clair took a sip of her coffee, glanced over at Nadine, and then back up at James before answering. "As I recall they didn't have a chance too. Not a one was ever found."

CHAPTER
18

AFTER MAGGIE hung the 'open' sign in the store window, she tried to focus on what to do next. The image of Frank looking up at her and taking his last breath flashed continuously, clouding every thought. Looking down at her hands, she could still see and feel Frank's blood, even though they were clean. She tried to focus. She worried if she had left any evidence that could be linked back to her.

Maggie's thoughts were interrupted when James and Larry came walking in.

"Hey guys, what can I get you today?" she asked them, forcing a pleasant smile.

"Hey Maggie, have you seen Frank?" James asked.

Maggie stiffened slightly, but remained calm. "No, I just got here a few minutes ago. I wasn't feeling well and overslept this morning. Did you try the hardware store?"

James nodded. "Yeah, we just left there. It doesn't look like he's opened today. Clair said she sent him over to your house this morning to check on you. She was concerned because you hadn't made it in to work.

Maggie expressed a puzzled look. "Well, I guess I could have been in the shower and didn't hear him knock. I didn't feel well this morning and overslept. Matter of fact I almost didn't come in today. I don't remember passing him on the road but I was in a hurry."

"I'm sure everything's all right," James replied. "Knowing Frank, he probably ran out of gas or got sidetracked somewhere along the way. Me and Larry will drive out that way, see if we see him."

Grabbing two cups of coffee to go, Larry handed the money to Maggie.

"What in the world did you do to your hands?" he asked, staring down at them. "Looks like you rubbed the skin right off of 'um."

Maggie, caught off guard, looked down at her hands and then up at Larry.

"That's what I get for shoveling in my garden without gloves. I was in such a hurry to put my plants out yesterday before it got dark, I didn't take the time to wear any."

"Well, we better get going. Don't worry about Frank; we'll track him down. Take care of those hands."

James did not say two words to Larry after leaving the restaurant. His disturbing conversation with Clair still fresh on his mind, he could hardly concentrate on the road. He wanted to know more. He could not understand why Shannon had not been more open with him about her traumatic childhood. He had promised her that he would not pry into her past, that he would wait until she was ready to open up. The more he thought about what Clair had said, the more he understood Shannon's reluctance.

"James, stop! Look over there, isn't that Frank's truck?"

The two men pulled to the side of the road and got out.

"Now that's what I call a flat tire," James said, kicking the wheel.

Larry opened the driver-side door, reached in, and pulled the keys from the ignition. "If old Frank bummed a ride, why didn't he take his keys?"

James shrugged. "Doesn't make any sense, does it?"

"And what do we have here?" Larry pulled a loaded gun out from underneath the driver's seat.

"That's Frank's gun for sure," James answered, eyeing it. "Or one of um,' anyway. Don't think Frank would leave his loaded gun under the driver's seat."

"No," Larry agreed, looking in the truck's bed. "And it doesn't make sense to have a jack and a spare tire in the back of your truck and not use um,' either."

James looked over at Larry and shook his head. "You thinking the same thing I'm thinking?"

"Yes sir, I am. Something just ain't right about this. I've got a bad feeling something's happened to old Frank."

Larry unloaded Frank's handgun, shoving the bullets into his pocket. "You know yourself; Frank would've taken his loaded gun with him. And he definitely knows how to change a flat tire."

"Yeah, I think you're right. It doesn't make sense." James walked around to the back of the truck. "Hey Larry, Frank and me have about the same size feet, right?"

"Yeah. Why you ask?"

James pointed toward the ground. "Well, look at these footprints leading away from the truck. Whoever left these had a much smaller foot than ours. Tell ya what, lock up your truck and we'll see where they lead."

James and Larry continued along the dirt road.

"What do ya know," James said. "Looks like the footprints are leading right up to Maggie's place."

"Yep, sure are."

"Are you thinking what I'm thinking?"

Larry scratched his head. "Yeah, none of this makes sense."

James removed his ball cap and kicked the dirt. "Maggie said she hadn't seen Frank, but yet his truck is sitting two miles from her house. The footprints we followed back here were definitely not his."

Larry seemed reluctant to speak. You remember those blisters on her hands?"

"Yeah."

"Well, didn't she say they were caused from gardening without any gloves?"

James nodded. "That's what she said."

Larry looked around. "I don't see any flowers or plants in her yard. Do you?"

"No, but it looks like someone's been digging over there," James said, pointing to a spot a few feet from the back door. "Looks like fresh dirt. What do you make of it?"

"Don't know. But I think it's time we pay the sheriff a visit."

SHANNON HELPED carry her mother's bags into the house and began preparing the guestroom while Katrina unpacked her things. While watching her mother, Shannon wondered what was going through her mind. She could not imagine being locked away from the world with little or no contact with the outside.

Katrina took a break and sat on the front porch enjoying the cool breeze while Shannon prepared them a snack. The sun was setting against an indigo sky, which gave way to glorious colors of ginger and crimson. The wind blew softly through her hair and across her face as she reclined in a lawn chair. Tucking her skirt underneath her legs, Katrina caught a glimpse of something disturbing. She starred at her hands and arms, sadly realizing that time had festooned them with brown age spots and wrinkles. She ran her fingers along the deep lines that ran up and down her face. The dress she had once filled out quite nicely now hung loose against her thin body. How could I have not noticed all this before? When did this happen to me?

"I know you must be starving." Shannon leaned over, handing her a sandwich and a drink. "There's more where that came from."

"How thoughtful of you. Thank you, dear. I know it's an awkward situation for both of us, but we'll work through it." Katrina took a bite and swallowed hard. "Things will be different this time, Shannon. You'll see."

AS MAGGIE approached her house, she met a wrecker pulling a vehicle. She held her breath. They were towing Frank's truck. Her mind raced. Had Larry and James found Frank's truck and reported it to the sheriff?

Once again, she ran into the house and started searching for any evidence of her guilt. She gasped when she noticed the paint on her bedroom wall and door appeared blotchy and streaked, due to the bleach she had used earlier. She fought to keep her emotions under control as she walked outside and passed Frank's grave toward the shed. After grabbing a paint roller and a gallon of paint, she hurried back inside. She pried open the lid and carefully applied a quick coat of paint. Exhausted and mentally drained she took a shower, and tried to relax.

Her head barely hit the pillow when a loud noise from the other room rang out. How ironic, she thought. Frank's gun would have come in handy about now.

What she saw would defy all logic. Springing to her feet, her legs trembled as she stumbled backwards against the wall. Maggie was face to face with the horror.

With his bloodshot eyes fixed on hers, Frank's ghost tilted his head as if in confusion. His pale white skin hung from his bones. Insects crawled in and out of the holes in his blood-stained tattered clothing. Thick, dried blood covered his hands. Raw skin hung from the ends of his fingers where his nails once were.

Why is this happening to me? I must be losing my mind!

"You seem surprised to see me, Maggie," Frank's ghostly image whispered in a gurgling voice.

Maggie stared into his dark hollow eyes. "This can't be!" she screamed, "You're dead. I killed you!"

"Yes, I might add. And just when I thought we had a connection. Make no mistake: we are still very much connected. It's true you took my life, but there's more to the story. Think about it. Think hard! Are you the one and only culprit responsible for my death? I'm afraid it's much more complicated than you realize!"

Sobbing uncontrollably, Maggie buried her head in her hands. I must be losing my mind!

"Maggie? Are you in there?" Sheriff Chesterton yelled as he pounded on the door. "I need to ask you a few questions."

Crouched in the corner of her bedroom, Maggie raised her head slowly, opened her eyes, and sighed a relief to find her nightmare over.

"Maggie, if you're in there I need you to open the door."

She struggled to get to her feet. She did not know how much more she could endure before losing her mind completely. She closed her eyes for a second, then took a deep breath and opened the door. "What's this about, Sheriff?"

"James and Larry came by the station and reported Frank's truck abandoned on the side of the road about two miles down from you. Seems he had a flat tire. Problem is, nobody's seen him since early this morning. I spoke with Clair and Nadine. They said they were concerned about you, sent Frank out here to check on you."

"I wasn't feeling well this morning and overslept. By the time I got up, I quickly dressed and left in a hurry. We must have just missed each other. You say you found his truck just down the road?"

"Yeah, a couple miles back. It appears he ran over a couple of good-size nails."

Maggie chose her words carefully. "You know, somebody probably gave him a ride and he's sitting at some bar right now boozing it up and swapping gun stories."

"Yeah, you're probably right." The sheriff murmured. He turned away and took a few steps forward. "Oh, one more thing, Maggie," he said, pointing in the direction of the footprints. "There seems to be footprints leading away from Frank's truck, heading in this direction. The strange thing is, they're too small to be Frank's. You haven't seen any trespassers out this way, have you?"

"No, none that I'm aware of. Should I be concerned?"

"I'm sure there isn't anything to be concerned about. I'm going to have one of my men patrol this area to be on the safe side. While I'm here, you mind if I take a look around?"

Maggie hesitated, but only for a moment. "I guess it would be alright, but you'll have to excuse the mess."

Sheriff Chesterton tipped his hat and stepped in. He walked through the house, going from one room to another, and stopped just short of her bedroom.

"Is that fresh paint I smell?"

Maggie glanced toward her room. "As of matter a fact it is, Sheriff. I thought it was about time that old room had a fresh coat of paint. I'm thinking about changing the wallpaper in the kitchen as well."

He followed her through the kitchen and was about to turn around when, out of the corner of his eye, he caught a glimpse of a mound of freshly dug dirt outside the kitchen window.

"You doing some yard work?"

Maggie was quick to answer, having rehearsed this scenario dozens of times in her head. "Oh, you must be talking about my new flower bed. I'm afraid it doesn't look like much now but a pile of dirt."

"Is that how you got those blisters on your hands?"

She glanced down at her hands as if it was the first time she had noticed. "Yeah, you'd think I'd be smart enough to wear gloves."

"Well," the sheriff tipped his hat, "I've taken up enough of your time. Guess I'll be going."

Looking back as he drove away, he couldn't help but wonder if Maggie was hiding something. She had answered his questions without hesitation, but her demeanor was all wrong. He noticed she had looked away too many times when answering his questions. Unconsciously she had wiped sweat from her forehead several times.

Knowing Maggie and her family since she was a young child, he could not imagine her being involved in anything illegal, much less having anything to do with Frank's disappearance. He said a silent prayer for Frank's safe return and hoped he had misread Maggie's behavior.

Exhausted from the search, James could not wait to get home and relax. Throwing his keys on the table near the door, he started to head upstairs.

"James, is that you?"

"Yeah, babe. I'm just going upstairs to relax a bit before dinner."

"Can you come into the kitchen a minute?" I'd like to introduce my—"

"Let me guess." James reached out for the woman's hand kissing it lightly. "This must be Katrina, your lovely mother."

"I was just about to cut us a piece of pie. Why don't you join us? Sit down and I'll cut you a piece."

"I'm not really hungry tonight, Shannon." He took his ball cap off, laid it on the counter, and ran his fingers through his hair. "I do apologize, but if it's okay I'm going to take a shower and lay down for a few minutes. It's nice to have you here, Katrina."

Shannon followed close behind as he walked out of the room.

"Are you upset because my mother's here? You knew it was a possibility."

"No. I'm glad to see your mother is well enough to come home. It's just been a strange day, that's all. Frank's missing, so me and—"

"What do you mean Frank's missing?" Shannon interrupted, eyes wide with shock.

"He never made it to work today," James explained. "Larry and I went by there earlier to get some supplies we needed and the store was locked up tight. Right after that, we saw Clair and Nadine and joined them for lunch. Oh, and get a load of this: they said that Frank had come by the boutique early this morning looking for Maggie."

"Why would Frank be looking for Maggie?"

"It's my understanding that he stopped by her store, and when he found it closed he got worried. That's when they agreed someone should go check on her and Frank offered. That's the last anybody saw of him."

Shannon frowned. "So why do you think he's missing? You know Frank. He's been known to take off from time to time."

"Yeah, but get this: me and Larry found his truck on the side of the road not far from Maggie's place. It was unlocked and his loaded gun was under the seat. Does that sound like Frank to you?"

"No, it doesn't. Did you report it to Sheriff Chesterton?"

James nodded. "Yeah. He's going to drive out to Maggie's and have a look around."

"You sound like you think Maggie might be involved," Shannon surmised.

"There were footprints leading away from Frank's truck. Larry and I followed them right up to Maggie's place and they weren't Frank's. I hate to say it, but my gut tells me Maggie knows something about this."

"There has to be a logical explanation, James. Let's wait and see what the sheriff says."

James nodded. "Yeah, maybe Frank caught a ride with a buddy and they're out boozing it up. But still, my gut tells me he's in trouble."

At the first hint of Frank's disappearance, the townspeople wasted no time making flyers with his picture and posted them everywhere. Frank might not have had many friends, but everyone was distressed to think that someone could just disappear without a trace from their sleepy little town.

People began to speculate on what may have happened. Rumors began to fly. Some said they had heard Frank's business had not been doing well, thought maybe he had decided to fold up and start over somewhere else. Others felt he may have cheated someone on a gun deal and had been murdered out of revenge. Everyone was on edge. The townspeople quickly became suspicious of any stranger that might happen through their little town.

CHAPTER
19

THE TOWNSPEOPLE of Patton held a festival in the downtown park every year about the same time. It included crafts and artwork, a pie-baking contest and a petting zoo for the children. Much of the proceeds went to the First Baptist Church of Patton. Overseeing the project for the past fifteen years was Edith's responsibility, one she thoroughly enjoyed. It was an event where townspeople could get together, feast, have fun, and gossip.

Shannon, like many others, looked forward to experiencing the festivities, and thought it was time Katrina got out and mingled with the community. Katrina had been reluctant to venture beyond the front yard since arriving back home. More importantly, Shannon hoped the festival would lighten up James's dark mood.

"Edith, I think you've outdone yourself this time." Clair leaned in close, savoring the sweet aroma. "That's a prize-winning blueberry pie if I ever saw one."

Nadine licked her lips. "I believe you're right. This is even better than last year. How do you do it?"

"An old recipe passed down for generations," Edith replied.

A large crowd of teenagers gathered at the dunking stand. Youngsters waited patiently in line for their chance to knock Sheriff Chesterton off his platform into the icy tub of water. It was his or her way of getting revenge for every speeding ticket or violation that they had been so unfortunate to receive.

Under a huge tarp, a local band set up their music equipment. One booth after another, adorned with local artwork and handmade jewelry, formed the perimeter of the festival. Even the illusive Lola managed to get in on the festivities.

"Don't tell me that old witch woman is taking a part in our festival," Nadine grumbled. "I'm surprised you would rent her a booth."

Edith shrugged "Why not? She paid her money like everybody else. After all, a large part of the proceeds go to charity, remember."

"I know where the money is going, I just meant—"

"Why don't we take a walk and look around for Shannon and James," Clair said, changing the subject.

Nadine took a bite of cotton candy, licked her fingers, and pointed. "Dear heavens! Is that Shannon's mother I see with her and James?"

"Where?" Clair searched through the crowd.

"Right there, by the dunking booth."

"Guess she did get out of that loony bin after all, huh?"

Clair snatched her cotton candy out of her hand and nudged her on the arm. "Nadine, I swear you'd better behave, or I'm going to dunk you in that ice water myself. Katrina, it's so nice to see you!"

"It's so nice to see you again too, Clair."

"Does it seem strange?" Nadine nudged her way in between the two women. "I mean, being able to walk around so freely and all?"

With a look from Clair that could have frozen a bird in flight, Nadine rephrased her comment. "What I meant to say was, I'm sure this is a big adjustment for you, being around all these people."

Katrina winked. "I only hope my medication doesn't wear off and cause me to have a violent episode."

Nadine blushed, and then lowered her head. The others tried to hide their amusement. It was not often someone could silence Nadine so quickly.

However, it would not be the last sarcastic comment Katrina would have to endure concerning her return home. Many of the townspeople were skeptical about her as well.

After half a pack of cigarettes and a couple of shots of vodka, Maggie staggered out of her car.

Katrina looked up just in time to see her stumble. "Shannon, isn't that your old friend Maggie?"

"Would you like to go over and say hi?" Shannon asked.

"I'm not sure what I'd say. It's been a long time."

"It'll be fine."

Excusing himself, James went to look for Larry.

"Hi, Maggie. You remember my mother? She's staying with me and James for awhile."

"Of course, I remember. It's nice to see you again, Katrina. You look great." She shifted her gaze toward Shannon. "Didn't I see James standing over here with you?"

"Oh, you know James. He didn't want to hang out with us women so he went looking for Larry. Are you feeling okay, Maggie? Your eyes are blood-red and your face looks flushed."

"Well, I haven't slept much lately," she said, retrieving a pair of sunglasses from her purse. "And the heat does bother me."

Shannon opened her purse and took out a bottle of pills.

"Here, take these."

Maggie turned the bottle around, looking for a label. "What are they?"

"It's just a sedative, much like the ones I've given you before. Take two right before bed."

Hesitant, Maggie stared at the bottle.

"You trust me, don't you, Maggie?"

Maggie flashed a slight smile, then slipped the pills into her purse.

James weaved his way in and out of the crowds of people, searching for Larry. Since Larry was an avid lover of country music, James had a good idea where he might find him, and he was right.

"I figured I'd find you here."

Larry nodded a greeting. "Hey there, James. Why so gloomy, fella? The band is half-ass decent, even though I'd rather be listening to Conway Twitty or Merle Haggard. Why, Edith even made an extra blueberry pie and said we could have a piece if we didn't cause any trouble today."

James kicked the dirt with his boot. "Sorry, Larry. Guess I'm just a little edgy."

"What's up?"

"Oh, I almost ran into Maggie over there. I hate feeling like this. The sheriff said there wasn't any solid proof connecting her to Frank's disappearance. You think maybe we overreacted?"

"James, my friend, if Maggie had something to do with old Frank's disappearing, and I don't want to believe it no more than you, but she'll mess up one way or another and it'll all come crumbling down."

James nodded. "Guess you're right. After all, I've known Maggie for a long time. You know the circumstances. Don't know what I was thinking. I've never known her to be violent or deceitful."

Larry patted his foot to the drumbeat and nodded. "Yeah, and around here, the way rumors and gossip fly, I'm sure she could use a friend about now."

As Larry and James continued to discuss Maggie's predicament, a crowd gathered around Lola's table. Close to thirty different styles and designs of quilts lay stacked in her booth. Lola had a way of drawing attention to herself, and no one could be more curious than Nadine.

"Hey Clair, what do you say we take a walk over to the old woman's table and take a closer look at those magnificent quilts? I might be able to find me a new bedspread."

Clair let go of a laugh that even embarrassed her. "Now you know better than that. You don't give a hoot about buying one of those quilts. You're just curious to see if she has anything intriguing to say about the future, or maybe even about you."

Nadine pursed her lips and stuck her chest out. "It must be nice thinking you know everything, Clair. Hell, maybe I ought to be asking you what the future holds, huh? So, are you coming with me or not?"

"No."

"Fine. I'll meet you at the bandstand in a few minutes. Oh! But I bet you already knew that."

It tickled Clair to death to aggravate Nadine. She knew just what buttons to push.

Nadine pushed her way through the line of people, finding herself standing directly in Lola's view. She had forgotten how old and frail the woman looked. Seeing her now made it difficult to believe she could be dangerous.

She started rummaging through the quilts on the table, trying to appear inconspicuous, when suddenly their eyes made contact.

"Nadine, my dear, would you be interested in one of my quilts?"

"I'm not sure. How did you know my name? I don't remember being introduced."

"Oh, my dear, I'd like to say my spirit guide told me, but I'd be lying. At the town meeting, remember? I heard you speak. You do like to talk, don't you? Isn't it annoying when others think they know you better than you know yourself? Always thinking they are right and you are wrong, but then again, maybe she's right. You're not really interested in my quilts, are you?"

"Well, there's nothing wrong with your hearing, is there? We go on like that all the time. Clair's a good friend of mine."

Lola smiled. "Yes, my dear, I know. You should really be careful what you say to others, though. They might get the wrong impression." She glanced to her right, and then to her left, leaned forward and whispered. "You would not want to upset someone already in a fragile state of mind, now would you? I think you know what I'm talking about."

"But how—you couldn't have possibly—"

"Dear, stop by my place sometime and we'll talk some more. Feel free to bring your little Chihuahua with you."

Nadine's eyes widened. For a moment, she thought sure Lola had put a hex on her feet, as they would not budge. When her brain finally signaled her feet to move, she pushed her way through the crowd with little regard to those in her way.

Lola knew Nadine would spread the word. She counted on it. She knew when talk of their conversation got back to James it would peak his interest in her as well. Lola needed to see James again, but it had to be by his own free will. James would be the key to locking away the evil that brewed like a dormant volcano in their close-knit community, and time was not on their side.

A few yards away, the others were gathering by the pie booth, waiting to hear who would take home Patton's prestigious blue ribbon. Just as the final judge prepared to call out the winner's name, silence broke.

"Clair! You're not going to believe what just happened!"

"Shush!" Clair placed her hand over Nadine's mouth. "They're about to give out the blue ribbon for the best pie."

"Oh, who cares? Edith wins every year, anyway."

Clair grabbed Nadine by the arm, pulling her aside. "Okay, what's so important it can't wait? And it better be good."

James and Shannon, along with Katrina, headed over to see what all the commotion was about.

"Alright, let me catch my breath," Nadine said. "You know I went over to the old woman's stand to look at her quilts."

"Yeah, so?"

"She looked right at me and told me I shouldn't be so rude to people I hadn't seen in awhile. She almost repeated your conversation and mine word for word. You know, there wasn't any way she could have heard us. Then, to top it all off, she told me to come by and see her sometime and to bring my Chihuahua. How could she know about Arnold?"

Clair sighed and shook her head. "What did I tell you about people like that? They work with people in the crowds. They find out things about you and—"

James raised his hand as if he were back in school. "Wait a minute, Clair. Surely you don't buy into all her crap, do you Nadine?"

Nadine raised a brow. "She is intriguing, in a spooky kind of way."

"Spooky kind of way? Are you nuts?" Clair laughed.

"Look!" Katrina jumped up and down with excitement. "They're pinning the blue ribbon on Edith!"

Nadine rolled her eyes and let out a sigh. "What a surprise. Doesn't anybody else think my encounter was just a bit strange and interesting?"

Clair had heard enough. "Come along now, Nadine. It's time we old women went home and got our beauty sleep."

Shannon glanced over her shoulder and then back. "Did anyone see where Maggie went?"

James glanced beside him. "No, she was just here a minute ago."

"Yeah, well, I'm sure she was just in a hurry to get home. By the way, James, are you ready? I'm getting a little tired myself."

"Uh, yeah. If you want to take your mother and head on out to the car, I'll be right there."

James looked over his shoulder toward Lola's stand and thought about his own recent encounter with her. Could she really foretell the future and predict atrocities beforehand, thereby potentially saving countless lives? What was really in that black book of hers? Did it hold some secret power or knowledge? Maybe an insight to the impending doom she so adamantly confessed?

Although frightening as he found these questions to be, he could not deny the underlying connection he felt with her, an unexplainable bond of some sort.

CHAPTER
20

MAGGIE POPPED the cap on the bottle of pills Shannon had given her. She tilted her head, downed a couple with a glass of water, and stood at the kitchen window staring out into the darkness. The image of Frank's cold, dead body lying within just yards of her back door haunted her thoughts. She pulled the shades shut, double-checked the locks, and returned to bed. She closed her eyes, but it only brought the haunting images closer. She flinched at the slightest sound.

Her mind fought to understand how she could have committed such a despicable act. She cursed herself, then God, and then prayed for forgiveness. She had to talk to someone, someone whom she could trust to help her understand. It was evident what she had to do. Tomorrow she would put away all of her doubts and fears and confess to everything.

WITH KATRINA settled in for the night, James and Shannon decided to grab a beer and sit outside.

Shannon knew James well enough to know something was on his mind.

She began massaging his shoulder blades, working her hands softly up toward the back of his neck. "Do you want to talk about it?"

He shook loose from her hands. "I'm sorry, babe. I'm just worried about Maggie. I think she could really use a friend."

Shannon frowned. "I don't understand. The last time we talked I was under the impression you thought she was involved in Frank's disappearance. What's changed?"

"You and I both know Maggie has never committed a malicious or violent act in her life. I should have never made such an assumption."

"Yes, but the fact is it's a real possibility she may know more than she's letting on. I know you want to believe she's a helpless, timid creature who can do no wrong, but maybe you don't know her as well as you think you do. Everyone has a dark side."

James gulped down the last of his beer and wiped the excess from his chin. "Maybe you shouldn't be so defensive. I thought she was your friend too. Innocent until proven guilty, right?"

"Well, sorry for sounding so judgmental. I forgot you once had deep feelings for her. Maybe you still do."

Her beer bottle tumbled over the edge of the porch as she stomped off and into the house. James would sleep alone yet another night.

Early the next morning, a nurse from Thebes came by to pick up Katrina for her therapy session.

Shannon, late for work, hurried out the door behind them. She arrived late at her office and found Maggie waiting anxiously in the lobby.

"What are you doing here?" Shannon asked.

"I need to talk to you. If you can work me in, I'd really appreciate it."

Shannon signaled Maggie to follow her. "Well, I've got a few minutes until my first appointment. Come on in."

Maggie took a seat in front of Shannon's desk and placed her hands in her lap.

"Okay, why don't you start by telling me why you're here. I'll just listen."

Reluctant to speak, Maggie fidgeted in her chair for a moment before answering. "Anything I tell you doesn't go beyond this room; It's confidential, right?"

"Yes, as your therapist I'm bound by a strict code of confidentiality."

Maggie stood up and began to pace the floor.

"Shannon, I've done a terrible thing. I don't know what to do about it. You have to believe that it was an accident. I never meant it to happen."

"Sit down and relax, take a few minutes if you need to."

Several long minutes passed in silence, then Maggie began to open up about everything. When she was through, she wiped her sweaty hands on her jeans and waited for Shannon to respond.

An eerie silence followed. "Say something, Shannon."

Shannon sat with her hands cupped under her chin and her elbows planted firmly on the desk. "How could this have happened? How could you have been so careless?" she demanded at last.

"I panicked! I never meant to—"

"You not only committed murder, you've attempted to conceal the evidence. Who else knows about this?"

"No one knows. I've told no one else."

Shannon reached into her pocket, pulled out a key, and unlocked her desk drawer. "I'm going to give you some more Valium. Go home and don't talk to anyone. Let me think this thing through."

I can't go to jail," Maggie whimpered, "I'll lose my mind!"

Shannon stood up and pounded her fist on the desk. "You have to take responsibility for what you've done. We're not children anymore and I'm not going to cover up for you this time. You understand what I'm saying."

Maggie ignored the voice in her head, the one telling her to leap across the desk and place her hands around Shannon's throat. Instead, she nodded. "I understand perfectly."

Shannon wondered what James would think of his Maggie now. This would be the one time her patient-to-doctor confidentiality clause would mean nothing to her. She could not wait to tell him about Maggie's confession. She had a strong feeling Maggie had been trying to get James's attention for some time. If Shannon knew James at all, he would be appalled by Maggie's actions and would want nothing more to do with her. At least that's what she was counting on.

MILES AWAY in Thebes, Katrina prepared to deal with her own nightmares. A new therapist had been assigned to her case by the name of Dr. Ellory Mead. His primary specialty happened to be hypnosis. He found that under hypnosis a patient could sometimes recall even the most traumatic memories, which otherwise might stay buried in their subconscious psyche, therefore helping the patient considerably in their recovery. Although a relatively new procedure, when combined with medication and therapy, brought about much success.

Katrina had been under hypnosis for a few minutes when she began to respond to his questions. Her body began to tremble as her heart rate elevated. "I feel as though I'm suffocating!"

"Just try and relax, Katrina," Dr. Mead said.

"I can hear a loud noise; sounds like glass shattering, and then a short, high-pitched squeal...then silence. I'm in what looks like—yes, it's a kitchen, and my baby girl has blood on her hands. She's holding some sort of object."

"Look closer, Katrina. What do you see?"

"I—I don't know what to do. She's just standing there staring at me with this glazed look in her eyes. I don't know if she's cut...I can't understand what's happening! There's blood everywhere. Oh my God!"

"It's okay, Katrina. Breathe in and then breathe out slowly. You are back in your bed, safe from any harm. You are going to awaken now, as if from a good night's sleep, feeling relaxed and refreshed."

Katrina opened her eyes and took a moment to focus. "How did I do, Doc?"

"Excellent, Katrina! You just lie there and relax. I'll be back momentarily to discuss your progress."

Dr. Mead had been granted access to Shannon's files and, after going over them once again; it now appeared that Katrina's account of the incident while under hypnosis contradicted Shannon's statements years earlier.

CHAPTER
21

LARRY CONTINUED stocking the beer cage, expecting a busy night at the bar. Ordinarily he looked forward to a busy night but he was not feeling up to par. A piercing pain rushed through one side of his temple and out the other with the slightest movement. Tossing back a third dose of aspirin, he continued.

He set a case of beer on the bar and misjudged the distance, accidentally knocking over a couple of mugs. Squatting down slowly, he began picking up the pieces of glass off the floor when he suddenly got the distinct feeling he was not alone. Broken glass carefully cradled in his hand, he stood up and looked towards the back room. He could not remember if he had latched the back door after taking out the trash. Easing his way around the end corner of the bar, halfway to the back room, he heard a familiar voice.

"Better be careful, Larry. You'll cut yourself. Bring me a beer if you're coming this way."

"My God, is that you Frank!" He dropped the broken glass and pushed open the double doors leading to the stock room.

"You know it's true, these beer crates aren't really that comfortable. Now don't be frightened, Larry. I know I don't look too good. You don't know what I've been through."

Larry struggled to remain standing. The image that stood before him mirrored a rotting corpse, an unconscionable horror.

"You didn't know you had this ability, did ya, brother? I mean the ability to talk to the dead."

Larry pressed himself up against the wall as if a magnet had taken hold of his body. "This is not happening!"

"It's like this: I'm stuck here for a while. It's still not quite clear to me, but it seems I've been in some sort of accident involving a gun. Kind of ironic, is it not?"

Larry looked around as if he thought someone would jump out at any moment and yell, "April fools!"

"Focus, Larry. If it'll make it any easier, close your eyes and just listen to what I have to say. I don't have much time. The old woman was right. There is an evil lurking here in Patton, and it's closer than you think. I'll see you again, Larry, but until then, remember: things aren't always as they seem."

A loud bang on the front door sent Larry crashing to his knees. In the time it took for him to assemble the courage to look back, he found himself staring at an empty crate. Forcing one foot in front of the other, he proceeded to the front of the bar.

"Larry? You in there, partner? Answer the door!"

"Uh, yeah, I'm coming! Hold on."

After several feeble attempts, the key finally connected with the lock.

"My God, old man! You're ringing wet with sweat and you're as white as a bar towel. What's up, good buddy? If I didn't know better, you look like you've just seen a ghost!"

"My friend," Larry said, shaking his head. "You're not going to believe what just happened."

"Well here, sit down before you fall down."

James pulled up a barstool and listened as Larry told of his bizarre encounter.

"You don't believe me, do ya, buddy?"

James searched for the right words. "I believe something frightening happened to you, but listen to what you're saying. Frank's ghost? Think about what you're saying."

Larry raised his hand up, reached around to the back of his neck, and began trying to massage away the knot that had formed. "I know it sounds crazy. I wouldn't believe me, either."

"Listen, man." James reached out and patted him on the shoulder. "We've all been stressed out by everything that's happened lately. First with the murders, and then Frank's disappearance. I'm just saying it's normal for your mind to play tricks on you when you're under a lot of stress. You're vulnerable, that's all."

"I know you're right." Larry nodded. "I'm just tired. Hey, whaddaya say we just forget I said anything?"

"It's forgotten," James said, winking.

Larry reached in the beer cage and grabbed a couple of beers. "Have a drink with me. It's on the house."

James stopped by Shannon's office after leaving the bar. He wanted to surprise her. Her secretary informed him that she had cancelled all of her appointments early and left. He headed home, hoping nothing was wrong.

The front door was wide open. He hurried up the stairs, could hear the shower running. He stepped inside the bathroom door.

"Dammit, James!" Shannon said. "You almost scared me to death! What are you doing?"

He leaned against the bathroom door, arms crossed. "I was just about to ask you the same question. I stopped by your office and your secretary said you cancelled all of your appointments for the rest of the day. Are you sick?"

Shannon raised her voice above the running water. "It's a long story. I was confronted with some startling news by one of my patients. You'll never guess which one. Anyway, I had to take a drive and collect my thoughts about what I heard. I'd been driving a while when I realized I'd better turn around. That's when I got stuck."

"The car got stuck?"

Shutting the water off she grabbed a towel that hung on a hook just outside the shower, wrapped it around herself, and opened the bathroom door. "I guess I turned too sharp and managed to get my tires stuck in the clay. I walked at least a mile before this nice man stopped to help. Luckily he was able to wench my car out."

James pursed his lips. "Huh, that's some story. Did you get his name?"

"No, I think he was just passing through."

"Sounds like you've had a hell of a day." James leaned back on the bed. "I've got some rather startling news myself, but you go first."

"Well, Maggie came by my office bright and early this morning," Shannon said, wrapping a second towel around her hair like a turban. "Said she needed some advice. She wanted a guarantee that what she was going to tell me would be confidential. I assured her it would be."

James arched a brow. "Are you sure you should be telling me this then?"

Shannon yanked the towel off her wet head and threw it on the floor. "It doesn't really matter. Before long, everyone in Patton will know Maggie confessed to Frank's murder."

"What the hell?" James yelled, sitting straight up on the edge of the bed.

"Well, she says it was an accident. The morning Frank came by to check on her, he startled her. Half awake, she mistook him for an intruder and shot him with the very gun he'd given her to protect herself. What's even worse, she says she panicked and hid his body behind her house."

"Dear God! How did you react? What did you say?"

"I tried to calm her down. I explained to her the only way she could deal with this was to come to terms with what she had done. I gave her Valium and told her to go home and pull herself together. She has no choice but to confess."

James stared at Shannon, wide-eyed and mouth agape. "This is unbelievable! I can't imagine what she must be going through. I was hoping she wouldn't be involved. She's definitely going to need all of our support."

"Maybe we ought to find out all the facts." Shannon snapped back. "You know, it is possible she could be lying. What if it wasn't just an accident? Everybody knows she never thought too highly of old Frank."

James jumped to his feet. "In that case, half the population of Patton would have probable cause. I don't believe it was anything but an accident."

Shannon leaned across the bed towards James. "Innocent until proven guilty, right? Well, only time will tell."

Katrina arrived back just in time to overhear part of their intense argument. Trying to intervene she suggested they both cool down before it got too far out of hand.

Shannon tightened the strap around her robe and cut her eyes toward Katrina. "For once will you mind your own business!"

"I just don't want you both to say something you'll regret later."

"Oh, and we both know you're an expert on that subject." Shannon muttered, turning away.

Katrina could see she was getting nowhere so she turned the focus of the conversation on herself.

"My therapist tried something different today, hypnosis. Have you used that on any of your patients, dear?"

Shannon never took her eyes off James. "No, Katrina. I've read some literature on the procedure. It's a very difficult technique to learn."

"James, would you be offended if I spoke with my daughter alone for a minute?"

"Why no, certainly not. I think I'll take a drive, clear my head."

Shannon followed close behind as James headed down the stairs. "Just where do you think you're going this late anyway?"

Ignoring her question, he hurried out the door.

"Come sit with me a minute, honey, and I'll tell you what happened to me."

"Sure, why not." Shannon flopped herself down on the couch.

"While under hypnosis, Dr. Mead took me back in time. The horrible incident I recalled today under hypnosis was quite different than how I had remembered it. It involved you, Shannon."

Shannon took a deep breath and blew out. "Katrina, I can't talk about this right now."

Katrina nodded. "I—I know. I just thought maybe you could set aside a time when we could—"

"That's not a good idea," Shannon stood up and blurted out. "I'm not the one you need to be discussing this with."

"Of course, dear. I understand," Katrina whispered, bowing her head.

"You know everything is not always about you," Shannon said, staring out the window as if she thought James might reconsider and return home.

"I'm sorry, Shannon. I didn't mean to upset you any further."

"You don't know the half of it." Shannon headed towards the stairs. "I'm tired and I'm going to bed. I suggest you do the same."

Katrina wanted to call her back, wanted to drop to her knees in front of her daughter and beg for her forgiveness, for every wrong she had ever done to her. In that moment she realized, for the first time in her life, her daughter's happiness and well being meant more to her than her own.

CHAPTER
22

GROGGY FROM the Valium and other sleeping pills she had taken earlier, Maggie staggered into the bathroom. She leaned over the sink and stared into the mirror. She did not recognize the image staring back at her. Everything she had done in her life right up to this moment had gone wrong. She had not fought hard enough to keep the man she loved. She thought of herself as weak and pathetic and could not escape the childhood abuse of her own father. The torment and anguish she felt due to being responsible for Frank's death consumed her.

Positioning the razor blades in a perfect line at the head of the tub, she laid back, letting the warm bubbles surround her body. She knew it was the coward's way out, but being brave had never been one of her virtues. Her life was of very little significance, or so she thought. It was time to remove the mask that she had worn for most of her life. The masquerade was over.

Twisting her hair in a bun, she pulled each strand tight. Her hands surprisingly steady, she slowly reached for the blade. She started to begin what would ultimately be the end, when suddenly the ringing chimes of the front doorbell interrupted her. Quickly, she grabbed her housecoat and headed for the door. Through the tiny window of her front door, she could see James waiting impatiently on the steps.

"Come on, Maggie, open the door. I know you're in there."

She opened the door. "What are you doing here, James?"

Maggie's blood-shot eyes and somber appearance heightened James's concern. "I'm sorry if I came at a bad time, but I talked to Shannon and I know everything." He gently placed his hands on her shoulders. "I'm here if you need a friend."

Maggie buried her head in James's chest and sobbed. "I've really messed up this time, James, but you have to believe me. I swear it was an accident."

He raised Maggie's head from his chest, softly wiped away the tears from her cheeks, and looked directly into her eyes. "I believe you, Maggie. It was a horrible accident and you panicked."

With James on her side, Maggie now had a sense of hope. Thinking about what she had almost done just seconds earlier, she wondered if James could truly be her angel of mercy.

"Listen to me, Maggie," he said, raising her head from his chest. "I've heard some good things about a defense attorney by the name of Michael Burns. I think it's time you give him a call."

With a little coaxing, James handed Maggie the receiver and dialed the number. The man listened closely as Maggie confessed her ordeal. He asked if she fully understood what the consequences of her confession could mean. After she hung up the phone up, she said a silent prayer and hoped she had done the right thing.

A few minutes later, Maggie glanced at the clock on the wall. "How long has it been since we called?"

"He should be here any time," James assured her. "You know you'll have to show him where you buried Frank's body."

Maggie could not bear the thought of having to go anywhere near the site again. Pointing toward the back yard, she motioned James to go look. He opened the back door and stepped outside. A moment later, she heard him yell. He was standing near the mound of dirt, looking confused.

Maggie ran to him and fell to her knees and screamed. "How can this be happening? It's not possible!"

The makeshift grave she had so painstakingly dug and filled now lay open and empty.

Suddenly the sound of a car door slamming shut echoed from the driveway.

James flashed Maggie a panicked look and grabbed her hand. "When we get inside, lock yourself in the bathroom and don't come out."

James wiped away the sweat from his forehead with the sleeve of his shirt and ran a comb through his disheveled hair. After ignoring several knocks on the door, he took a long deep breath and exhaled before answering.

"You must be Michael Burns," James said, forcing himself to remain calm.

"Yes, I'm Michael Burns," the man in an expensive three-piece suit replied. "And you are?"

"I'm James King. First let me say I'm so sorry you had to come all the way out here like this. There's been a huge mistake. Maggie's a dear friend of mine, but she's been having some mental issues. In fact, she's seeing a therapist."

Irritated, Mr. Burns lit a cigarette and exhaled. "I hope you don't mind if I smoke."

"Of course not," James said, handing him an ashtray from the end table.

The man took another drag from his cigarette and flipped the ashes. "And just who would that therapist be?"

"A lady by the name of Shannon White."

The attorney nodded. "Yeah, I've heard of her. You know, a prank of this sort is very serious. By the way, just where is your sick friend?"

"In the bathroom, relaxing in a hot bath," James replied without missing a beat. "I can assure you, Mr. Burns, it wasn't a prank. Maggie sometimes has problems with distinguishing fantasy from reality."

With furrowed brow and narrowed eyes, Mr. Burns looked him over. "I don't appreciate being called out in the middle of the night on some lame-ass story like this."

James's face blushed a bright red; he cleared his throat a couple of times and hunched his shoulders. "This really is embarrassing. Again, I can't apologize enough."

"You can bet I'll check out your story."

"Like I said before, Maggie's a dear friend, but she does have issues."

"Well, if she's that sick she needs to be in a mental facility under close watch."

James looked toward the bathroom and nodded. "I've called her therapist and I'm sure she'll know what to do."

"Yes, you said Shannon White."

James extended his hand. "Again I apologize for your inconvenience.

Mr. Burns ignored James's gesture to shake hands and without hesitation replied. "On the phone Ms. Simmons stated to me that she had accidentally killed someone, and had buried their body on her property."

"I know how it all sounds," James said, looking at the floor and scratching his head.

"Then you don't mind if I take a look around outside."

Not wanting to add further suspicion James obliged, "Of course not. After you."

James led the way and the two men walked around to the back of the property.

The gaping hole in the ground stood out like a sore thumb. Mr. Burns walked slowly up to the edge of the opening and peered down into the empty space.

"I couldn't believe it myself," James said. "She fed me the same exact story, said she had accidentally killed an intruder and buried him out here. But as you saw in the house, there wasn't any sign of a struggle and there's definitely nobody in this hole."

Mr. Burns lit another cigarette, straightened the brim of his hat, and then shook his head. "I thought I'd heard and seen it all, but this scenario is one for my books. Well, Mr. King, it's like I said: I will be contacting Ms. White and following up on this."

Watching him drive away, James felt a sick feeling in the pit of his stomach. He could not believe what he had said. He had not only blatantly lied with a straight face to a respectable defense attorney, but at the same time had involved Shannon. Knowing his ass was on the line, he wanted some answers.

He tapped a couple of times on the bathroom door. "Maggie? You can come out now."

Before venturing out she peeked through the crack of the door, thinking the man might still be there. "What did you tell him?"

"I lied my ass off to that attorney and I'm not too sure he bought into it."

"What'd you say?"

"In short, that you were a close friend that was having some mental problems, and that you were under a psychiatrist's care. I told him you were experiencing a delusional breakdown when you made your statements to him. I involved Shannon in this mess, something I should have never done."

Grabbing James by the arm, Maggie pleaded with him to help her understand. "I feel like I'm going insane. None of this makes any sense. I killed Frank and I dug that hole and put his body there. It happened exactly like I said!"

James did not doubt that Maggie believed she was responsible for Frank's death and the so-called cover-up that followed, but he had his own doubts as to her story being legitimate. He now questioned her sanity.

"Maggie, I know you've been troubled for some time. I've known you for many years and you've always looked down on yourself. You've always jeopardized everything good in your life. It's like you have an underlying passion to destroy everything that's remotely good in your life. You said you had a disturbing nightmare right before Frank allegedly entered your room. Is it possible the events played out in your mind instead of in reality?"

Leaning back on the couch with her head in her hands, Maggie sat silent, hanging onto his every word. Distraught, she looked up once again into his eyes for guidance.

"Tell me what to do, James. I don't know what to believe anymore."

James pulled her close to his chest. "We'll get through this. I'm going to talk to Shannon, explain what happened tonight, and see what she suggests. Until then, don't speak to anyone about this."

Maggie assured James that she would be okay. She would wait for his instructions. She longed for him to stay with her through the night, but she knew it was out of the question. Just knowing he was on her side and cared enough to get involved meant the world to her.

After watching him leave, she walked into the bathroom and stared for a moment at the razor blades still lined up neatly on the tub. She picked them up carefully and placed them back into the medicine cabinet. Although thoughts of suicide had diminished, she could not dismiss them completely. However, James had given her hope and for now, she would try to hold on.

When James got home, he found Shannon asleep on the bed. Not wanting to wake her, he turned quietly to leave, but the outline of her body through her sheer nightgown stopped him in his tracks. It had been some time since they'd made love. He hungered for her touch; the sweet smell of her perfume lingering in the air excited him. He leaned in closer, sliding his hand up under her nightgown and softly caressed her thigh, hoping for a reaction.

Startled, she jerked away, grabbed a pillow and placed it between them. "Damn it, James. You scared me to death!"

James chuckled. "Well, I definitely wasn't going for that kind of reaction."

"You woke me from a deep sleep. What did you expect?" She rubbed the sleep out of her eyes and reached for her watch that lay on the nightstand. "Where have you been, anyway?"

"I stopped by Maggie's to—"

"You stopped where?" She could not believe what she was hearing.

"If you'd calm down for just one minute and let me explain. I went over there to let her know she could count on us for support. I advised her to talk to an attorney before turning herself in. We called an attorney out of Sedgewickville—"

"You can't be serious!" Shannon shouted back. "Yeah, she says it was an accident, but what if she's lying? You know she's always been a little quirky. In my opinion, she's downright psychotic."

James clenched his fists and stormed out of the room, which only infuriated Shannon more.

"You don't know what you may be getting us involved in!" she shouted after him. "In the short time I talked to Maggie, I was under the impression she was extremely unstable. You seem to forget I lived most of my life terrorized by a psychotic individual! I think in the profession I'm in, I can clearly say I'm a hell of a lot more qualified than you to make that evaluation!"

James turned and stomped back into the room. "I may not have a degree in psychology, but you just referred to your own mother as a psychotic individual. You couldn't even say her name."

"Oh, I get it. Shannon formed a tight fist with her right hand and pounded on the wall. You want to try to turn this around. Don't you try to psychoanalyze me. You're the one that came home hot and ready for a night of passion after leaving your ex-girlfriend's house. What's the matter, James? Did she turn you down? Were you looking for me to boost your self-esteem?"

James tried to finish explaining the strange circumstances that had taken place at Maggie's, but he could not get two words in over her shouting.

"I can't believe you both would involve me in this mess!" Shannon shouted.

James threw his hands up. "I'm done arguing with you." This time she would not follow him.

Not able to reach any common ground, James knew it would only get worse if he stayed. Sleeping in the van would be more comfortable than continuing to quarrel all night. He had never known her to be so inconsiderate. He wondered if she really doubted Maggie's true innocence, or if the sudden bouts of jealously were clouding her judgment.

Katrina, awakened by their loud arguing, crept down the hallway and stood outside their bedroom door.

"What's going on, Shannon? Is everything okay? I thought I heard a loud noise."

Shannon shoved the bedroom door open and a piece of plaster fell to the floor. "It's none of your business, Katrina! Go back to bed!"

"Is there something I can do? You look so upset."

"You can't even help yourself, now go back to bed!"

Shannon ended the conversation by slamming the bedroom door in her face, leaving Katrina alone in the hallway.

Katrina had hoped her daughter could somehow see past her illness and learn to confide in her. In reality, she knew the chances of that happening were slim. Both women shared only memories of despair and misery.

AT HOME, Larry fought with his own dilemmas. The truth being his episode with Frank's disappearing ghost had rattled him somewhat. He wanted to tell Edith about the encounter but could not bear to think what her reaction might be. He needed to be alone with his thoughts, so he decided to take a drive.

As he drove by the old Patterson's place, he saw a light on in the farmhouse. Overcome with a definite feeling of being drawn there, his car began to steer toward the main house. With no control over his vehicle, all he could do was watch as the steering wheel mysteriously turned on its own. Once the car stopped, the driver-side door opened as if by an invisible hand. Convinced he must be hallucinating, Larry sank back in the seat, took a deep breath, and closed his eyes.

"Come on in, Larry," Lola called out, stepping out on her porch. "I've made us a pot of tea."

When he heard her voice, Larry opened his eyes and got out of the car. He could not believe what was happening. Something beyond his control had lured him there.

"I'm sorry, ma'am. I must have made a wrong turn."

Lola stood holding the screen door open. "Nonsense. You've wanted to visit me for some time. Come inside. I've made us some tea."

His common sense told him to get back in the car, turn around and leave, but curiosity and an overwhelming desire kept him moving forward.

Larry walked in behind her, leaving the front door open and the screen door unlatched. He had never seen so many candles twinkling at one time. The steady flicker of the light lit up the entire room. An old wooden rocking chair sat alone in the corner. In the middle of the room sat a broke-down couch directly across from a weathered coffee table. On top of the table lay a large black book trimmed in gold.

"Beautiful book, isn't it, Larry?" She placed a cup of tea in his hand. "Your spirit guide brought you here. I'm told you encountered the dead man's spirit, but still you denounce your unique spiritual abilities. Do you see your gift as a curse?"

The saucer rattled against the teacup in Larry's hand. He shivered as a chill ran over his body. "Ma'am, I'm just an ordinary man. I don't believe in all this voodoo and I'm certainly not into any sort of witchcraft. Now if you will excuse me." Crouching forward, he placed his teacup on the table and stood up to leave.

"Your friends are in danger and you have the ability to foresee the impending disaster, yet you make a mockery out of your gift! We have much more in common than you know. You have always had this ability, even as a young child. Your Cherokee heritage is as mine: strong and pure. Listen to your spirit guides and believe, for they will steer you in the right direction."

Pointing to the black book, Lola motioned him to pick it up. "Look, for inside is the knowledge you need to understand this evil that lurks among you."

Larry took two steps back. "No offense, but you're scaring the hell out of me and I think the best thing for me to do is leave."

He fumbled his way to the door, knocking the table over and sending the book crashing to the floor. Once outside he did not look back. He put the car in drive and spun the tires, throwing gravel halfway down the driveway.

Leaning down with the support of her cane, Lola maneuvered the table upright. Caringly, so as not to tear a page, she gathered up her bible from off the floor and gently placed it upon the table.

In the same sense that an architect's blueprint is his bible, or a medical dictionary is a doctor's bible, this was Lola's bible. Its contents contained crucial information about people and places from the past, present, and future. The type of information not from this earthly world but rather from a spiritual dimension light years away. With each new adventure to an unfamiliar destination, the contents of Lola's bible would change.

Time was running out. She would do all she could to save the innocent from the evil about to lunge on their small community by giving them signs and pointing them in the right direction. However, her assignment was proving to be much more difficult than expected.

CHAPTER
23

CLAIR AWOKE that morning belting out "Joy to the World".

She waltzed around the storeroom with a mop, feeling that even Nadine's tardiness would not provoke a negative response from her.

Nadine thought she would slip in quietly, but it appeared there would be no need, Clair was in a jovial mood.

"Okay, I know you've either lost your mind or you've stumbled on a magic potion to regain your youth," she said with a grin.

"You know what I think, Nadine?

"No, and I'm not so sure I want to know."

I think we should mark a forty percent discount on all our new handbags. What do you think?"

"Okay, you're really worrying me now. I'm going to go get a straitjacket, so just wait right here."

"Don't be silly, Nadine. Matthew and his wife Barbara are coming for a visit and they're bringing my grandson Zachary."

Nadine smacked a palm to her forehead. "Now it all makes sense!"

Clair smiled. "I know it's only been a few months ago since they were here, but it seems like a lifetime."

"You think that youngest one of yours is ever going to get married and settle down?"

"Oh, you know Scottie. He is a bit of a womanizer. However, when it comes to running the farm he takes after his father, rest his soul. Truth is, he hired some of the finest farmhands around this area. If Buddy were still living he would be so proud."

"Well, Clair, I for one can't wait to see them again."

Putting her arm around Clair, Nadine pulled her close. "Oldest son an architectural engineer raising a fine son, youngest boy running the family farm. I'm sure he's looking down from Heaven beaming with pride."

Across the street, Maggie tried to keep herself busy by arranging and rearranging the candy aisle. She'd cleaned the storeroom windows so many times not a smudge could be detected. She had hope that by continuing some sort of normal routine, she might block out all the craziness.

Business started slow. Even her regular customers were a no-show. She blamed the lack of business on the new store opening around the corner. With everything that had happened, she dreamed of selling out and starting all over somewhere new, somewhere far away from Patton. Maggie knew in reality that she could not run away from her nightmare, but it didn't hurt to daydream.

Counting her money drawer for the third time, she stopped and looked up when the door buzzer went off. Her excitement quickly changed to apprehension when she realized it was Shannon.

"Thought I'd stop in and see how you are doing, Maggie."

"I know what it must look like. I want to own up to what I did, but after what happened last night—"

"I know all about it," Shannon said. "James told me everything. You know, all you're doing is putting off the inevitable. Meanwhile, Frank's poor family and friends are still holding out hope he's alive. You could end their pain of not knowing."

Maggie stepped out around the counter. "That's just it, Shannon. Didn't James tell you? The body wasn't there! I can't explain it."

"You shouldn't have involved James. Have I not always been there for you? Have you forgotten about the ordeal surrounding your father's death? I've never told a soul."

"I could never forget what you've done for me,"

"You and I both know James still holds a soft spot in his heart for you. No, my suggestion is, if you want my help as your therapist, and as a friend, you'll distance yourself from James."

"But Shannon, it's not—"

Shannon placed the palm of her hand over Maggie's mouth. "This is neither the time nor place to be having this discussion. Make an appointment with my secretary and we'll talk further at my office. In the meantime, stay away from James."

Maggie felt a shiver of fear pass through her. She wanted to run, run as far away as she could. She watched until Shannon drove out of sight. She placed the 'closed' sign in the window and latched the door.

With hands shaking, she put the key in the ignition and stomped the gas pedal, almost sideswiping the car parked next to her as she pulled away. She kept hearing Shannon's voice saying to her "Have I not always been there for you?"

After several hours of endless driving, Maggie could no longer concentrate on the road. She pulled onto a side road and stopped. She laid her head on the steering wheel, sobbing.

Her conversation with Shannon had ignited the horror she had tried so desperately to repress. Memories of that fateful day long ago flooded her mind, drowning out all other thoughts.

The sight of her father's body lying motionless on the floor, blood oozing out of his mouth and nose, now played vividly in her mind. Blood spatter on the walls formed a random design like that of an amateur painter. In her mind it was like someone was running a film projector, slowly moving from one clip to the next.

She remembered confiding only in Shannon at the age of twelve. Revealing the diabolical and sadistic acts of abuse her father repeatedly subjected her to. She had told of her overwhelming desire to see him dead. Like a thief in the night, he had robbed her of her childlike innocence. Maggie remembered Shannon's first reaction upon learning the disgusting details and their conversation that came shortly after.

First Shannon had been silent, then with a grin on her face Shannon had asked, "Doesn't your father own a gun?"

"Yeah, he keeps it in a shoe box in the top of his closet." "Well, have you ever heard of self-defense? The next time he comes into your room uninvited, do what you have to do. Just make sure your mother isn't home."

The next night Maggie did exactly that. With her mother away, her father attempted to molest her, but this time would be his last. On Shannon's suggestion, Maggie pointed the gun she had secretly hidden under her pillow and fired, shooting her father in the chest. In shock, not knowing what to do, she called the one person she could trust. Shannon would come to her rescue.

Shannon had wiped the gun clean and placed it in his hand. She even thought to set a whiskey bottle half empty on the floor in front of him. With only Maggie in the house as a witness, Shannon convinced the sheriff that unfortunately Maggie had walked in at the ill-fated moment that her father shot himself. Hysterical, she had called her only friend to come right over. Maggie, in shock of course, let Shannon do all the talking.

As Maggie sat alone in her car, tortured by the memories of her childhood nightmare, she began to question Shannon's loyalty for the first time. After all, Shannon had suggested she murder her father and had been the mastermind in covering up the evidence. After all these years Maggie now wondered if Shannon had taken advantage of her fragile state of mind, manipulating her into committing murder? She thought about how for months afterwards Shannon insisted upon discussing the gruesome details. She acted as though reliving the nightmare gave her some sort of sick thrill.

No matter how much Maggie had wanted her father dead, she had never intended on being his executioner.

CHAPTER
24

ACROSS TOWN, Larry worked in the yard mowing the lawn and helping Edith in the garden. He tried to keep his mind occupied, moving tirelessly from one chore to the next. Every spare minute he thought of his disturbing visit with Lola the night before. Usually at suppertime, he and Edith would discuss the day's events and enjoy each other's company, but tonight Larry had little to say. With the night ending, Edith could not stay quiet any longer. She knew something was troubling her husband.

"Alright mister, what's going on with you?"

"What are you talking about, woman? I'm just relaxing in front of the television."

"You were quiet at supper and you haven't called to check on the bar all night."

Larry grabbed his boot sitting next to his chair and hurled it towards the wall. Missing his target, Edith's favorite vase fell crashing to the floor. "Can't a man just relax in his own home without something being wrong?"

Edith took off her apron, slung it in his lap, and stormed out of the room.

He lowered his head in shame, repulsed by his own actions. Yet, he could not bring himself to tell her what was bothering him. The odd meeting with Lola the night before, his bizarre conversation with a ghost. Oh yeah, she would without a doubt think he was going nuts. He was beginning to think maybe he was.

Working well into the night, Shannon continued to prepare notes for the next workday. She paused for a moment when she heard a truck pull into the drive. It was James.

James entered and placed his keys on the counter. He looked back outside. "Whose car is that in the driveway, and where's your car?"

"It's a loner from the insurance company. I had a minor mishap today when I was backing out of the grocery store parking lot. I hit a pole and banged up the bumper pretty good."

"You okay?"

She winked at him and suggestively leaned forward exposing a section of her bare breasts. "I am now that you're here. Listen, I'm tired of fighting with you. I understand your concern for Maggie's situation. She's my friend too. As a matter of fact, I dropped by the store today and we had a heart-to-heart conversation."

He took a drink then cleared his throat. "You went by and saw Maggie today?" He could not believe what he was hearing.

"I did, and I told her to come by here or to drop by my office as soon as she could. You know, James, I've known Maggie for a long time, and we've been through a lot together. It's only right that I be there for her now."

This was the Shannon he knew and loved. He set his beer on the table and went to her. Taking her in his arms, he pressed her body close to his and tenderly opened her lips with his mouth as his hands caressed her shoulders, making his way down to her breasts. He could feel her nipples rising with his touch. The sweet taste of her skin on his tongue heightened all his senses.

She gazed into his eyes, while firmly stroking his masculine chest, and while her body tingled with pleasure at his every touch.

No one had ever made love to her like James. No one ever came close. He was her world. Nothing else mattered; not her career, or Maggie, or anyone else. She could not bear the thought of ever losing him. She would do whatever it took to make sure that never happened.

The next morning a cool front moved in from the north that sent relief from the blistering heat to the people of Patton and the surrounding area. The wind picked up, turning over lawn chairs and umbrellas that lined the back yards of almost every neighborhood. Debris scattered by the wind and leaves from trees accumulated on rooftops and sidewalks. Ominous dark clouds enclosed the sun rising in the east, blocking the morning rays, making it difficult to distinguish daytime from night.

Maggie stood at her kitchen window, staring out at the empty hole that now overflowed from the drenching rain. She replayed the tragic events of that fateful day: the thunderous sound of the gun as she pulled the trigger, the hot smell of the gunpowder that lingered afterwards. Closing her eyes, she saw Frank's lifeless body, soaked with blood, lying on the floor. She recalled the panicky feeling of desperation as she swiftly and strategically tried to clean up the crime scene. Maggie knew there was no way she could have just imagined such an unthinkable act.

Deep in thought, she jumped when the phone rang. She looked over at the clock on the kitchen wall. It read 7:00 am. She could not imagine who would be calling that early. She picked up the receiver, struggling to hear the low whisper on the other end that was scarcely loud enough to understand.

"Have you checked your mail?" was all she heard, then silence.

Bewildered as to the identity of her caller, she became even more confused by what was asked. Apprehensive, she grabbed her robe and umbrella and headed out the front door down the walkway. She lowered the door to the mailbox, and looked inside. She pulled out a folded brown paper sack and quickly ran back up the walkway. Once inside, she set the sack on the kitchen table and, little by little, started to unfold the contents.

Taking out what at first looked like a meaningless piece of old fabric, she soon realized it meant much more than that. Gasping desperately to catch her breath, lips trembling, her body began to shake. Nauseated, Maggie fell to the floor in anguish. In her trembling hands, she held the bloodstained nightgown she had worn that tragic night. The same gown she had carefully thought to discard in a plastic bag. She was terrified! She nervously shoved it back into the bag, but before she could regain her composure, a loud knock at her front door startled her. Quickly she shoved the bag under a couch cushion, and then made her way to the door.

"Are you going to let me in, or are you going to let me drown out here in this pouring rain?"

"Is something wrong? Is it James?" Maggie asked, unlatching the screen door.

"Nothing's wrong with James. I'm here to check on you, Maggie."

Shannon unbuttoned her drenched coat and slung it on the corner of the couch. Soaked to the bone and shivering, she reached for the throw cover that lay across the back of the couch and wrapped it around her shoulders. She squatted to sit down, but not before Maggie could stop her.

"Why don't we go into the kitchen and I'll pour us some coffee? We can talk in there."

Shannon followed close behind. "I have some disturbing news to tell you. I take it you haven't read the morning paper?"

"No, I haven't had a chance. What happened?"

"Well, it seems a well-known defense attorney from Sedgewickville by the name of Michael Burns was involved in a fatal car accident yesterday. It appears he lost control and the car ran off the road, overturning several times. He was pronounced dead at the scene."

Dizzy, Maggie stumbled back against the stove sending her coffee cup crashing to the floor. She gasped to catch her breath as she bent down to pick up the broken pieces that lay scattered across the kitchen floor.

Shannon sat motionless, unmoved by the incident. "Didn't burn yourself, did you?"

"No, I'm fine. Just wasn't expecting to hear such startling news. That's all."

"I know it must be upsetting, especially given the circumstances. James told me about your close encounter with Mr. Burns. I had planned to speak with him, try to smooth over any misconceptions he might have had about you, but as it is I guess luck was on our side."

Maggie shook her head in disbelief. "That's not luck, that's horrible! How can you talk about something so tragic as if it was nothing?"

"Listen to me, Maggie. James is under the assumption that you're innocent and that you've concocted an imaginary story involving yourself in Frank's death. He thinks you have this overwhelming sickness to sabotage your life, brought on by some underlying guilt you've been carrying around."

"Is that what you believe, Shannon?"

"I'll tell you what I think: I think his past relationship with you has clouded his judgment as far as weighing all the evidence. However, I feel I can put our friendship aside, and as a psychiatrist help you to make a distinction between what is real and what is purely imaginative. Only if you trust me and do as I say."

"I do want to open up to you, Shannon, to try to figure out what the hell is going on. I'm just so confused."

"Well, let's see what we have so far." Shannon continued glaring coldly into Maggie's eyes. "First you admit to killing Frank, and now you're not so sure. My God, Maggie, you dug a hole in your back yard and confessed to putting Frank's body there. He didn't just get up and walk away. You've involved James in all of this and therefore we're breaking the law by not turning you in to Sheriff Chesterton. Have you forgotten I put my ass on the line years ago for you?"

Maggie leaned in close. "No, nor will you let me forget. I also haven't forgotten that you were the instigator."

Shannon jumped from her seat, moving so fast her chair scooted across the floor several feet. She grabbed Maggie by both arms and shoved her to the floor. "All I did was make a suggestion! You made the final decision! Maybe the guilt you've been carrying around all these years was due to killing your father. On the other hand, maybe he wasn't abusive to you at all! Maybe you imagined the whole scenario in that sick little head of yours. As a kid I believed what you said back then as the truth, but maybe that was my mistake. I'm telling you one more time: stay away from James!"

Leaving Maggie lying on the kitchen floor, Shannon stormed out of the house, slamming the screen door behind her.

Maggie pulled herself up and staggered into the living room. She locked the door and peered through the blinds, watching Shannon speed away.

CHAPTER
25

THUNDER CRACKED its whip every few minutes as rain bore on endlessly, hammering on the rooftops, flooding the streets and sidewalks.

"Storm woke you up too, huh?" James asked Katrina "Yeah, it's really coming down out there. Since I'm already up I could fix you and Shannon some breakfast if you like."

"I'm afraid Shannon left early this morning. Guess she wanted to get to work before the storm got any worse. I'd love a couple of eggs, if you don't mind?"

"I don't mind at all," she said, reaching in the refrigerator pulling out a carton of eggs. "It'll give us some time to talk."

James poured himself a cup of coffee and sat down at the kitchen table. "What's on your mind?" James asked.

"Lately I've been concerned about Shannon. Whenever I try to have a conversation with her, she always ends up cutting me short. She doesn't eat and barely ever sleeps. It seems like something is weighing heavy on her mind. Yesterday I asked her why she and Maggie had become so distant, and she almost bit my head off. She told me they hadn't been close for a while. She wouldn't talk about it. Do you know what's going on?"

James shook his head, took a sip of coffee, and gazed down into his cup. "I'm afraid I have a lot to do with that. I don't know if you're aware of it, but when I met your daughter, I was involved in a relationship with Maggie.

Katrina dropped the spatula in the frying pan, turned around from the stove, and gave him her full attention.

"I know how it must sound," James said, looking up from his coffee cup. "But our relationship was already in trouble. Maggie and I always seemed to bring out the worst in each other. "I know it sounds cliché but when I met Shannon, I knew that she was the one."

Katrina was not sure how to respond. Turning back around to the stove, she flipped the eggs and placed them on his plate. Placing the plate in front of him, she pulled out a chair and sat down. "Well, I certainly have a better understanding of the situation between my daughter and Maggie now."

James placed the fork on his plate, looked over at Katrina, and leaned back in his chair. "I guess I've been making matters worse here lately."

"You and Maggie aren't—"

"No!" It's nothing like that." James proclaimed. "It's just that, well, recently as her friend I've been advising Maggie on something she needed help with. Unfortunately I think I might've went about it the wrong way."

Katrina placed her hand on top of his. "Well maybe both of you just need to get away for a couple of days, spend some time alone.

"No. I've tried convincing her to do that. She's always got an excuse as to why she can't get away."

"Here's an idea, why don't you make a reservation for the weekend at that nice little bed and breakfast over in Sedgewick-ville. Surprise her."

"Maybe I'll do just that." James grinned. "Lord knows we could both use the time away."

With no relief in sight, the rain continued to submerge every inch of Patton, rising up out of the ditches and overflowing into the fields.

"I told you it was going to rain today," Nadine said, taking her shoes off and rubbing her legs. "I can always tell when a storm is coming by the aching in my joints."

"Could you move your shoes out of the way!" Clair yelled, almost tripping over them.

"Did we get up on the wrong side of the bed this morning?"

"I'm sorry, Nadine. It's just there was some kind of mix-up at Matthew's architectural firm, so the kids had to cut their visit short and head back."

"Oh, I'm sorry to hear that. You know you could always take some time off from the boutique. Go visit them. I'd be more than happy to run things here."

"I appreciate your offer and I might sometime soon."

"Is there something else bothering you?" Nadine asked, concerned.

"I don't know, it's just that, well, the kids were such a pleasant distraction from all the unpleasant and strange things going on around here."

Nadine leaned forward and lowered her voice. "Speaking of strange things, have you noticed Maggie doesn't have two words to say here lately? The last time I saw Shannon leaving her store, she appeared to be extremely upset over something. You don't think there's a little love triangle going on involving James and Maggie, do ya?"

"Any other time I'd say you were way off base, but I noticed a peculiar change in Maggie's personality right after Frank's disappearance. As far as James and Maggie go…well, you and I both know they were involved with each other at one time."

"You don't really think Maggie could be involved in Frank's disappearance, do you?"

A few seconds passed as Clair considered her answer. "The only thing I'm sure about is, from the time that senseless murder happened to that poor little family, it's been nothing but one misfortune after another. Makes a person not want to trust anyone."

CHAPTER
26

LARRY WOKE up covered again in sweat and was trembling, each nightmare was worse than the one before. Taunted by visions of Frank's rotting corpse was becoming a nightly ordeal. His loving relationship with Edith was growing cold and distant as well. Feelings of confusion fueled by his frightening nightmares, not to mention his strange encounter with Lola, had Larry seriously questioning his sanity. While Edith slept, Larry quietly dressed and slipped out the back. He could think of only one person who might be able to help him make sense of what he was going through. Shannon had helped him overcome his psychological fear of losing his arm just a few years earlier. He prayed she could see him through this ordeal as well.

The storm had begun to subside, but the streets were still treacherous. Larry pulled around to the side of the clinic and parked. He sat for a moment trying to remember exactly why he was there. How had he come to this point in life? The point of no return, it seemed. Wasting no more time, he finally opened his truck door. He looked from side to side to see if anyone was around who might recognize him. The last thing he wanted to do was cause any kind of embarrassment for Edith. When he thought it was safe to go, he quickly made his way up the walk and up to the front of the building.

The receptionist was handing him a stack of papers to fill out when Shannon walked in.

"Hi, Larry. Are you looking for James?"

"No, Shannon." Larry stepped forward. "I'm here to see you."

"I've got another hour before my next session. Come on in and have a seat."

Larry sat with both hands folded in his lap and head hanging low. He could not believe it had come to this. He was not even sure how to begin. "I'm here because I didn't know where else to go. I've had some things happening to me I can't explain …not logically, anyway."

Shannon settled in the chair behind her desk and prepared to take notes. "Take your time, Larry. I'm sure I can help you make sense of whatever it is."

Larry slowly lifted his head to speak, but what he saw next left him speechless and horrorstruck. Shannon's appearance had changed. Deep-set menacing eyes stared back at him with burning intensity. Her features no longer appeared to be human, but mimicked that of a wild animal ready to devour its prey. His breath became visible as a bitter chill ran through his body. He closed his eyes and prayed the image would disappear.

"Mr. Jacobs? Mr. Jacobs? Dr. White is ready to see you now." Larry opened his eyes and looked around to see the waiting room empty. He looked down at the clipboard in his lap still full of forms not yet filled out. Once again, the receptionist called his name. "Mr. Jacobs, are you alright? Can I get you a glass of water?"

Larry, visibly shaken, laid the clipboard on the counter and stepped back. "I'm sorry, I'm not feeling so good. I think I'm going to have to reschedule."

He barely made it back to his truck before getting deathly ill. He took a handkerchief out of his pocket and wiped the excess vomit and sweat from his face. He grabbed his chest as if he thought any moment his heart could leap from its cavity. He became weak as the veins in his neck began to pulsate. He feared he could no longer distinguish reality from fantasy. He kept hearing Lola telling him to trust his instincts, and his instincts were telling him that what he had witnessed depicted pure evil.

DUE TO bad weather, James had no choice but to give his crew the day off. With several construction sites underway, he prayed the rain would let up soon. He looked at the endless stack of folders scattered about on his work desk, and decided now might be a good time to file them away. While thumbing through his filing cabinet, he came across some blueprints of an unfinished home he had drawn up sometime earlier. He had hoped one day it would be his and Shannon's dream home.

After pouring himself a cup of coffee, he leaned back in his chair, admiring his drawings. Suddenly, someone beating franticly on the outer door of his office interrupted his train of thought.

"James, open up!"

James flung the door open. "What's going on, Larry? Has something happened?"

"Yeah, something's happened to me. I'm telling ya, I think I'm about to lose my mind."

"Okay, just have a seat, take a deep breath, and tell me what's happened."

Larry pulled up a seat and caught his breath. "To make a long story short, the other night I decided to take a drive and ended up at Lola's. That's when—"

"Why on earth would you go there?" James asked, leaning forward, looking him straight in the eye.

Larry shrugged. "It's like I had no control over my car. I know that sounds crazy, but it's like it had a mind of its own. She knew I was coming, James. She says I'm not imagining Frank's ghost. It's real. She had this book and—"

James held up a hand. "Slow down, Larry. I know what you're going to say. She wanted you to look at her book. She told you that it would give you this magical insight into foretelling drastic and horrible things to come. Don't you remember? She told me the same thing."

"It only gets worse," Larry said. "Today I went to see Shannon. I thought maybe she could help me."

"That's great!" James smiled. "I'm sure Shannon will be able to—"

"No, you don't understand! One minute I'm sitting in her office getting ready to pour my heart out, the next minute I'm looking up at this—I don't even know how to explain it. She—she turned into this hideous-looking monster right in front of my eyes. The next thing I know I'm back in the waiting room, clipboard still in my lap full of forms that I haven't filled out, and the receptionist is calling my name."

James stood up, poured them a cup of coffee, and thought for a moment. "That's it, Larry. You must have fallen asleep while you were waiting. You had a nightmare, old man. That's all."

"It wasn't just a nightmare!" Larry protested. "I know what I saw was real, and I know what I felt was real too."

"Listen to yourself!" James threw his hands up in the air. "Shannon a monster? Did Lola feed you this crap? You can't honestly believe what you're saying!"

The two men stood glaring at each other.

"Enough is enough," James sighed. "You can't continue with this nonsense."

Larry turned away without saying a word and walked straight to the door. With his hand on the doorknob, he paused and looked back. "I'm sorry I bothered you, James." He exhaled deeply. "Just forget I was ever here."

James watched as his friend drove away. He didn't know what to think of Larry's peculiar behavior, and thought certain Lola must be the cause for putting such nonsense in his head.

Larry, on the other hand, had walked away feeling humiliated and hurt from his best friend's reaction. He worried James would never take anything he said seriously again. Most of all, he was getting damn tired of having to defend his own sanity. He could not rationalize the bizarre events he had experienced in Shannon's office, but to him it did not make them any less real. He did not know how, but he was certain that, in time, whatever evil he had been confronted with would be revealed.

Katrina felt apprehensive about her scheduled appointment with her therapist and decided to work off some nervous energy. After sweeping, mopping, and vacuuming every room of the house, she started a load of laundry and then began the task of dusting every piece of furniture.

When she opened the door to her daughter's room, she was amazed to see the multitude of books and magazines that lay stacked on the floor and piled high on the dresser. Grabbing an armful at a time, she tried carefully to keep them in order as she set them aside. Unfortunately, the last stack slipped out of her hand. Aggravated, she looked down at the mess she had made and caught a glimpse of a magazine cover that sent chills down her spine. The title read Brutal Unsolved Murders. It depicted an image of a young woman who had been viciously stabbed and beaten to death. Even more disturbing, she found many others of the same nature hidden underneath countless stacks of legitimate literature.

Katrina wept at the thought that her daughter took interest in such disgusting publications. Her mind filled with anguish over what she should do. There was only one thing she could think of: confront Shannon about what she had found and pray that she had a logical explanation.

Expecting Shannon home at any moment, Katrina quickly finished dusting and carefully placed her daughter's books back the way she had found them. When she was finished, she shut Shannon's bedroom door behind her, turned around, only to come face to face with her daughter.

"Were you just in my room, Katrina?"

Caught off guard by her daughter's sudden appearance from out of nowhere she stepped back, and leaned against the door. "I just thought I'd straighten up a little for you. I know how busy you've been lately."

"I hope you didn't move anything," she said, reaching around Katrina and opening the bedroom door.

"I'm sorry, Shannon, but I was moving a stack of books from your dresser when they slipped out of my hand. I have to say I was shocked at some of the material I saw."

Shannon squinted at her mother for a few seconds as if she were trying to read her mind. "What on earth are you talking about?"

"I'm talking about those trashy magazines that exploit innocent victims who have been viciously murdered."

Shannon's face grew red with anger. "What makes you so sure those are mine? For all you know they could belong to James."

"So are you saying those belong to James?"

"What I'm saying is, it's none of your business who they belong to. Don't you think you have enough on your own plate to worry about?"

"I didn't mean to upset you I was just concerned that—"

"From now on our room is off limits and I expect you not to bother James with your foolish concerns!"

Katrina's bewilderment at her daughter's reaction only made her more suspicious of her. Memories of Shannon as a little girl flashed across her mind. She remembered how her daughter often tried to lie when caught red-handed. However, Katrina's clouded memories of hers and Shannon's past were becoming much clearer with the help of her therapist, and the past was a very different color than the one Shannon had always painted.

"I feel I must involve James," Katrina said, making her way toward the doorway. "I feel like there's something you're not telling me, something really wrong going on here."

"Don't push it, Katrina." Shannon lunged at her mother swiftly turning her around and grabbing both her wrists. "I'm having a hard enough time coping as it is to maintain a control over this… this thing inside of me."

"You're hurting me, Shannon!" Katrina squirmed to break free. "Release me this instant!"

Shannon clenched her jaw and grinned. "Oh, I'm going to let go of you, alright. Something I should have done years ago."

JAMES DECIDED to lock up early and head on out. After hearing Larry's outlandish story, he couldn't concentrate on his paperwork, much less anything else. With a little time to spare, he decided to pay Maggie a visit.

When he pulled into the driveway, he got the distinct feeling of despair and uneasiness. The closer he got to the front door the stronger the feelings became. After knocking and getting no response, he called out to her.

"Maggie, are you there? It's me, James. "Open up."

The front door was locked. He turned to leave and then heard a whimpering sound coming from inside the house. He wiped away the rain from the window with the end of his shirtsleeve and peered inside. There was Maggie, crouched down in the corner of the living room, continuing to ignore his plea.

"Maggie, open this door or I'm going to break it down!" he shouted.

She made her way to the door, unlatched the lock, and collapsed into his arms, weeping hysterically.

While stroking her tear-soaked cheeks, James gazed tenderly into her eyes. "I'm here now, Maggie," he whispered. "Everything is going to be fine. Calm down and tell me what's wrong."

"James, someone is stalking me," she sobbed. "They're calling me, leaving things in my mailbox—"

"Hold up. What kind of things? Who's been calling you?"

"This morning early I received a phone call. I couldn't make out who it was, they were mumbling. The voice on the other end asked if I had checked my mail." She lost her composure once again and began to sob.

"It's okay, Maggie. What did you find?"

"A brown paper bag, and my nightgown; the one I wore the morning of the accident. It was covered in blood. Frank's blood. I don't understand; nothing makes sense."

"Listen carefully to me, Maggie," James said, taking her by the shoulders. "If indeed it happened the way you said it did, someone must have been watching you that morning and saw everything, and now they're trying to blackmail you."

Maggie wrapped her arms tightly around James's waist. "What am I going to do, James? What am I going to do?"

James wasn't sure how to answer, but one thing he knew for sure: it was not safe to leave her alone.

"You're coming to stay with me and Shannon for awhile until we can figure out the best way out of this mess."

Jerking away from James, Maggie shook her head. "I can't. You don't understand. Shannon—"

"I won't take 'no' for an answer," James interrupted. "We'll get your things later."

Maggie placed herself between James and the door. "Listen to me a minute, James. Shannon has made herself perfectly clear about how she feels."

James shook his head. "No, no, you're mistaken. She's had a change of heart and realizes how much your friendship means to her. You'll see."

"Listen to me, James, she was here today."

James blinked. "Shannon was here today?"

"Yes, and she was outraged that I had involved you both in this mess. She's concocted a notion that I'm trying to lure you back into a romantic relationship, and that's not the half of it."

"Listen, I don't know what's going on in her mind, but I do know I'm not leaving you here alone. Now let's go."

CHAPTER
27

CLAIR STOOD at the storefront window, staring out at the rain. "Tell you what, Nadine, why don't we close this place down early today?"

Wasting no time, Nadine reached for her purse. "I didn't think I'd ever hear those words come out of your mouth, but I must say it's music to my ears."

"Well, there's no logic in staying open in this kind of weather." Clair shrugged. "Nobody's going to go out today unless they have to." As soon as the words came out of her mouth, the bell on the door went off, signaling the arrival of a customer.

"I'm sorry ladies, were you about to close?" Lola tapped the end of her cane on the floor.

Nadine glared at the old woman. "As a matter of fact, we were."

"Please excuse Nadine," Clair spoke up. "It's been exhaustingly slow today due to the bad weather. What can we do for you?

"I was needing to buy some extra candles," Lola said. "Maybe a box or two."

"Well, we have a few scented ones on the back wall," Clair replied. "Nadine, would you mind grabbing a few off the shelf and bringing them up front?"

"What's the matter?" Nadine asked Lola with a sneer. "You don't have electricity where you live?"

"Nadine!" Clair snapped.

"What?"

"Just go get the candles."

Nadine slammed her purse on the counter and headed toward the backroom.

"I must say you have many beautiful things in here," Lola remarked, looking around.

Clair nodded. "Yes, well we're a little store but we do try to accommodate our customers needs.

"These are the only candles I could find," Nadine said, slamming the box down on the counter. "They come three to a box priced $2.95, so if that's all ya need, I can check you out over here."

Ignoring Nadine, Lola took Clair by the hand and slipped her a note.

"It seems I won't be needing them candles after all," the old woman whispered, "but thank you for your time."

Nadine raced out around her. "Here, let me get the door for you."

Lola walked slowly towards the exit, tapping her cane loudly against the floor with every step. She paused at the door, glancing back over her shoulder. "You really should see a doctor about that arthritis of yours," she said, before disappearing into the rain outside.

Nadine couldn't lock the door fast enough. Clair quickly turned away, unfolded the note, and began to read:

Behold your visions, for they will reveal the truth

"Did you tell her about my arthritis?" Nadine said, stomping her foot and pointing her finger at Clair.

Clair blinked, eyes still glued to the note. "What?"

"Did you tell her about my arthritis?"

Crumbling the paper in her hand, she tossed it into the waste-basket. "Why would she care about your arthritis? Not everyone wants to hear about your aches and pains."

Nadine walked over to the window and stared down the road. "I'm telling you, there's something very strange about that woman. How in the hell did she get here? Furthermore, how in the hell does she travel about? It's as if she just appears and disappears. She probably wanted those candles for some kind of voodoo crap."

"You and your imagination," Clair said. "Let's just go."

Clair could think of only one thing: dropping Nadine off and paying Lola a visit. But first, after dropping Nadine off, Clair decided to go home, take a shower, and relax before going to Lola's. She was now having second thoughts. Sure, she was curious as to why Lola had slipped her the note and what it all meant, but at the same time apprehensive about being alone with her. After an hour of contemplating the idea of whether she should go or not, she rolled over on the bed, looked at her car keys laying on the dresser and thought, it's now or never.

Clair parked her car at the end of the long, narrow drive and sat for a moment. She thought about the young couple and their small child that had lived in the house at one time. Back then the old place had been full of life and laughter. That is, until the tragic accident. One afternoon their five-year old daughter wandered into the pond out back and drowned.

She convinced herself it was now or never, and proceeded slowly up the drive. After shutting off the motor, Clair got out of the car and flinched when chimes dangling from the overhang on the porch gave off an eerie jangling sound. She cautiously made her way up the porch steps. Something caught her attention out of the corner of her eye just as she was about to knock on the door. She cringed when a small, dark shadow darted back and forth in front of her.

She stumbled back on the porch railing as the door opened and Lola appeared. "Come in, my dear, I hope Mila didn't frighten you."

"Who?" Clair asked.

"Mila."

Leaping out from behind her, Lola's cat scurried into the house., Clair laughed at herself for being so paranoid.

Once inside, Lola motioned Clair to have a seat. "I hope you don't mind, dear, but I took the liberty of making us a fresh cup of tea."

Clair felt almost hypnotized as she watched the multitude of flickering candles scattered about the room.

Lola eased herself into a rocking chair, sitting directly across from Clair. The candlelight shining on the old woman's weathered face helped soften her appearance.

With hands clenched tight in her lap, Clair sat, anxiously waiting for Lola to explain.

"Clair, my dear, you're here today because I knew if I could get the town's biggest skeptic to believe in what I know to be true, maybe together we can save your friends from this evil soul who lurks among you."

Not wanting to show fear, Clair gathered up all of her trepidation and buried it deep. This was her opportunity to expose Lola for the phony she truly was.

"If you have these powers of foreseeing the future, and these great premonitions of what's to be, then why don't you just go straight to the source of this so-called evil and confront it yourself?"

Lola pursed her lips and frowned. "How dare you mock me! You cannot possibly imagine what I'm capable of. My spirits have chosen you, the biggest skeptic of them all, to help me convince your friends of this evil that lies in waiting. When these trials and tribulations are over, you and your people will never again dispute the knowledge and power of your own spirits…the ones you so blindly try to ignore."

Clair could no longer contain her fear. Every inch of her body trembled with terror. She had never before heard someone speak with such conviction about something so unfeasible.

Lola leaned forward, gently placing a large black book, trimmed in gold, on Clair's lap.

"I mean you no harm, child."

All traces of anger disappeared from the old woman's face. Once again, she appeared fragile and helpless. Lola's dark, piercing eyes gave way to a look of urgency and a need to be trusted.

Looking into her eyes, Clair fell into a trance.

"Open the book, my child," Lola commanded. "Look closely at the pages, for it will show you your past, present, and future, as well as those of your friends. It too will reveal the wicked one's name, and the prophecy which must be fulfilled in order to destroy the evil that is lurking ever so near."

As if hypnotized, Clair opened the book and began to turn its pages slowly, one by one. Images of herself as a toddler curled up in her mother's lap appeared. A calm came over her when in the distance, she suddenly heard the faint sound of her father's voice reading the Bible. She relived her father's passing, then her mother's, her wedding to her beloved husband Buddy, and the birth of her precious sons, followed by the premature death of her soul mate. Every aspect of her life she revisited with each turn of the page. Friends, loved and lost, past and present. Her body sat in Lola's presence, but her mind and soul traveled in another dimension. To her dismay with a turn of a page, she began to experience feelings of loathing, despair, and agony. It was no longer her life she saw but someone else's life, a life of confusion and disarray. Someone she knew very well and trusted. Holding her stomach, she crouched forward as a gnawing pain pierced her insides with thoughts of murder, revenge, and pure evil.

Fighting to block out the distressful image, Clair closed her eyes and imagined it had all been a bad dream. After several grueling minutes, she forced her eyes open. Disoriented she rubbed her eyes and called out to Lola, but received only silence in return. With trembling legs, she struggled to stand. The hair on the back of her neck stood up as she glanced over at her car keys lying on top of her nightstand.

I need a stiff drink, she thought. She walked from room to room turning every light on in the house. Entering the kitchen, she opened the liquor cabinet, pulled out a bottle of bourbon, unscrewed the metal lid, and quickly took a drink. Clair sipped her drink and tried to recall if she had ever had such a vivid nightmare.

CHAPTER
28

IT WAS late in the evening when James and Maggie pulled into the driveway. James coaxed Maggie out of the car and led her into the living room.

"Guestroom is down the hall, second door on your right. Try to get some rest. I'm going to go upstairs and explain to Shannon what's going on," James said.

"She's going to be furious," Maggie replied. "She'll never go for it."

"I'll make her understand," James said. "You'll see. Everything's going to be alright. I promise."

Upon entering their bedroom, James found Shannon lying in bed. Not wanting to startle her, he leaned down next to her and whispered, "Shannon, are you awake? I need to talk to you."

"I must have dozed off," Shannon murmured, trying to focus.

He bent down and kissed her, gently brushing a strand of hair away from her cheek. "I'm sorry I'm so late getting home."

"Where have you been?" she asked him.

James hesitated before answering. "We need to talk."

Shannon yawned. "Can't it wait until tomorrow?"

James shook his head. "I don't want you to be upset, but I stopped by Maggie's to check on her and found her in an awful state. She was crouched down in the corner of her living room crying. Seems someone is stalking her, making prank phone calls, and get this: someone left a bloody nightgown in her mailbox. And it only gets worse. She swears it's the one she wore the night of the accident."

Shannon frowned. "What did you go and do now, James?"

James bit his lip. "Well, I was concerned about her safety, as I knew you would be too, so I talked her into staying with us until we could figure this all out."

Shannon jolted from the bed, yanked open the bedroom door, and leaned over the staircase to see Maggie sitting quietly on the couch. Turning around, she walked back into the bedroom and glared daggers at James before stomping into the bathroom and slamming the door behind her.

James was thinking he should've canceled the reservation at the B & B. He knew they weren't going to make it. "Baby, I know I'm asking a lot, but we're Maggie's friends." He leaned against the bathroom door. "I know I involved us in this mess, but what's done is done. Together maybe we can help her through this. I'm sure she'd do the same for us." He stumbled to catch his footing as Shannon, enraged, flung the bathroom door open.

"After all I've been through, you want me to welcome another lunatic into our home?"

When Shannon had her mind made up about something, James knew there was little he could say to change it. However, this was one argument he was not going to back down from.

"I love you, Shannon, you know that. We'll figure this out. We just have to stick together. She needs your guidance right now more than ever. There's no proof she's killed anyone, let alone Frank. I think someone is setting her up, trying to frame her for Frank's murder. Hell, we don't even know if he is dead!"

"You mean our sweet little Maggie might actually have enemies?" Shannon snickered.

"What I mean is," James said. "She could use your expertise in helping her understand why she invented this crazy scenario in her head to start with."

"You know the stress I've been under lately. I have more patients at work than I can handle, I can't remember the last time I had a good night's rest, and now you want to throw this all on me!"

James pulled Shannon close, wrapping his arms around her.

She pushed him away, turned, went to the bed and sat on its edge, her head lowered. "You know, not every story has a fairytale ending, right?" she murmured.

"Baby, listen to me," James said, kneeling at her feet. "When all of this is over we're going to get away from here for a little while, spend some time alone."

Shannon leaned back, curled up on the bed, and pulled the cover over her head.

JAMES WOKE up groggy; he'd been asleep for a couple hours. Every muscle in his body ached. What he needed now was a strong cup of coffee and an aspirin. Shannon appeared to be sleeping peacefully, something he had not witnessed in awhile. Not wanting to disturb her, he quietly slipped out of the room. Turning the television on, he headed into the kitchen to make a pot of coffee. Walking back from the kitchen, he stopped dead in his tracks. His jaw dropped when he heard the news report. There had been a development in the case of Frank's disappearance.

Shannon, still half asleep, came walking into the living room.

"What are you doing?"

"I'm sorry, baby. I didn't mean to wake you. I couldn't sleep, so I made a pot of coffee and thought I'd catch the morning news. It seems the news station received an anonymous letter containing information about Frank's disappearance."

Shannon sat at the table, poured herself a cup of coffee, and leaned back in her chair. "Is that it? Did they reveal what kind of information the letter contained?"

"No, just that the letter had been sent to Sheriff Chesterton's office to be investigated."

A blood-curdling scream rang out from the other room, cutting their conversation short. Tripping over each other, they rushed to find Maggie, distraught, standing in Katrina's bedroom doorway. Katrina's lifeless body lay covered in blood on the bed. James rushed to her side.

"Oh my God! What have you done, Katrina? Shannon, call an ambulance! Shannon, did you hear me?"

Shannon stood in the doorway, eyes fixed on her mother's body.

"Now, Shannon!" James yelled once again.

"Is she—" Maggie moved closer to the bed.

James felt for a pulse, but knew it was too late. "She's gone. Why would she do something like this? It makes no sense!"

Maggie sobbed and staggered backwards. "Oh God, James, this can't be happening!"

"I don't understand, Maggie. Did you hear something? What made you come into her room?"

"No, uh, I guess I was still half asleep. I thought I was going into the bathroom."

"Listen to me," James commanded, "go check on Shannon, and make sure she doesn't come back into this room. She doesn't need to see her mother like this."

James kept his eyes focused straight ahead. He could not allow himself to look at Katrina another moment.

The paramedics arrived within minutes, but it was clear there was nothing they could do. Draping a sheet over her body, they waited for the coroner to arrive.

Sheriff Chesterton was the next to arrive after hearing the call come over the police scanner.

"It's bad, Sheriff. It's really bad." James pointed down the hallway. "The paramedics say there's nothing they can do."

"Slow down, James. There's nothing they can do for who?"

James glanced over at Shannon and Maggie, and then pulled him aside. "It looks like Katrina killed herself."

"You stay here with the girls," Bill said. "Try and keep them calm."

Sheriff Chesterton could not allow his emotions to take over. His job now was to secure the room and evaluate the situation. Pulling the notepad from his pocket, he began to record his findings. He noted the razorblade in Katrina's right hand and the deep, gaping slit in her left wrist. Glancing around the room, he established no apparent struggle had taken place.

Staring down at Katrina's body, he felt a sense of déjà vu. Almost eighteen years earlier, he had been called out to the scene of an apparent suicide. Unfortunately, he had known that victim as well.

Everything had been relatively quiet that summer night until a call came in reporting a shooting at 209 Lester Street. Familiar with the location, as well as the troubled family, he remembered thinking the worst.

Upon entering the house, he had observed two young girls, the daughter of the victim, obviously in distress, and her friend, who appeared quite lucid. Upon questioning them, it had been determined that the victim's daughter had witnessed her father's suicide. Hysterical, she had called upon her friend for support before calling the authorities.

Sheriff Chesterton never forgot that grim summer night years ago. Now he stood looking at what appeared to be another heartbreaking act of desperation involving a member of his community. In an ironic twist, he would once again be interviewing the same two young women.

Sheriff Chesterton looked at Katrina's body one last time before the paramedics gently raised it onto the gurney.

Shannon stood motionless as they wheeled it out of the room. She finally went to the gurney and pulled the sheet back from her mother's face. She took one last look, then turned away.

James rushed to her side, wrapping his arms around her.

Maggie sat motionless, staring off into space. The eerie sound of silence now replaced the earlier cries of hysteria.

After several more silent moments, Sheriff Chesterton put his personal feelings aside and began the daunting task of questioning. He sat next to Shannon and placed his hands over hers. "Shannon, I can't express how sorry I am for your loss."

Shannon's demeanor changed suddenly from distraught to resentment. "I took her out of that asylum and gave her a second chance. I should've known it would come to this. No one could ever make her happy."

"You don't mean that, baby," James said. "We all know how much you loved your mother."

"He's right, Shannon." Maggie reached across James and took her by the hand. "None of this is your fault."

Shannon leaned forward towards Maggie, her body red-hot with anger. "You know nothing of what I've been through. Who are you to tell me how I should feel?"

"Let's all take a deep breath," Sheriff Chesterton said, jumping in. "You've all been through a traumatic ordeal, foremost Shannon."

Maggie backed away to the far end of the sofa. She understood all too clearly where Shannon was coming from. She felt guilty, knowing her presence there only added to her friend's unimaginable grief.

James felt helpless, having never witnessed such a tragedy before. He was anguished over the thought of his and Shannon's ongoing arguments playing a part in Katrina's demise.

Sheriff Chesterton could no longer put off his inevitable line of questioning. He began to speak. "I've got to ask everyone some questions, but I promise to make this as quick and painless as possible. I need to know who the last person was to see Katrina alive."

James and Maggie looked at each other, then at Shannon. Raising her head from James's chest, Shannon collected her thoughts before answering.

"I'm not sure of the exact time, somewhere around 7:30 last night. She said she didn't feel well; she was going to lie down. She asked me to call and cancel her session with Dr. Mead, her therapist. That was the last time we spoke."

"Did she make a habit of canceling her sessions?"

"No, this was the first time."

The sheriff hesitated for a moment. "Had she been depressed or unusually upset recently?"

"No, that's why this doesn't make sense," James spoke up. "Shannon had left for work earlier that morning, so Katrina offered to make our breakfast. She appeared to be in good spirits.

"So she didn't come across as depressed or upset in any way?"

James shook his head. "No, Bill, not at all."

"Again, I'm sorry you had to find your mother this way," the Sheriff said, directing his attention to Shannon.

Maggie burst into tears.

"Uh, sheriff," James quickly added, "It was actually Maggie that found her first."

"You see, Sheriff," Maggie said, wiping her eyes. "Shannon had been thoughtful enough to send James over to ask if I'd join them for supper. They know how lonely I get over there by myself. Anyway, it just so happened that earlier I'd heard a strange noise outside my house, and I panicked. Shannon suggested I should stay over."

"What are friends for?" Shannon sneered, cutting her eyes towards her.

Sheriff Chesterton sensed something was not quite up to par. "So how did Katrina seem at supper?" he asked, moving along.

"Mother didn't join us at supper," Shannon explained. "I didn't want to disturb her."

The sheriff flipped the paper in his notepad and leaned forward. "Okay, now tell me what exactly was the circumstance that led to her being found?"

Once again, Maggie's eyes welled up with tears. "I'd gotten up to use the bathroom, and still being half asleep, I mistakenly opened the door to Katrina's room. I—I couldn't believe what I saw." She paused to catch a breath. "There was so much blood!"

"I'm sorry I have to ask these questions. I promise I'm almost done."

"We know you're only doing your job," James said.

"Shannon, although everything points to your mother taking her own life, you should be prepared. There could be an inquest to perform an autopsy."

"My God! Isn't it obvious what happened?"

"I'm sorry, Shannon, if I've upset you. If I have any further questions, we can do this later. Once again, I'm so very sorry for your loss."

Sheriff Chesterton would weigh all the facts before coming to any conclusion. He had done enough investigations to know that in his line of work things were not always as they appeared.

Having a long day ahead of him, he headed back to the station. Paperwork would keep him bogged down most of the morning. However, he could not shake the sense that something was missing, an aching, stabbing sensation that just would not let up, a feeling that he had overlooked something important.

CHAPTER
29

ARRIVING AT work, Nadine found the boutique locked up tight. She looked down at her watch, then smiled when she realized she had actually made it to work early. Once inside she began pricing the new shipment of women's scarves that had arrived the previous day. She was counting the startup cash when she looked up and saw Clair coming in the door.

"Oh my God, woman, you look like you were kicked by a mule!"

"Don't start, Nadine!" Clair said, tugging at the neckline on her sweater. "I didn't get three hours' sleep last night and my head is pounding."

"That's clear to see. Those bags under your eyes look like two giant pillows."

Clair slowly turned away from Nadine, took a few steps, and then stopped short. Turning back toward Nadine she thought for a moment, and then asked, "Can I ask you something?"

Nadine nodded. "Sure."

"Have you ever had a nightmare so vivid that when you woke up it felt like you had truly experienced it?"

Nadine thought about it. "Well, once I dreamt I was held captive on this ranch with three of the best-looking men you've ever laid eyes on. One of them kept referring to himself as Little Joe. Come to think of it, I had been watching an episode of Bonanza right before I went to sleep."

Clair raised an eyebrow. "Are you making fun of me?"

"All I'm saying is you must have had a nightmare. That's all it was…a bad dream. But if it'll help you to talk about it, I'll listen."

Clair ran over to the wastebasket and began pillaging through the trash.

"Clair, you're acting like a crazy woman." Nadine pulled the wastebasket from her hands. "You're scaring me."

Clair continued unfolding each wadded-up piece of paper. She dropped to her knees and franticly searched through the scattered mess, as if looking for something that would save her life. Jumping up triumphantly, she waved a piece of wrinkled paper in one hand. "I found it! This is it!"

"Great." Nadine said, scratching her head.

"Nadine, get me a chair. I feel faint."

"What in the world has got you so upset? Let me see that piece of paper." Nadine eased the note out of her hand. "Behold your visions for they will reveal the truth."

"What the hell does that mean?"

Clair swallowed hard. "Lola did come into the shop yesterday, didn't she?"

"Yeah, don't you remember? She was looking for some candles but ours were too expensive for her taste. Not that she has any taste! What the hell does any of this have to do with her?"

Before Clair could reply, Nadine shook her head, as if having a moment of clarity. "Wait a minute. She slipped this piece of crap to you while I wasn't looking, didn't she?"

Clair shrugged and bowed her head. Unsure what to say, she took a deep breath and, at the risk of sounding like a lunatic, she began to explain the disturbing events of the night before.

"I tell you, I think I'm going crazy, Nadine. Everything happened just as I said it did. I know I was there at that farmhouse and I know what I experienced was real. I just can't explain how it could have happened that way. Don't just stand there! Say something!"

For a moment, Nadine stood speechless, powerless to respond immediately to Clair's outrageous tales of premonitions and out-of-body experiences. After a few minutes of dead silence, she finally responded. "Here's what I think," she said, tapping her fingernails on the ceramic countertop. "By giving you that note, which doesn't make any sense, I might add, Lola knew it would peak your curiosity, then she put some kinda hex on you with that voodoo crap of hers. Of course you'd have nightmares after all that."

Hoping for some sign of a logical explanation, Clair listened closely to Nadine.

"Well, doesn't that make more sense? Didn't I tell you that old woman was bad news?"

Clair sighed "All right, explain this to me then. Why would I envision Shannon as the evil one? We've known that girl practically all her life. She's done nothing but help people. My God, she even took her mother out of that mental hospital and welcomed her into her home."

Nadine thought for a moment and then snapped her fingers. "Deception."

"What?"

"Deception! She's using deception and trickery to try to turn you against Shannon. Hell, sounds like she might be trying to turn all of us against each other."

"That makes no sense. For what reason?"

"I don't know," Nadine sighed. "Maybe just for the fun of seeing our little community in turmoil. All I know is, from the moment she set foot here in Patton, there's been nothing but trouble."

"I know, but—"

"No buts!" Nadine fired back. "Wasn't it you that said people like her work through trickery? It's true she had me fooled for a while, but you convinced me how foolish it was to believe in such nonsense. Are you saying that you, the biggest skeptic of all, now believe it's possible she has some great supernatural powers?"

Something Nadine said lit a spark in Clair. "Lola said the same thing," she murmured, dumbstruck.

"What are you talking about?" Nadine threw her arms up. "Have you not heard a word I've said?"

Clair took her by the arm and pulled her close. "Lola said if she could convince the biggest skeptic of all, being me, to believe in her power of foreseeing the future, in return it would become clear."

"What would become clear?" Nadine asked.

"The person we've all took for granted as being our friend, a pillar of the community. Maybe Shannon's using deception to cover up her phony innocent act."

"Oh, okay." Nadine turned away, shaking her head. "Now you're really scaring me."

"Listen, I was wrong. There is something very genuine about Lola. I can't understand it all but I know what I saw and felt last night was real."

In the middle of their discussion, a light tap on the storeroom window interrupted them. Looking up, they saw Edith standing outside the door pointing at her watch, then to the clock on the storeroom wall. Engulfed in conversation, the girls had not noticed they were fifteen minutes late opening the store.

"Clair, if I was you I wouldn't mention this to anyone else." Nadine turned the key in the lock and opened the door. "They might send for those people in white jackets to come pick ya up."

"If they've not come for you by now, I figure I'm safe." Clair chuckled.

Edith entered with a worried frown. "Is something wrong? I've never known you girls to open the store late."

Clair placed the 'open' sign on the door. "I do apologize, Edith, it's just I didn't sleep well last night and got a late start."

Edith nodded. "I know the feeling."

"You too?"

Edith thumbed through the scarves on the table in front of her. "I can't sleep for Larry getting up and down all hours of the night. Something's bothering him but he won't talk to me about it."

"I hope he's not coming down with something," Nadine said.

Edith shook her head. "No, it's more like something heavy is weighing on his mind, but when I suggested maybe talking to Shannon might help, he almost bit my head off."

Clair's curiosity peaked. "That is strange. Wonder what could've happened to make him react that way."

"I didn't ask, didn't want to push it." She moved along to the dress rack. "I thought I'd pay Shannon a visit. Maybe she can shed some light on what's going on."

"I'm not so sure you ought to do that," Clair said.

"And why shouldn't I?"

"Uh, I'm just saying—"

"What Clair means," Nadine spoke up, "is you know how men are. They don't like us women getting into their business, even if we're just trying to help."

Clair nodded. "Yeah, that's what I meant."

"Well, maybe you're right," Edith said. "I'm sure he'll come around soon. Changing the subject, did you here the news this morning?"

"No," both women answered in unison.

"Well, it seems someone sent the station an anonymous letter saying they had information about Frank's disappearance. You know Charles and Ester Felker from church? Their boy works down at the station. I swear he was just in diapers not long ago. It's hard to—"

Impatient to hear the point of the story, Nadine interrupted. Yeah, you were saying something about an anonymous letter?"

"I'm sorry. I do get sidetracked sometimes." Edith straightened her scarf and adjusted her glasses. "They couldn't say what was in the letter, only that the person sent it on to Bill down at the police station, and you know Bill, he takes his sheriff duties seriously. I'm sure he'll get to the bottom of all this soon."

Nadine's eyes widened. "Well, I for one think it's odd that he happens to come up missing right after he'd gone to check on Maggie. And did you hear they found his truck not too far away from her house?"

Edith shook her head and glanced over at Clair, then cut her eyes back toward Nadine. "Why on earth would anybody think that girl would want to harm Frank?"

"From what I've heard, Frank had been sweet on Maggie for some time but it was clear the feeling wasn't mutual. You know Frank; he could be a little forward sometimes. Maybe he came on a little strong and Maggie had to use force."

"Okay, that's enough speculating." Clair pulled a dress from the rack and handed it to Edith. "I'm sure Edith isn't interested in hearing any more gossip."

"Clair's right, Nadine," Edith said, admiring the dress off the rack. "You really shouldn't spread such idle rumors. Next thing you know they'll be saying one of us was involved, whoever they may be!"

CHAPTER
30

HOPING TO get some answers from Katrina's doctors, Sheriff Chesterton headed seventy-five miles south towards Thebes. On the way out of town, a disturbing memory filled his thoughts as he passed by the old Hillcrest asylum. In the past, on more than one occasion, he had helped the Sedgewickville police in escorting dangerously disturbed psychotic criminals to its doors.

One of Sheriff Chesterton's first tasks on the force included transporting one of the most notorious insane criminals to ever come out of Sedgewickville, Edward Ray Brantley. At the time, Mr. Brantley was a forty-one-year-old husband and father of two young children.

On the day of January 6th, 1951, the official police records described three horrifying and brutal murders at the location of 938 Ganes Boulevard. The first victim found was Brantley's young wife, twenty-eight-year-old Emily. Her lifeless body was discovered lying in the doorway of their children's bedroom. She was covered in blood, her head nearly decapitated, her throat cut from ear to ear. Beyond the doorway lay the children, three-year-old Mary Elizabeth and five-year-old Beth Ann. Both children had sustained blunt force trauma to the backs of their heads, a blow hard enough to cause immediate death, as the coroner would later state.

Brantley's defense would be that he suffered from severe paranoia along with delusional thoughts that his family was evil and must be destroyed.

Back then the majority of patients assigned to Hillcrest was often given extensive electric shock treatments on top of invasive lobotomies.

Upon entering Hillcrest for the first time, Sheriff Chesterton remembered observing numerous patients restrained in straitjackets. Patients walked the halls in a zombie-like state. He also remembered the vivid scars that marked their foreheads; a clear indication that a lobotomy had been performed. Truly disturbed at the time by seeing another human being forced to sustain such treatments, he quickly reminded himself as to why Brantley had been brought there. He had left Hillcrest that day with a guilty feeling of pleasure in knowing the ill-fated torture that most likely lay ahead for Edward Ray Brantley.

After witnessing the horror at Hillcrest, Sheriff Chesterton had his own preconceived ideas about mental facilities in general. He wondered if Katrina had been subject to the same kind of extreme treatments as those confined to Hillcrest. If so, how could she have endured such pain for so many years? Knowing Katrina and her family and being aware of their dysfunctional and turbulent lives, he hoped that now maybe she would find some peace.

He took a second glance at the directions he had mapped out previously. The building in front of him looked nothing like he had expected. Massive in size, it stood three stories tall, surrounded by a magnificent landscape adorned with a variety of blooming flowers. Once inside, he was pleasantly surprised to find a color scheme of warm soothing colors, a stark contrast to that of Hillcrest.

As he walked to the front desk, a young woman in a crisp white nurse uniform approached him with a smile. "Hello, I'm Nurse Wilkins. Can I help you?"

"Yes ma'am, you can. I'm Sheriff Chesterton and I have an appointment with Dr. Delacruz and Dr. Mead."

The nurse nodded. "I'll inform them that you're here. In the meantime, please make yourself comfortable," she said, escorting him to a chair.

He lifted a magazine from the table in front of him, he thumbed through the pages while trying not to look nervous. He had interviewed countless people before, but this day he was finding it difficult to pull his thoughts together.

A short time had passed before Nurse Wilkins walked over and patted him on the shoulder. "Dr. Delacruz can see you now. Follow me and I'll show you to his office."

He followed her down a long corridor and into Dr. Delacruz's office. The doctor immediately stood up from his chair, introduced himself, and shook the sheriff's hand.

"As I said when you called me this morning, I'll do what I can to answer your questions, but you understand that Katrina's medical files are confidential."

"I understand," Sheriff Chesterton nodded. "As the sheriff of Patton I'm obligated to investigate every aspect of her death. So, any information you can give me as to your opinion of Katrina's recent state of mind would be helpful."

Rubbing his head, Dr. Delacruz leaned back in his chair. "Dr. Mead would be more of an authority to comment on that. As an outpatient, Katrina had been seeing him regularly for her therapy sessions."

Hesitating for a moment, Sheriff Chesterton took his hat off and slammed it on the desk. "Weren't you Katrina's doctor at one time? Do you not collaborate with each other on your patient's well-being?" he demanded.

Dr. Delacruz frowned. "I can assure you, we wouldn't have released Katrina from this facility if we hadn't been confident that she was ready to return to society." The doctor tilted his head and straightened his tie. "At the time of her release, she had shown no sign of suicidal tendencies or violent behavior. And, with the agreement that her daughter regulate the medications that she was prescribed, we felt confident she would be able to adjust."

The sheriff leaned forward. "Exactly what medications are we talking about, Doc?"

Opening his file cabinet, Dr. Delacruz searched through his charts until he came to Katrina's file. "I see here that Katrina was still being prescribed several medications as treatment for her illness, along with a mild sedative due to her insomnia."

Conversation stopped as both men stood up to welcome Dr. Mead into the room. "I apologize for my tardiness. I'm Dr. Mead, and you must be Sheriff Chesterton."

Reaching out to shake the doctor's hand, the sheriff hoped the surprised look on his face wasn't too obvious. Unlike Dr. Delacruz, Dr. Mead did not look old enough to hold a degree in medicine, much less a degree in psychology.

"Don't let my baby face fool you, Sheriff." He patted his smooth cheek and smiled. "I'm well qualified in my profession."

Not easily embarrassed, the sheriff blushed.

"I have to say I was saddened and somewhat perplexed at the news of Katrina's sudden passing," the doctor added solemnly.

Hoping Dr. Mead could give him the crucial answers he needed to seal the case, Bill did not waste any time.

"Dr. Mead, you say you're perplexed. Please explain."

"It is in my professional opinion that Katrina had been making great progress in her therapy sessions. Her bouts with depression were diminishing and she stated recently that her insomnia had lessened dramatically. It is troubling to hear she has taken her own life."

Bill smiled slightly. Confident he was finally getting somewhere, he moved forward with his questioning. "So, is it your opinion that she wasn't in a suicidal state of mind?"

For a moment all conversation ended as both doctors glanced nervously at one another, as if they suddenly realized what the sheriff was looking for.

"Let me be the first to clarify something," Dr. Mead said, sitting straight up in his chair and cupping both hands underneath his chin. "Katrina entered our hospital ten years ago diagnosed with undifferentiated schizophrenia with suicidal tendencies. During that time, she received electro convulsive therapy along with insulin shock therapy. As Dr. Delacruz will confirm, after supplementing a range of medications we were able to stop the further invasive treatments. Although she became well enough to receive outpatient treatments, such as her psychoanalysis therapy, there is not, nor can there ever be, a guarantee a patient such as Katrina wouldn't relapse back into her once dark, imprisoned shell."

Tired and mentally drained, Sheriff Chesterton slowly stood up from his chair, walked over to both doctors, and shook their hands.

"I do thank you gentlemen for taking the time out of your busy schedule to see me."

Had Katrina fallen victim to the illness that not long ago had consumed her mind? Had she believed taking her own life was the only way she could ever truly be free? These questions haunted him.

As he walked down the corridor to exit the lobby, he stopped for a moment and took one last look at what Katrina had called home. It made him sad to think that if she had not been released… had still been there under her doctor's care…maybe, just maybe… she might still be alive.

CHAPTER
31

EARLY MORNING and already the radio stations were reporting a heat advisory for Patton. Larry unfolded his favorite lawn chair in the shade and sat down with a cold glass of freshly squeezed lemonade. With Edith out shopping, he could relax without the constant feeling of her watching his every move. He was tired and irritable, hadn't felt like his old self for a while.

Larry lifted his cap, wiped the sweat from his forehead, and downed the last drop of lemonade. He closed his eyes and began to say a prayer, only to be interrupted seconds later by a loud noise coming from down the street. He cringed when he realized what the loud noise was.

Larry had three loves in his life: Edith, his 1968 Torino Squire station wagon, (with simulated wood-grain side panels and chrome roof rack) and his bar.

When Edith got out of the car, he could tell by the disgusted look on her face that it was not going to be good.

"Larry, how many times have I asked you to take a look at the brakes on this car? You promised you would take it in for repair weeks ago. I swear I thought I'd never see the day!"

"Woman, you know I've been busy. Anyway, it hasn't seemed to stop you from driving it."

Swallowing hard to keep from saying something that she would regret, she chose to ignore his sarcasm by not responding. She into the back seat, gathered up her packages, and walked towards the house.

Disgusted by his own actions, Larry hung his head. It would be just one more thing he would have to apologize for. He had put off his responsibilities far too long.

He pulled the car into the garage and turned on the AM radio, flipping through until he found his favorite station. He couldn't resist singing along with John Denver to "Take Me Home, Country Roads."

He had been underneath the car but a few seconds when the radio suddenly changed stations. The twangy chords of "The Devil Went Down to Georgia" caught him by surprise.

"Edith, is that you?"

"Ah, don't you just love that song?" said an eerily familiar voice somewhere above him. A chuckle followed the song's chorus. "I do believe the devil is right here in Patton."

Larry's blood ran cold. "This isn't happening," he told himself. "It's just a figment of my imagination. Frank's dead, and that's that."

"You really are beginning to hurt my feelings," the voice said sadly.

Slowly sliding out from underneath the car, Larry moved cautiously forward, heart pounding with dread. He prepared himself for yet another chilling encounter as he approached the driver-side door. Frantic, he yanked it open, expecting to see Frank's ghostly image inside, but instead found nothing. He turned off the radio and sat back in the driver's seat with a sigh of relief.

"I must say, Larry, you're really letting yourself go. When's the last time you had a shave?"

Not wanting to look behind him, Larry stared straight ahead. "I'm having a hallucination and in a minute it will pass," he said as calmly as though he was merely commenting on the weather.

"Oh, I assure you, I'm not a hallucination, but you don't have to look at me to hear what I have to say. This will be the last time I come to you, Larry, so I need you to listen carefully. Last night another tragedy happened in our town."

Larry took a deep breath and exhaled. "Frank, if you're supposed to be some dead spirit guide here to give me information on how to stop this so-called evil person, then why not just give me their name and address and I'll alert the sheriff. Otherwise leave me the hell alone."

"It doesn't work that way," Frank replied. "I was sent to help guide you in the right direction. You remember the stranger in your bar that night? The stranger that killed that innocent family? You said he gave you a bad feeling, but you couldn't put your finger on it. You sensed his true evil, but you distrusted your instincts. You've seen pure evil face to face, but once again you choose to doubt yourself. I can tell you this evil will pursue its victims with painstaking precision, not unlike that of a starving lion stalking its prey. So, stop second-guessing yourself and accept this gift you've been given. Use it wisely."

Larry didn't have to turn around and look; he knew Frank's spirit had left. The dread in his heart was replaced with a feeling of sadness. Frank's ghost had become an almost everyday fixture in his life; not one of eager anticipation, but an odd feeling of familiarity. Somehow, Frank's spirit had finally broken through to him, and now he was experiencing a warmth and peace of mind that had been eluding him for weeks. No longer was he consumed by fears of his own madness. He had known for some time about the gift Frank had spoken of, but he had locked it away deep in his soul, not wanting others to know.

Shannon didn't waste any time packing away her mother's things. With a strange, eerie calm about her, she sifted through Katrina's belongings, sorting her clothing into one pile and miscellaneous items in another.

"Shannon, baby, you don't have to do this right now."

"James is right," Maggie said. "There will be plenty of time later."

A sneer came over Shannon's face as she glared at Maggie. "Now is as good a time as any."

"I need you to call Jackson's Funeral Home and tell them I'll be making arrangements as soon as the morgue releases Katrina's body," she said, turning toward James.

James and Maggie listened with disgust as Shannon spoke nonchalantly of her mother's passing.

The quicker she could put Katrina's things out of sight, the easier it would be to let go of her mother completely. She had no desire to reminisce about the past. What she needed now was time away; time away from the both of them, time to pull herself together and work on a plan. She knew just the perfect place.

"I REALLY don't think it's a good idea for you to take off by yourself," James said, pulling the car keys from his pocket. "But if you insist, promise me you won't be gone long."

Shannon nodded, taking the keys. "I just need time alone to sort out a few things. I'll be back before you know it."

As Shannon made her way down the winding dirt road, her heart began to race. She slid the palms of her sweaty hands back and forth around the steering wheel. She finally stopped the car and cautiously reached for the door handle as if it would scorch her fingers at the slightest touch. On trembling legs, she braced herself against the car and removed her sunglasses to get a better look. Straight ahead was her childhood home.

She picked up a dried roof shingle, one of many that lay scattered about, and threw it into the dense weeds that replaced the once green lawn surrounding the property. Nothing looked like what she remembered.

She stepped across broken planks that lined the rotted porch, turned the doorknob, and with a few good yanks, she was inside. Something deep within was urging her on.

With her fingers wrapped around the stair railing, Shannon took the first step. She made her way towards the top of the stairs, then paused halfway for a moment when hearing what sounded like laughter coming from her parents' old room.

A warm, unexpected feeling of familiarity and calm came over her. The tick-tock of the old grandfather clock at the bottom of the stairs echoed a soothing sound. Family photographs once again adorned the wall leading up the staircase. She had stepped back in time. For a moment she swore she heard her best friend, Star, barking for attention as his little metal tag jangled back and forth on his collar.

She raced up the softly lit staircase towards the sound of her mother's laughter.

"Mama, I think I found Star!" she said, shoving her mother's bedroom door open and rushing in.

Her mother's eyes dark and distant shot a piercing look of disgust. "How many times have I told you not to barge into my room without knocking?"

She could no longer hear the soothing sound of the grandfather clock. The soft light that had guided her up the stairs had vanished. Her brain told her legs to move, but they wouldn't listen. She stood motionless, eyes fixed; she gaped at the image of her mother half naked and the stranger lying next to her.

An intense rush of heat and anger engulfed her body. The same feelings of rage she had experienced so many years earlier boiled to the surface. She stumbled backwards out of the room slamming the door behind her. As quick as the images had appeared, they vanished back into the disturbed corner of her tormented mind.

Shannon's childhood had been shrouded with intense hatred and disgust over her mother's adultery, festering and boiling over, peeling away layer after layer any empathetic feelings she might have had for her.

With Katrina's release into her care, Shannon's deep wounds had once again been exposed. The moment their lives crossed paths again, Shannon's mental stability had begun to diminish.

Slouched down, she sat in the darkness with her back against the dilapidated staircase. If only Katrina could have stayed comatose, locked away securely out of her life, maybe things would have been different.

The danger of losing everything she had accomplished and acquired—her practice, the love of James, respect from the community—only fed her obsession to move forward, manipulating and removing any obstacle in her way.

She drove back home in a trance, ignoring all speed signs and stoplights. She imagined what James and Maggie were doing alone in the house. She pictured the two of them making love, lying naked in each other's arms. She could hear the sound of their laughter and see the smirks on their faces as they relished the fact that they had made a fool out of her.

At last she envisioned herself standing on a cliff, daring each of her feet to move one step closer to the edge, all the while praying someone to stop her. Not to rescue her from what would be certain death, but to help her put an end to what she believed had been (and would forever be) a life of torment and despair.

CHAPTER
32

SHERIFF CHESTERTON sat at his desk, surrounded by paperwork. Hands shaking, he opened the autopsy results on Katrina and began to read. The coroner concluded the cause of death to be an apparent suicide. Breathing a sigh of frustration, he took his glasses off and rubbed his tired eyes. With no clear evidence of foul play, he had no choice but to release Katrina's body for burial.

Exhausted, he was about to call it a night when Deputy McCain adverted his attention.

"Sheriff Chesterton, I think you'll want to take a look at this."

"Can it wait until tomorrow?"

"Uh, no sir, it's quite urgent."

Handing Sheriff Chesterton an envelope, he explained, "The KFVT news station received this anonymous letter earlier today. As you can clearly see, it doesn't have a return address, but it has Patton's postmark."

Putting on his reading glasses, the sheriff began to read. "The content of this letter is my admission of guilt. No longer can I control my despicable acts of violent behavior. Nevertheless, as much as you would like me to divulge my identity, I will not. It is up to the great Sheriff Chesterton of Patton to do that."

Pausing for a moment, he took a deep breath, desperately trying to keep his composure. He then continued reading. "Although he has had more than one chance to catch me, he has sadly failed. You see, Sheriff Chesterton and I go way back. Now I must say, for the sake of poor Frank Phillips' family and friends, he was just in the wrong place at the wrong time. This sickness of mine takes over and I have no control. I do fear that if I'm not caught soon this irreversible madness that empowers me will ignite into a raging inferno."

Sliding the chair away from his desk, the sheriff stood up abruptly. "How many people have had access to this letter?" he asked.

Removing his hat, Deputy McCain scratched his head. "Uh, it's unclear, sir."

"What do you mean 'unclear,' Deputy?"

"Well sir, no one at the news station could be sure. They have several employees that work in the mailroom, not to mention it ended up on three different newscasters' desks in the process."

The sheriff slammed the letter down on his desk. "Inexcusable." Clenching his fists with anger, he growled, "First thing bright and early I want you to go back down to that station and get the names of every person that had any contact with this letter. And furthermore, make it clear that anyone divulging its contents to the public would only further obstruct our investigation."

Dropping his head, Deputy McCain nodded. Wanting to make one last desperate plea on his own behalf, he tried to explain. "Bill, can I just say, sir—"

"No you may not. Do as I ask."

Alone at his desk, the sheriff read the letter repeatedly until his eyes began to blur. Physically and mentally drained, he sat back; shoulders slumped, rubbing his tired eyes. He had felt secure in making the right choice of becoming a law officer so many years ago, but now he questioned his decision.

Following his father's example, he had joined the police academy right out of high school. His father had been a sheriff for thirty-one years before retiring, only to pass away from a fatal heart attack the following year. As a child, he had idolized his father and would often try to imitate him.

His mother, a homemaker, took pride in her husband and his line of work, but often voiced her concern. Being the only child, his mother had been especially protective of him. She was not excited to say the least when her son announced his decision to join the force. However, after a lot of persuading from her husband and an immeasurable amount of imploring from her son, she finally gave her blessing.

He stared down at his trembling hands. The deep lines around his mouth and sunken eyes from lack of sleep aged him ten years. It was times like these he wished for companionship. Sure, he had dated more than a few lovely women over the years, but his work had always taken center stage. Truth being he could never bear to put a woman he had feelings for in the position of worrying night after night about his safety.

Too tired to think anymore, he put the letter back into the envelope and filed it away under lock and key. He turned off his desk lamp, then took one last glance around the room before closing his office door.

CHAPTER
33

FOR THE tenth time, James looked at his watch and tapped on its back, positive it must have stopped.

"I'm sure she'll be back any moment." Maggie handed him a hot cup of coffee. "I'm sure she knows how worried we are about her."

"Does she? James frowned. "I'm beginning to wonder if she really cares. I'm starting to think I don't really know her anymore. I thought I did!"

Maggie patted his shoulder. "You're just upset and exhausted, that's all. None of us are thinking clearly."

James sighed. "Maggie, look at me. I need to ask you something, and I need you to be honest."

"Ask me anything."

"I can't believe what I'm about to ask."

Maggie leaned in closer, caressing his shoulder.

"Something's not right with Shannon, but I can't put my finger on it," James said.

"Exactly what do you mean 'not right'?"

"I mean for a while now she's been distant, not just with me but with everyone she knows. I overheard her arguing with Katrina more than once. A few times it got so bad I thought I was going to have to step in."

Maggie hung onto his every word.

"I'm worried, Maggie. The other day I tripped over a stack of her files from work; she has them strewn all over the bedroom floor. When I started straightening things up I came across some disturbing magazines."

"What kind of magazines?" Maggie asked.

"Those true crime magazines, the ones you pulled off your shelf at the store because they were so explicit."

"You mean those trashy magazines that showed all those gruesome murders? I've never known her to be remotely interested in anything like that."

James shrugged. "Yeah, well, like I said, she's not been herself lately."

"Did you—" Maggie began then stopped.

"Ask her what was going on? Oh, no! She would've accused me of snooping and made up some lame excuse as to why she had them."

"James, I have to tell you something." Maggie's lips began to tremble. "Shannon's made more than one threat towards me."

James stared at her in surprise. "Threat? What kind of threat?"

"Remember I told you she came by the house the other day?"

James nodded. "Yeah, vaguely."

"She made it clear that under no circumstances was I to come anywhere near you ever again. I tried to tell you earlier that she thinks we're having an affair. She thinks it's been going on for some time."

"That's ridiculous!" James snapped.

"Her excuse for stopping by was to ask me if I'd heard about the sudden death of that attorney, you know the one we called out to the house that night?"

"Oh yes, Mr. Burns. I read about that in the newspaper. Terrible senseless accident."

"Well, Shannon could barely contain her excitement as she told me the gruesome details. She said the accident was fortunate in that how we had involved her in our little scheme of things; she wouldn't have to answer any of his questions. James, I think she might have been involved somehow."

"Oh my God!"

Maggie held up a hand, signaling James to calm down. "I need you to listen to me closely. What I'm about to tell you I've never told anyone else."

Opening up to him about her father's sexual abuse, she then revealed Shannon's connection.

"I'm so sorry, Maggie." James pulled her close, wrapping his arms tightly around her. "I can't imagine the pain you've been going through all these years. And for Shannon to have played on your vulnerability at such a critical time in your life is inconceivable."

"You can never speak of this to Shannon. Promise me!" Maggie pleaded. "She already thinks I'm trying to seduce you every time we're near each other. She's made that clear."

Maggie buried her head in James's chest, her warm, wet tears soaking through his shirt and into his skin. A burning heat of passion flowed rapidly throughout his body, making him weak with desire. The sweet scent from her body heightened his excitement to a degree he had never imagined possible. Instinctively reacting to his touch, Maggie's body trembled, leaving her craving for him to fulfill her hungering desire. They could no longer deny their lust for one another.

Aware only of each other, they were oblivious to the presence of a voyeur just outside the window.

A murderous rage swept over Shannon, searing her soul to the core, eating away at her insides. She doubled over in pain and nausea and fell to her knees, her mind racing with thoughts of revenge.

Struggling to recover from the anguish that was devouring her, she pulled herself up off the ground while trying to steady her trembling legs. She pulled her tangled hair back into a bun, and wiped her face and dusted the dirt off her pants. Wanting to make sure they heard her approaching, she went back to the car and slammed the door.

"Shannon, where have you been?" James tugged at the waistband of his pants.

"I told you, I took a ride to clear my head. Do you feel all right? You look a little flushed."

"We were worried sick about you," he said, directing the focal point back to her. "You've been gone a long time."

"Where's Maggie?" she asked, looking past him into the other room.

"She's in the kitchen making a pot of coffee. Are you going to tell me where you went or are you going to keep me guessing?"

Shannon forced a smile and kissed him on the cheek as she headed toward the kitchen.

"I'll take a cup, too, if you don't mind," she said to Maggie.

Standing at the stove with her back to Shannon, Maggie reached into the cabinet for a cup. "I'm so glad you're here. We were really beginning to worry."

"I'm so sorry. I just needed to be by myself, clear my head. I never meant to upset either of you. Can you forgive me?" Shannon's mouth smiled but her eyes did not.

It didn't take Maggie long to catch on to Shannon's phony act. Trying to figure out what she was up to would be more difficult. Knowing Shannon was an expert at playing head games, she thought the best thing she could do would be to play along

"Don't give it another thought, Shannon. Just know I'm here for you."

At this point Shannon could hardly restrain herself. The picture of them both entangled in their lustful embrace had been scorched into her brain.

"Are you alright?" Maggie asked in a pretentious voice. "You look a little pale."

Her false pretense of concern only infuriated Shannon more. Up until now, she had been unable to make eye-contact with Maggie, but now as she looked closer, she spotted something peculiar.

"I'm sorry, I don't mean to stare, but did you know some of the buttons on your dress are missing?"

Looking down at her dress, it became embarrassingly clear. During her and James's rowdy love session two of the top buttons on her dress had popped partially off, exposing her breast. She stammered to come up with a conceivable excuse.

"I knew I shouldn't have worn this old thing. I've had trouble with these buttons before. I can't believe I didn't notice it myself!"

"Don't be embarrassed." She reached across the table and patted Maggie's hand. "A little needle and thread will take care of that. Anyway, it's been so kind of you to put your personal dilemmas aside so that you can be here for James—I mean, for the both of us. I can't imagine the pure hell you're going through feeling responsible for Frank's death. Is it true someone's trying to blackmail you into coming forward?"

The sarcasm in Shannon's voice was obvious. What troubled Maggie the most was where the conversation might be headed. Had she caught a glimpse of their little liaison through the open blinds? Had she perhaps been hiding in the bushes outside the window, spying the entire night? Maggie thought either scenario could be possible.

"Shannon now's not the time to worry about me. You need to focus on taking care of yourself. You really should try to get some sleep."

Shannon watched as Maggie dashed out of the kitchen, reveling in the fact that she had made her squirm. Her main objective now was to see Maggie and James suffer the same pain and humiliation they had brought upon her.

James popped his head in the kitchen doorway. "Sheriff Chesterton's on the phone. He says it's important that he speak with you."

James stood at the edge of the doorway, trying to eavesdrop on the conversation, but couldn't make out a word Shannon was saying.

When she finally hung up, he approached her. "Are you okay, Shannon? What did he have to say?"

"I've decided not to have a funeral service," she said, without turning around. "Tomorrow I'll arrange for my mother to be cremated, and anyone wanting to give flowers can contribute to the psychiatric ward in Thebes."

James stared at her in disbelief. "Are you sure? If you're worried about the cost of—"

"It has nothing to do with money. She answered with an air of impatience. "She wouldn't have wanted a long, drawn-out funeral and neither do I. The sooner we put this behind us, the quicker we can move on."

James's jaw dropped. He could not believe what he was hearing. Gone was the sensitive, loving woman he had fallen in love with. Standing before him was a cold, calculating human being. He wanted to run, run back into Maggie's arms, and get as far away as he could.

"It's late," she muttered. "I'm going to bed. Are you coming?"

Without looking back, she headed towards the bedroom. Not wanting a confrontation, James dropped the issue and followed.

Once upstairs, he lingered in the shower, taking his time and hoping she would fall asleep. He couldn't get his mind off Maggie. He closed his eyes and pictured the way her hair fell over her shoulders, and he could almost feel the soft crease in her lower back leading up to her delicate neck. Just the thought of her body pressed against his stoked a burning inferno of desire in his belly.

As he stepped out of the shower, he reached for a towel and wrapped it around his waist, listening for any sign of movement coming from beyond the door. Hearing only silence, he opened the door and peeked around the corner to find Shannon sleeping soundly.

He carefully slid on top of the sheets, keeping as much distance between their bodies as he could. Little sleep would come to him that night. Visions of his and Maggie's lovemaking filled every waking moment.

CHAPTER
34

DOWN AT the local beauty parlor, the usual chatter of trading beauty secrets was replaced by rumors and speculation concerning Katrina's death. The people who had known Katrina most of her life knew of her troubled past and were not surprised. To a few, including Clair, the thought of Katrina committing suicide made no sense.

Clair anxiously wrapped the phone cord around her finger, as she waited for Nadine to answer.

"Nadine, you're not going to believe what I just heard on the morning news."

"I was just about to call you," Nadine replied. "Isn't it tragic? You know that poor woman had been troubled for years. Doesn't it make you wonder? Maybe she should've stayed in that psychiatric place a while longer."

"Doesn't it seem a little suspicious, Nadine?"

"Suspicious, what do you mean?"

"Well, the way I heard it, she was making great progress. Why now? Something doesn't add up."

"Surely you don't think—Oh Clair, tell me you don't think Shannon had something to do with her own mother's death!"

"I don't know what to think anymore," Clair sighed. "Hell, I think maybe sometimes I could use a rest in one of those places."

"A sanitarium! Does this kind of talk have anything to do with earlier? I told you that old woman was trouble from the start. We don't know anything about her, where she came from, or how many other people's lives she screwed with using that evil witch-craft of hers."

"I know you're right, Nadine, but—"

"But nothing!" Nadine yelled into the receiver. "It's time we had a little meeting and find out just what she's been trying to pull. I can bet you your head isn't the only one she's been trying to fill with nonsense. I'm going to call Edith and Larry and I know this isn't the time to bother Shannon, but I'll pass it by James and see what he thinks."

"What about Maggie?" Clair asked.

"Maggie too." Nadine answered. "I think it wouldn't be a bad idea to include Bill as well. You know he's not only an old friend but being sheriff and all, he might have some idea of how we can put a stop to that old woman's crap."

Hanging up the phone, Clair felt as if the roles had been reversed. She had always been in control, not one to jump to conclusions. Usually Nadine needed guidance. Not too long ago she was telling Nadine what a fool she was to believe in such nonsense, not to play into Lola's supposed psychic abilities. Clair thought maybe Nadine was right; maybe it was time to find the underlying cause of the madness, once and for all.

The forecast for Patton called for a partly sunny day in the high nineties, but the weather cannot always be predicted accurately. Rain hammered down on the cobblestone roadway leading up to county hall. Riding together, Nadine and Clair parked as close to the entrance as possible, popped their umbrellas open and rushed inside.

"Do you think anyone will show up in this kind of weather?" Clair shook the rain off her umbrella.

Nadine nodded. "I think I made it clear how important it was. I'd hope a little rain wouldn't stop 'um."

"You think they'll be upset to find out the real reason you called this meeting?"

"I told them it was about an important issue concerning our community," Nadine said, grinning slightly. "That's not a lie!"

Clair rolled her eyes and handed her the coffee pot. "Here, you start the coffee and I'll set up the chairs."

One by one, drenching wet, people began to make their way in. Edith and Larry were the first to arrive.

"What on earth is so important that it couldn't wait?" Larry pulled his handkerchief out and wiped his face. "It's raining cats and dogs out there, did you know that?"

Edith nudged Larry. "I'm sure whatever it is, it's important. Nadine wouldn't have called us down here on a day like this if it wasn't. Right, Nadine?"

Handing them cups of coffee and a towel, Nadine nodded. "It's very important and as soon as the others arrive we'll begin."

Nadine had barely spoken these words when James and Maggie came rushing through the door.

"I'm sorry to call you at a time like this," Nadine said, taking their wet coats and setting them aside. "I appreciate you taking the time out to be here. How is Shannon holding up?"

James shrugged. "You know Shannon. She thinks in her line of business she should always be in control."

Edith placed a hand on his shoulder. "If there's anything we can do to help, please don't hesitate to ask."

"Thank you, Edith. It's just at this point I'm not sure what any of us can do for her."

"Are they sure it was a suicide and not foul play?" Larry mumbled.

Edith nudged Larry and gasped. "What a question to be asking!" She leaned in close to James's ear. "He really hasn't been himself lately."

"It's okay, Edith, don't worry about it."

Clair put her coffee cup on the table and pulled her chair closer to James. "It must have been horribly traumatic for Shannon to find her mother in such a manner."

"Well, actually Maggie had the misfortune of seeing her first."

Everyone's attention now turned towards Maggie. They didn't have to say a word. Their blank stares said it all. Maggie knew that if she didn't give them an explanation, and fast, rumors would soon start flying.

"Earlier that night I had a scare by what I'd thought was possibly an intruder. I know I should've called the sheriff's office, but instead I bolted out and headed to James and Shannon's place. Taking them up on their kind offer to stay, during the night I accidentally wandered into Katrina's room thinking it was the bathroom."

Clair held her breath. She could tell by Nadine's wide-eyed look what was coming next.

Nadine drew a deep breath and exhaled. "Well, my dear, you must have been traumatized, two frights in one night."

Maggie did not have to be a mind reader to tell Nadine's response lacked sincerity. They were all aware of her and James's past, and knowing James and Shannon's relationship was strained, Maggie was certain they were questioning her motives as well.

Edith walked over to Maggie and softly placed her hand on her back. "I can't imagine your horror. I'm sure Shannon feels blessed to have such a loyal and caring friend so close by, especially at this time."

Unlike Nadine's snide remark, Maggie knew Edith was sincere, yet she found herself feeling extremely uncomfortable. Edith's heartfelt show of emotion spurred feelings of shame she had suppressed. She knew if Edith were aware of what had really taken place, her opinion of her would be one of disgust.

Sheriff Chesterton was the last to arrive. Walking in to find Edith and Maggie embracing, tears flowing, he could only speculate the worst. Seeing his concern, James hurried over to explain. "Everything's all right, Bill. We were just discussing the circumstances surrounding Katrina's death and things got a little emotional."

The sheriff nodded. "It was a traumatic situation. It'll take her some time to accept it, but she'll never forget, I'm sorry to say. How's Shannon holding up?"

James shrugged. "Your guess is as good as mine. I thought I knew her better than I knew anyone, but now I'm not so sure. She's decided instead of a funeral she's going to have Katrina cremated."

Nadine waved her hands, trying to get their attention. "I don't mean to interrupt, but I'm sure you're curious as to why I called this meeting, so if everyone will take a seat I'll begin."

With everyone in place, Nadine began to reveal why she had called them all together. The room was silent as she described her own encounter with Lola. She then gave the floor to Clair, who began to tell her own extraordinary tale of terror involving Lola, holding nothing back.

"So, I'm sure you can all understand my dilemma," Clair concluded. "I'm telling you people, there's something to what Lola has been trying to convey to us, something beyond the norm."

Sheriff Chesterton shook his head and smirked. "Well, that certainly is some story."

Clair screamed at him. "You think I'm making all this up!"

"I didn't mean any disrespect," he replied hastily.

Clair's eyes slowly widened. "I'm just as confused as the rest of you guys as to exactly what did happen to me. All I know is that's how I remember it."

"Well, that's why we're all here, to try and figure out these peculiar happenings amongst ourselves," Bill said, standing up to address the crowd. "As sheriff of this community I intend on getting down to the bottom of all this."

Larry squirmed in his chair next to Edith. Pulling his ball cap off, he wiped the nervous sweat from his forehead, stood up, and began to speak. Their stories were mere fairy tales compared to what he had witnessed. Nevertheless, hearing their stories of uncertainty and fear involving Lola helped him feel connected. Feeling like an outcast, he had distanced himself from the others for some time, only speaking to James occasionally, and now their friendship was in question.

James sat silently across the room, lifting his head now and then as he listened to Larry. The thought of having to reveal his personal accounts and details of his experience with Lola terrified him.

Suddenly everyone's attention turned towards the back of the room.

The doors had been flung open as if by a violent gust of wind, but the air was still. None of them were prepared for what they saw next.

In the middle of the doorway, looking quite frail and thin, clenching a large black book in one hand and leaning against her cane with the other, stood Lola. With no apparent help from any human source, the doors slammed shut behind her, startling every-one. Up until now, the sheriff had listened to what he had thought were stories of nothing more than hysteria that had no premise, but even he couldn't deny what he had just witnessed.

"Ma'am, this is a closed session so I'm afraid you'll have to leave."

The deep wrinkles around Lola's mouth tightened with anger as she glared at the sheriff. "Rest assured that time is near, but not before I give all of you my final warning."

Sheriff Chesterton tugged at the band of his uniform pants as if they were about to slide off his narrow hips. "Around here we don't take threats lightly, so I think—"

"Is that what you think?" Lola glared across the room. "Do all of you think I'm here to make threats? Or maybe you think I'm here to confuse or manipulate you into turning against one another."

Nadine's polyester shirt, drenched in nervous sweat, clung to her like a second skin. Her hands trembling, she pulled out her handkerchief, took off her eyeglasses and gently wiped her stinging eyes. The intensity of Lola's fierce stare frightened her to the core.

Maggie stood and acknowledged her presence. "Maybe we should listen to what she has to say. After all, she seems to be the focus of this meeting."

All eyes were on Maggie. They could not believe she was inviting her to join them. She didn't appear frightened at all. Truth was, besides Edith, Maggie was the only other one in the group that had not been a subject of Lola's quest. Neither woman had any reason to feel frightened or intimidated by Lola. That is, not until now.

Edith took Lola by the hand, helping her into a chair. "Maggie's right, Bill. You of all people should agree she's innocent until proven guilty. Although I'm still not certain what law she's supposed to have broken."

Placing her feeble hand on top of Edith's, Lola gazed up at her. The deep wrinkles in her face, which had been highlighted by anger moments earlier, relaxed, creating a softer, less daunting appearance.

"You, my child, out of all who are here today, are by far the most pure of heart. You judge me not as a threat and so I shall not judge you."

Looking across the room, Lola noticed Maggie's eyes were focused on the book she held close to her chest. James and Larry sat quiet and still in their seats, heads lowered, eyes glued to the floor, as if somehow it would make them appear invisible. Nadine and Clair huddled close to Sheriff Chesterton; all curious as to what Lola would say next.

Lola lowered the book from her chest into her lap, positioning it so as everyone could see. Placing her cane against the leg of her chair, she laid both hands on top of the book, closed her eyes, and began chanting softly. A sweet scent of lavender and honeysuckle swept through the entire room as the temperature rose slightly. The harsh light from a hundred-watt bulb mounted directly in the center of the ceiling began to flicker, giving off the faint luminescence of a soft-lit candle. Overhead, tiny circular balls of light bolted in and around each other. Lola opened her eyes as if awakening from a deep trance. Looking around the room, she focused on Larry and began to speak.

"You, of all who are here, possess the strongest link to the supernatural world. You always have. Your spirit guides brought us together, for they knew in my possession I hold the book of knowledge, knowledge of not only the past and present, but the future as well. To you I offered the book as insight into this demonic presence that is lurking ever so near, yet you resisted."

Lola tilted her head to one side, pointed her finger first at Clair and then to James and continued, "I summoned you both as well, offering the same insight into this wickedness you try so firmly to disregard as foolishness, and now innocent lives have been sacrificed."

Lola reached for her cane slowly, balancing herself as she stood up from her chair, as if out of pity, and looked directly at Maggie. "The turn of events that shall follow will forever transform the lives of each and every one in this room today. Lies and deception have devoured innocent souls throughout eternity, unleashing one's darkest demons to play havoc on unsuspecting souls."

Maggie could stand it no longer. "Are you saying that by choosing not to believe in your supernatural powers and disregarding your earlier warnings, that now we're all doomed for disaster? If you were truly sent here to help us then we deserve a second chance!"

Reacting to Maggie's bluntness, James nervously bit down on his lower lip, drawing blood. Every one listened patiently, fearfully anticipating Lola's response.

The sweet scent that floated softly in the air swiftly disappeared as the soft glow of light transformed into one of near darkness. Overcome by a feeling of heaviness, each of them became anchored to their chairs by some unseen force, making it impossible to move. Imprisoned in the darkness and overwhelmed with panic, they struggled to keep some kind of composure. Unable to move, sitting in pure darkness, they listen as Lola bid them farewell.

"Guided here by my spirits, I came to your little town to warn you of impending doom. Many years you have closed your eyes, chosen not to see the evil that lay dormant within your circle. Evil takes on many different forms. This evil hides itself behind a mask of what appears to be on the surface a nurturing and caring soul. This wickedness has shown itself to you many times, yet you are fooled. As for your second chance to unmask this malevolence, you have had many. Remember me as you will, but as for yourselves you have been shown a spiritual awakening into a realm only few ever see." The eerie silence following Lola's last words were almost as frightening as what they had experienced prior.

Suddenly the invisible chains they had felt strapped around their legs, binding them to their seats, loosened, and they were free again to move. Sheriff Chesterton would be the first to venture from his seat as he fumbled his way through the darkened room until he finally found the light switch. Mentally drained, the people stared at one another, dazed and in shock from what they had witnessed.

"Okay, can somebody tell me what the hell just happened here?" Nadine cried out, breaking the silence.

"Okay, everybody, just stay calm," the sheriff spoke up. "There has to be a logical explanation for what just happened."

"You've got to be kidding me!" Nadine shouted. "After everything we just witnessed! You might be the expert here but I think this is a case even you can't solve."

Clair agreed, "This is one time I think Nadine is right."

"They're right, Bill," Edith said, clenching Larry's arm. "I've read my Bible enough to know what just happened here. Good or bad, it can't be rationalized."

Bill nodded, looking pale. "I'm going to take a look outside."

"I'll come with ya, Sheriff," James said.

"Me too."

"Oh no you won't, Larry," Edith said, yanking at his shirtsleeve. "You can stay right here with us womenfolk."

It didn't take long for James and the sheriff to return. They did not have to say anything; the bewildered look on their faces spoke louder than words.

"Let us all guess," Nadine frowned. Suppose she disappeared into thin air?"

James looked over his shoulder and shrugged. "Well, it would appear that way. But you've got to admit, that's no stranger than everything else we've witnessed here today."

Sheriff Chesterton waved his hands in the air. "Okay, let's all just try to stay calm for one minute and focus."

"You stay calm!" Nadine shouted. "We all know what happened here today can't be explained by human logic. I'm not sure myself what it all means, but I've got a good idea of who Lola was referring to."

All eyes were on Nadine as she focused her attention toward Maggie. "If you'd all stop and think about it a minute, think back to when all this craziness began, you'd have to agree it started when poor Frank disappeared. Who was the last to see him alive? Oh, that's right, that would be you, Maggie, and everyone knows you've been acting a little peculiar these days."

Maggie jumped to her feet. "How dare you point the finger at me!"

James placed himself between the two women. "Hell, if you want to go there, let's point the finger at Larry. Everyone knows his behavior lately has been more than a little odd!"

Larry bolted from his seat, shoving his chair halfway across the room. "I'd point at who I think the real culprit is, but she doesn't appear to be here today."

James clenched his teeth, trying desperately to keep his temper under control. "You'd best just leave Shannon out of this," he growled.

"See what you started!" Clair said, pointing her finger accusingly at Nadine.

Edith motioned Larry to take his seat. "Okay, that's enough! Don't you all see what's happening here? We should be pulling together, not accusing each other of things we can't possibly be sure of."

"Edith's right," Sheriff Chesterton nodded. We've all witnessed an unusual if not to say a bizarre episode of events. Right now, I want each one of you to go home and stay there. And I'd recommend that we all keep what happened here today to ourselves as well."

"You mean act like nothing ever happened?" Nadine asked in a trembling voice.

"In a word, that's exactly what I mean, Nadine. I'm going to do a little investigating and I'm going to start by going out to the old Parker place."

Sheriff Chesterton held the door open until everyone had made it out. Cautiously he watched over them as they made their way to their vehicles and pulled away. Hesitating before shutting the door, he took one last look around and shivered when he thought about what had just happened. In his line of work, becoming a victim to fear could mean the difference between life and death, and up until that moment, he thought he had handled himself rather well. He thought of the oath he had taken as an officer of the law 'to protect and serve at all cost.' Determined not to succumb to his fears, he could not help but wonder what price he would have to pay.

CHAPTER
35

GROGGY, SHANNON rolled over in the bed and reached for James. Realizing he was not there, she assumed he must have woken early and went downstairs. After a search of the house, she realized Maggie was missing as well. Her body trembled as her blood began to boil with rage. She closed her eyes and pictured James and Maggie somewhere secluded, their bodies entangled in passion. Perspiring, she doubled over in pain, her stomach aching with nausea.

She sat on the cold tile floor in the corner of her bathroom, curled up in a fetal position, arms wrapped tight around both legs as she rocked back and forth. Silently she cursed everyone and everything, including God.

Now, completely delusional, she believed that her life had been cursed at birth. Her mother's indiscretions had driven her father to alcoholism, she was sure of it, and his premature death had prevented her from having the father-daughter relationship she had so longed for. Now the only two people she had completely given her loyalty and trust, had chosen to kill her slowly with their betrayal. In the end, she could see everything she had worked so hard to accomplish vanishing before her eyes: her honorable status in the community, her psychiatric practice, and any genuine sanity that she may have ever had.

Her wallowing in self-pity and paranoia was cut short by the sound of footsteps coming up the stairs. On her hands and knees, she crept across the floor. She bolted the door.

As the doorknob turned, she jumped at the sound of James's voice.

"Shannon, you alright in there?"

She turned the shower faucet on full blast. "Yeah, I'm fine. Just getting into the shower."

"I was going to fix breakfast but we were out of everything. I didn't want to wake you, so I made Maggie come along to help. You know how I hate to go grocery shopping."

"Yeah, I bet you were grocery shopping," Shannon mumbled to herself.

James leaned against the closed door and yelled above the running shower, "When you get done with your shower come downstairs and we'll have breakfast."

Food was the last thing on Shannon's mind, but she was not about to let them know the despair and torment they had put her through. She jumped in and out of the shower, wrapped her hair up in a towel, grabbed her robe, and headed downstairs. Rounding the corner heading towards the kitchen, she hesitated for a moment when she heard what sounded like whispering from the other side. She stood still as a statue, straining to hear what they were saying.

"Do you think she bought it?" Maggie asked in a low voice.

"Well, I hope for our sake she did," James replied.

Maggie kept her voice at a whisper. "Whatever we do, we can't let her know where we were or what we were doing."

"I just feel so guilty lying to her, but you're right. After everything that's happened, she'd never understand."

Her hand to her chest, Shannon was sure she felt her heart stop. She prepared herself for the agonizing pain in the pit of her stomach, but it did not come. She expected to break out in a nervous sweat, but was stunned to find that instead her body felt cold, her hands steady as a surgeon's. Gone were the feelings of heartache and panic. In their place, was a ghostly sense of calm flowing through her body, tingling every nerve.

Through the crack in the door, she watched as the lovers sat silently at the kitchen table, sipping their coffee and occasionally gazing up at one another.

She heard a voice in her mind whisper: "You know what has to be done. We didn't come this far to lose it all." Shannon took a deep breath and slowly opened the kitchen door.

James jerked his head up as she walked in, and plastered a grin on his face. "There you are.! Come sit down and I'll fix you a cup of coffee. Fixed your favorite: pancakes and bacon. Better have some."

Placing a passionate kiss on his lips, Shannon wrapped her arms around his neck. "You're too good to me," she purred. "What would I ever do without you?"

Her false act of sincerity did not fool Maggie for a second. "Shannon, you look so tired," she remarked casually. "Are you sleeping at all?"

Shannon kept her pent-up rage in check. "I know I've not said it enough, but I couldn't ask for a better friend. I'm not sure if James told you, but I've made a difficult decision concerning Katrina's burial. I've decided to have her cremated."

Puzzled, Maggie glanced over at James. "No, he didn't mention."

"Mother wouldn't have wanted a long, drawn-out funeral, I'm sure of it. Anyway, I'm supposed to meet the funeral director later today, and I know you both may not understand but I'd really like to do this alone."

James set his coffee cup down and scooted his chair close to Shannon. He gently took her hand and said: "Shannon, are you absolutely sure? I don't think you need to do this alone."

"I'm positive, James. It's something I need to do alone. But I do need to ask something of you, Maggie."

Maggie's face tensed, "Uh, sure, Shannon. Anything."

"Well, I've decided to take some time off from my practice, and James needs to get back to his business. So, I know it's asking a lot, but I'd really appreciate it if you could stay just a little longer."

Immediately all tension left Maggie's body. "I'd be more than happy to stay close as long as you need me. I'll have to hire someone part-time to help out at the store, but it shouldn't be a problem."

Shannon snickered silently with delight as she reached across the table and patted Maggie's hand. "You'll never know how much this means to me. Now if you'll excuse us, I'm going to take James upstairs and have him give me one of his famous backrubs."

James's eyes drifted over to Maggie, but only for a moment. How much longer could he carry on with this charade? To confront Shannon with his suspicions, to attack her lack of loyalty to him or question any of her motives concerning her most recent behavior, could spell disaster at this time, this he was certain of. Torn apart by his passion and rekindled love for Maggie, he had crossed the line, leaving himself to question his own behavior and lapse of judgment and restraint.

Shannon leaned over the back of James's chair, kissed him gently on the neck, looked directly across at Maggie and said, "Yeah, Maggie, I only hope one day you can find a man as loyal and devoted as I have."

A bolt of lightning shot through Maggie's body, attacking every nerve ending, exploding into a wave of disgust. She knew Shannon's invitation was nothing more than a way for her to keep a close eye on her and James. At that moment, she began devising a plan. The plan would be to give Shannon just enough rope to hang herself.

It was clear to Maggie; James had suspicions about Shannon's possible involvement in Katrina's premature death. Her sudden outburst of radical behavior had only fueled the fire. If Maggie had learned one thing about Shannon in all the years of knowing her, she had learned how easy it was to influence one's mind by manipulating their thoughts. Turning James and the others against Shannon would be easy. Hell, part of the plan had already been laid out, starting with the anonymous letter to Sheriff Chesterton.

Frank's death had been an unfortunate accident. Given the same circumstances, it was understandable that one might panic under such duress. What Maggie had not counted on was that someone had been hiding in the shadows, watching and waiting, waiting for the precise time to move the body along with the evidence, but for what reason? She could only draw one conclusion: they were playing a sick game of cat and mouse, trying to confuse her, make her think she was losing her mind, and it had almost worked. She knew of only one person who had the expertise and twisted mind to pull it off. Maggie had lost James to Shannon before, but it would not happen again. The wheels were set in motion and all she had to do was play her bluff.

CHAPTER
36

SHERIFF CHESTERTON parked his patrol car a short distance from the old farmhouse. He stepped from his car, and struggled for a moment to catch his hat as a brisk wind blew in from the north. Hat in one hand and the other on his holster, he cautiously walked up the path. When he got to the old wooden porch, he hesitated, wondering if it would collapse under his weight. A gust of wind ripped across the front porch, hurling a broken shutter straight into his path, barely missing him. He cringed to think how close it had come to striking him in the head.

Carefully he made his way up the steps of the the porch and to the front door. He raised his hand to knock on the door, but it opened without warning as if to welcome him in. Scarcely inside, he was immediately overcome by a damp, musty odor. A thick film of sludge covering the windows blocked out the sunlight, making it virtually impossible to see inside. After announcing himself a few times and receiving no response, he took out his flashlight and shined it throughout the room.

Electrical outlets dangled from their sockets, signifying that there hadn't been any electricity for some time. Furthermore, the room appeared empty, not a sign of furniture anywhere. With a tight grip on his holster, he made his way carefully up the dilapidated staircase. Finally reaching the top of the stairs, he took a deep breath, shined his flashlight in front of him, and continued on. Cobwebs shrouded the doorways; vermin droppings covered the filthy rotted wood floors like a thick carpet.

Done exploring, he was about to make his way back downstairs when he heard footsteps at the foot of the stairs. Aiming his flashlight, he drew his gun with his finger on the trigger.

"Hold up, Bill! It's me, Larry!"

"Son of a bitch, Larry! I almost shot ya. What the hell are you doing here?"

"I couldn't just go home and sit, not after everything that happened. I dropped Edith off and followed you here."

"If I'd thought I needed backup I would've called my deputy. Now let's get out of here."

Once outside, Sheriff Chesterton started towards his vehicle. Larry stood dumfounded, looking back at the old house. He could not believe what he saw. A short time ago, he had visited Lola there and it looked very different from the rundown two-story shack it now appeared.

Larry ran to catch up with the sheriff. "You don't understand, Bill. I was here. It looked nothing like this. I sat in that living room surrounded by candlelight across from her. Hell, she made tea in that very kitchen and brought it to me. You saw it; it looks like it's been abandoned for years.!"

The sheriff frowned. "You sure of that? 'Cause right now I'm not sure of anything. How's that make me sound? Being the sheriff, I'm supposed to know what's going on in my town. Hell, I ain't got a clue!"

"What are we gonna do, Bill?"

"Go home, Larry. Go home and pray a miracle happens to explain all this mess."

Larry watched the sheriff as he drove out of sight. He didn't want to go home and he certainly did not want to wait on some miracle to happen. What he did intend to do was follow his instinct, or as Lola would say, his spirit guide.

After making a quick trip to Sedgewickville to drop off the station wagon, Larry drove his rental back, stopping by the bar only long enough to make a quick phone call. Rehearsing his lines over again, he waited, hoping James would be the one to answer.

"Hello, James speaking."

"James, this is Larry. Listen friend, I know we haven't seen eye to eye lately and I feel very bad about that. I've made some nasty remarks about Shannon, but you know it was just an old fool talking. Right?"

"I've said some crazy things myself, Larry."

"Well, what I'm trying to say is, if it's alright I'd like to come by and personally tell Shannon how sorry I am about her loss."

"I'm sure she'd like that," James replied, "but she's not here right now. She's down at the funeral home."

"Did she go alone?" Larry asked.

"Yes, against my better judgment. She made a firm decision to do this alone. I'm not sure if I mentioned it but she decided against a funeral service. She's having Katrina cremated, probably as we speak."

Larry was stunned, not by what James had said, but by how his plan seemed to be coming together. He now had the perfect opportunity.

"Larry, are you still there? Hello? Hello?"

Larry felt bad hanging up on James, but his main priority was getting to the funeral home as quickly as possible. A force was leading him, guiding his thoughts and sense of direction. He couldn't explain it, didn't need to. He knew who was guiding him in his quest.

As Larry turned the corner, he looked up the street and spotted Shannon's car parked in plain view. He found an empty spot across the street, parked his rental, slumped down in the driver's seat, and waited. As luck would have it, he did not have to wait long.

He watched as she tried to steady an object in one hand while attempting to unlock her car door with the other. He could not help but wonder if the object might be Katrina's remains.

After several attempts, she finally succeeded and pulled onto the road. She passed the turnoff towards home and proceeded out of town.

Not wanting to be detected, Larry followed a safe distance behind. Shannon headed high up into the hills, winding around through the valley, passing the exit to the main highway. Larry's curiosity peaked into high gear when she suddenly turned off on an unmarked side road. He knew the road well because years ago it had been Patton's original dump site.

Stopping just a short distance from the entrance, Shannon parked her car. Surrounded on all sides by mounds of trash and rusted debris, Shannon walked directly towards a huge hollowed-out tree.

With a little maneuvering, Larry managed to hide his car in between some thick brush and overgrown weeds. Mystified, he watched as she knelt down and pulled an object wrapped in plastic from the hollow trunk. Larry's adrenaline surged with her every move. Her suspicious behavior gave him more than enough reason to notify the sheriff.

Crouched down among the bushes, he patiently waited until Shannon was no longer in sight. He wasn't certain what she was up to, but he was convinced she was up to no good. Wasting no time, he quickly started his car and stomped on the gas. The tires roared as they spun in place, throwing thick clods of mud in every direction. In desperation, Larry put the gearshift in forward and frantically tried to nudge his way out. He leaned forward, putting his head against the steering wheel and cursing aloud.

The tires were buried deep in mud. After thirty minutes of trying to free them, he gave up. Aggravated, he slumped down by the back tire and contemplated his next move. Darkness set in along with a murky fog.

CHAPTER
37

MAGGIE WALKED into the living room to find James sitting on the couch shaking his head.

"What's the matter James?"

"I'm not sure," he murmured. "I got the strangest phone call from Larry earlier."

"Strange?"

"Yeah, he started out by apologizing for his rude comments about Shannon and then asked if he could come by and give his condolences in person. When I told him she wasn't here, she was at the funeral home, he suddenly hung up on me."

"Who knows about Larry?" Maggie said, shaking her head. "You know he's been acting peculiar these days."

"Enough about Larry," James said. "I'm still trying to figure out what the hell we all witnessed earlier today and what it all means. I tell you, between that and trying to deal with Shannon's odd behavior, I'm not sure how much more I can take!"

Maggie wrapped her arms around James's neck, pressing her body close to his. "Let's just go, get away from all this craziness. I love you, James, and I know you feel the same."

Caught off guard, James was unsure how to react. Gently breaking their embrace, he pulled away.

Maggie's chin quivered. She hadn't anticipated this sort of reaction. "You do love me, don't you, James?"

"I do love you, Maggie, but it's not that easy," James sighed. "I have obligations."

"To who?" Maggie frowned. "Shannon?"

James nodded. "Yeah, to Shannon, you, our friends. You still have this thing involving Frank's death hanging over your head, and no matter how crazy it may sound, it's our obligation to determine if Lola's warnings hold merit. You're the one person I can trust to be honest with me. Your love and honesty is what's keeping me sane."

Maggie sat speechless, looking into James's trusting eyes that led deep into his loving soul. His truthfulness and vulnerability seeped through to her soul, devouring all thoughts of deceit. It all became painfully clear in her desperate plea to win back James's love; he had become nothing more than a pawn in her deadly game to destroy Shannon. She thought of Lola's words, her warnings. To save her own soul she must now let go, break free from Shannon's web, even at the cost of losing James and her freedom.

She fought back the tears, forcing down the lump in her throat. "James, there's something I need to confess. In the last few months, I've done some things, made some terrible choices. You need to know—"

James jumped to his feet. "Did you hear that?"

"What?"

James peeked out the window. "Sounded like a car door."

"Is it Shannon?" Maggie asked, peaking over his shoulder.

"Yeah, she's coming up the walk."

Maggie disappeared out of the room while James grabbed a book from the coffee table, pretending to be engrossed in the pages.

As soon as Shannon walked in the room, he was immediately struck by her unkempt appearance. A few hours earlier, she had left the house elegantly dressed in a black pinstriped suit, every hair in place, but now she appeared quite the opposite. Kicking her heels off just inside the door, he noticed what appeared to be dried mud an inch thick on the soles of her shoes.

"Are you alright?" he asked, looking her up and down. "You look a little worse for wear."

She set her mother's urn down on the table in front of him. "I'm just glad it's over. I know I must look a fright, but I am exhausted."

"I wish you would've let me come with you."

"Like I said, I'm just glad it's over."

James had thought about questioning the caked mud on her shoes as well as her untidy appearance, but thought it now to be trivial.

"Where's Maggie?" Shannon asked, looking around.

"Uh, I think she's in the bathroom, maybe not feeling so good."

"Really? I better check on her."

His pulse began to race when he glanced down at his book and realized it had been upside down the whole time. He thanked God she hadn't noticed.

Truth was, Shannon couldn't care less how Maggie was feeling. She had a good idea what they had been up to while she was away, but their little charade was nearing the end.

Shannon pressed her ear against the door. "Maggie, you alright in there?"

"I'll be right out."

After gathering her hair back into a clip, Maggie splashed cold water on her face. Legs trembling, she leaned against the sink to steady herself from falling. Her bottled-up emotions were now playing havoc on her body, as well as her mind, but for now she had to somehow shake those feelings. She dabbed a bit of color onto her pale lips, took one last look in the mirror, then slowly opened the door.

"Are you sure you feel all right? Shannon said, looking her over. "You look awful pale."

Maggie nodded. "I'll be fine. I think I just have a touch of the stomach flu. How are you feeling?"

"Like I told James, I'm just glad it's all over with."

Trying to be subjective, Maggie looked to Shannon for some sign of sincere emotion, something to help change her mind about the way she felt about her, but she saw nothing.

"What do you say I give you a ride back to your place?" Shannon offered. "You can pick up your car and I'll help you pack some things."

"Uh, I don't know Shannon."

"Nonsense the fresh air will do you good. Let me change real quick and I'll tell James what we're doing."

"And what are we doing?" James asked, eavesdropping at the door.

"Well, Maggie and I were discussing how she needed to go home and pack a few things to bring back."

"Great, I'll come with you."

Taking James aside, Shannon softly whispered, "Don't take this the wrong way, but we could use some girl time alone. You understand, don't you?"

James couldn't help wondering what she was up to. He knew Shannon held an underlying grudge against Maggie, and for good reasons. Shannon was no fool, and he knew by now she had caught on to his so-called innocent act of friendship towards Maggie. He wanted to come clean about his feelings for Maggie, although he knew now was not a good time; he knew he was just putting off the inevitable.

He cupped her face in his hands. "We need some time alone too, Shannon. With everything that's happened, we haven't had much time to talk, and there are some important issues we need to address."

Shannon could tell by his demeanor and tone that he was serious. She felt certain he wanted to confess his feelings for Maggie, but if things went as planned there would be no need.

Shannon smiled and nodded. "I promise the minute I get back we'll talk all night if you like."

CHAPTER
38

IT WAS just about dusk when Nadine and Clair rounded the last curve leading out of Sedgewickville. Fog was beginning to thicken, making visibility nearly impossible.

"Maybe we should've listened to Sheriff Chesterton earlier when he advised us to go straight home," Nadine said, biting her nails.

"For once I think you're right." Clair agreed. "I'm just glad the rain has let up a bit."

"I'm sorry," Nadine sighed, as she continued biting her nails. "I just wanted to get out of Patton for a while. Just didn't want to go by myself."

"Don't be silly, Nadine. After everything that happened today, going home by myself was the last thing on my mind."

"Clair?"

"Yeah?"

"Did you notice Lola directed her attention towards Maggie when she started talking about lies and deception?"

Clair nodded. "Yeah, it was quite obvious."

Nadine stared out the passenger side window and lowered her voice. "Just between me and you, do you think—"

Stomping on the brake, Clair struggled to keep both hands on the wheel. After sliding a few feet, they came to a dead stop on the shoulder of the road.

"What the hell!" Nadine shouted. "What are you doing, Clair? I may not want to go home alone but I'd like to get home in one piece!"

Clair looked back over her shoulder. "Did you see that?"

"See what?" Nadine said, looking back too.

"I could've sworn I saw someone trying to flag us down back there."

Nadine raised an eyebrow and shook her head. "You know how this fog can play tricks on your eyes. Anyway, why would someone be walking out in this weather?"

"Shh, did you hear that?" Clair said, raising a finger to her lips.

Latching her car door, Nadine nervously looked over at Clair. "All I want to hear is you starting this car and us getting the hell out of here!"

Before Clair could turn the key, a loud tapping sound on the passenger side window startled both women.

"Clair, is that you?" came a man's voice from outside.

"Larry!" both women called out.

"Thank God! I was beginning to think I'd have to walk all the way into town."

"You just about gave two old women a heart attack!" Nadine said, putting her hand over her heart.

"I'm sorry," Nadine, "My car broke down a ways back and then the fog set in."

Clair motioned him to get in the back seat. "Get in before someone runs you over."

Clair drove towards town and the women listened in awe as Larry explained his predicament.

Looking at Larry through the rearview mirror, Clair shook her head. "Let me get this straight: you drove to Sedgewickville, rented a car, and followed Shannon on a hunch that you might catch her in the act of doing something illegal."

Nadine could not keep silent. "Does Edith know what you're doing?"

"First of all, no. Edith doesn't know, and second, it was more than just a hunch. Have either of you been listening to me? Neither of you can deny what happened in that room today with Lola, and you both know as well as I do she's been trying to give us one warning after another of an impending evil. Now I know you don't want to believe it's someone we all know and have trusted, but after what I witnessed tonight I believe Shannon may hold the answer."

Clair and Nadine looked at each other, both wondering what the other was thinking. Clair could not deny her own eerie feelings of suspicions when it came to Shannon. She thought about the apparent nightmare she had had in which she encountered ghostly images of Shannon in all her evil. At the time, it had seemed so real, but after discussing it with Nadine, she had doubted herself. After listening to Larry talk, she was now more confused than ever.

He had given Nadine something to think about as well. She had hastened to lay the blame of guilt and suspicion on Maggie, and wished now that she hadn't been so quick to judge. She wished she had given Lola the benefit of the doubt. Maybe then she could've seen her warnings more clearly. One thing was sure: they were both thinking the same thoughts about Larry. They had known him for a long time and knew he would never pursue anything so passionately without just cause.

"Let's say for a moment all of this made sense. Now what?" Clair asked.

Larry thought a moment. "Well, before I had the misfortune of getting my car stuck, I'd planned on heading to the sheriff's office and trying to catch Bill."

"Are you sure that's a good idea?" Nadine asked.

"Nadine's right," Clair said. "What reason are you going to give for following Shannon? You said yourself you couldn't see exactly what she pulled out of that tree trunk. She could always say she was just there dumping some trash. After all, it is a dump site."

Larry snickered. "Yeah, an old dump site that nobody ever uses. And as sure as I have one good arm, I'd be willing to bet it was the gun she used to kill Frank." Stunned by Larry's remark, the women gasped.

"What on earth makes you think that's a possibility?" Clair asked.

"I can't explain it," he said. "Call it intuition, a gut feeling, or something supernatural. Whatever's been pointing me in the right direction is telling me Shannon has something to do with Frank's disappearance. I can't shake it."

Pulling around back of the police station, Larry was the first to spot Sheriff Chesterton's patrol car.

"You can let me out here." He opened up his car door and leaned in towards Clair's window. "I can understand if you girls don't want to be involved in all this. Just forget you ever saw me tonight."

"Like hell," Nadine yelled, jerking open the car door. "I wouldn't miss this for anything."

Sheriff Chesterton was sitting at his desk sifting through piles of paperwork when they walked in. He knew something was up by the frazzled look on Larry's face, and he was sure Clair and Nadine was not there to visit either.

"Bill, I'm so glad I caught you here!" Larry said, panting. "I've got something to tell ya, but you got to promise to hear me out."

"Yeah, this you gotta hear Sheriff," Nadine said, pulling up a chair directly in front of his desk.

Clair placed her hand softly on the sheriff's shoulder. 'Bill, what Larry's about to tell you may sound far-fetched. It did to us at first, but I think Larry may be on to something."

The sheriff threw up his hands. "Okay, everybody, let's just calm down and take a seat. Now Larry, what's got you in such an uproar?"

"Well, you know after we left the old Parker farm—"

"Was Lola there? Did you get to talk to her?" Nadine blurted out.

"Will you let me finish?" Larry snapped.

Clair nudged Nadine on the arm and gave her a stern look.

"Okay, Sheriff, like I was saying before Nadine interrupted, after I left the old Parker farm something strange came over me, and it was like something was leading me, telling me what to do. Next I drove to Sedgewickville and rented a car."

The sheriff threw up his hands. "Hold up, Larry. Why did you need to rent a car? Something happen to yours?"

"No, just listen! I followed Shannon out to the old dump-site and—"

"Hold on," Bill interrupted again. "Let me get a couple of aspirin and a cup of black coffee, or do I need something stronger?"

Sheriff Chesterton leaned back in his chair, put his feet on the desk, and listened as Larry explained the events that followed. He too had known Larry for many years and had never seen him this excited or determined about anything. He also knew Larry to be a well-rounded person, but what he was witnessing now was a desperate man.

After Larry finished his story, the sheriff sat straight up in his chair, moved the files on his desk to the side, and placed his badge on the center of the table.

"If I played into this outlandish tale of events and followed through, I might as well turn in my badge. You know that I have to follow certain procedures."

Larry frowned. "Are you saying you've never followed up on a case using your gut feeling that you just may be right? All I'm asking you to do is go over there, snoop around a bit, and ask a few questions."

Scratching his head, the sheriff hesitated for a moment, then gave into Larry's persistence. "If I do this, you have to promise me you'll accept the outcome."

"I solemnly swear, Bill."

"I'm not through. You also have to promise you'll never follow your hunches and go investigating again without informing me first."

Larry smiled, gave a wink and a nod and held up his hand. "I promise."

The sheriff glanced over at Clair and Nadine who, for the last twenty minutes, had been hanging on their every word.

"Now if these good ladies don't mind maybe they will give you a ride home. I'm sure Edith is home waiting and wondering just where you have been all this time."

Following Clair and Nadine to the door, Larry paused for a moment, turned around, and looked back. "You'll let me know what happens, right?"

Bill nodded. I'll keep you closely informed."

The sheriff didn't know where to start. He had always tried to follow the book, but after everything he had witnessed, and was still witnessing, the bizarre circumstances made it virtually unfeasible. Larry had heightened his curiosity as to why Shannon would have been poking around in a closed dumpsite. He thought back to the peculiar behavior that Shannon had portrayed immediately following her own mother's death. Although he had suspicions about her involvement in Katrina's death, he had never connected her to Frank's disappearance. He had his own suspicions about that, and Maggie played a major role. It seemed lately the more he thought he was on the right track, the further away from the truth he ended up. With the clock ticking, he didn't want to waste time. Finishing the last drop of coffee, he pinned his badge onto his uniform, placed his gun in his holster, and headed out the door.

James and Shannon lived not far from the station, but the dense fog made for a long, strenuous drive. Arriving at their house, he noticed Shannon's car missing from the driveway. Before he could knock, James met him at the door with a worried look on his face.

"Something wrong, Bill?"

"No, nothing like that. I couldn't help but notice Shannon's car is gone. I can't imagine anyone going out on a night like this if they don't have to."

"Well," James shrugged. "It wasn't quite this foggy when they left."

The sheriff's eyes widened with curiosity. "They?"

"Yeah, Shannon took Maggie back to her house to pick up some things. She convinced her to stay here for a while, keep her company while I'm at work. Matter of fact, I was just trying to call but didn't get an answer. You know women when they get together. Probably too busy yakking to answer the phone."

"Yeah, you're probably right. The sheriff tilted his head slightly and squinted his eyes. "Forgive me if I'm wrong James, but I got the impression Maggie and Shannon's relationship was somewhat strained."

"It was, but you know sometimes it takes a tragedy to bring people together."

"Let me explain why I'm here, James. A concerned citizen called into the station today, said they saw someone messing around up there at the old dumpsite. The description they gave of the vehicle leaving surprisingly matched Shannon's vehicle. Do you have any idea why she might have been up there?"

"That's the craziest thing I've ever heard. Shannon was here all day except when she went to the funeral home to witness her mother's cremation."

"I know it sounds crazy, but this person was adamant about what they saw."

James reached for the phone. "We can clear this up once and for all."

After trying the line three different times and getting no response, James slammed the phone down. Uneasy, he walked over to the window, first looking out one way and then the other.

"James, I think I might better drive over there, check things out."

"You know, that's a good idea, Bill. I'll come with you."

The sheriff had hoped to speak with Shannon alone. What good reason could she have had for snooping around in a closed dumpsite? No, he knew the odds of clearing this mystery up anytime soon was near to none.

Not to mention his witness had gone as far as to rent a car and then follow her to the location in question, and all because something supernatural had told him to. The only proof of anything out of the ordinary taking place revolved around an imaginary tale of events told by an old unstable man with a vast imagination...or did it?

CHAPTER
39

SHANNON KNEW everything had to be perfectly timed and coordinated if all was to go as planned. Maggie was putting a damper on things. From the minute they arrived, she had locked herself away in the bathroom. After several minutes, skin pale white and moving at a slow crawl, Maggie emerged. Partially bent over, holding a wet rag to her forehead, she slowly made her way to the foot of her bed and laid back on it. Raising her head, she glanced over at Shannon. "I can't do this tonight. I'm just too sick."

Standing in the doorway, unresponsive, Shannon glared back. She stood motionless with her arms straight at her sides, fists clenched. Her features appeared lifeless, eyes cold and dark.

"Shannon, what's wrong with you?" Maggie asked, swallowing a nervous lump in her throat. "Why are you looking at me like that?"

Shannon smirked. "Oh, I'm sorry. Am I scaring you?"

"Yeah, you are!"

"Well, you should be scared!" Shannon said, taking a closer step toward her.

Pulling herself up, Maggie slowly eased her way towards the head of the bed. Her entire body quivered. "What's gotten into you?" she demanded. "Why are you acting this way?"

"To tremble out of fear is quite different than to tremble out of excitement, isn't it?" Shannon smirked.

"What are you talking about, Shannon?"

"I'm talking about the way James made you tremble when he held you in his arms and made passionate love to you. Don't try to deny it. I've known for some time."

Maggie doubled over in pain from the jagged sword of guilt and anguish that had been buried deep inside her for so long. The repulsive touch of her sadistic father's filthy hands groping and devouring her innocence manifested, conjuring up images of inconceivable horror. Her childhood ripped away and discarded like worthless trash. Tears trickled down, staining her cheeks with the blood of Frank's death as the memory of that fateful night flashed before her.

Due to unforeseen circumstances, she had been given a second chance of love with James for a short time; he had filled the void that consumed her entire existence. However, like everything else in her life, that too had been surrounded by false pretense and scandal. Blinded by her love for James and the obsession to tear them apart, united with her own desperation and despair, she had set forth a plan to frame Shannon for Frank's death, starting with the anonymous letter to Sheriff Chesterton.

A blast of excruciating pain ripped through her body, so severe that she almost lost consciousness, and then it was over. Gone were the pain, guilt, and humiliation. Truly some sort of a divine intervention had occurred. A sensation of strength and power prevailed; she was ready to face any torment Shannon had in store.

Shannon saw Maggie's miraculous recovery as a taunt and it only infuriated her more. "It was you who sent the anonymous letter to Sheriff Chesterton!"

"It was." Maggie's eyes sparkled as she nodded.

Shannon pounced on her. Grabbing her by the back of her hair, she held her down on the bed. "You stupid bitch! What made you think you could play such mind games with me? I'm a professional at playing mind games!"

"Is that what you did with your mother?" Maggie replied as she struggled to break free from her hold. Is that how you drove her insane, with your mind games?"

Maggie's ears rang as Shannon slapped her across the face, but she didn't flinch. Loosening Shannon's grip, she managed to get off the bed and onto her feet. Much to Shannon's surprise, Maggie stood facing her eye to eye.

"Let this amateur try to describe for you a play-by-play of your deceitful and pitiful life. You smothered your father for attention when he chose his love for alcohol over you. You blamed your poor mother to the point of drugging her body and manipulating her mind. That I'm sure of. Even as a kid, you were morbid and vindictive. I wouldn't be surprised to find out you had slaughtered that innocent animal, not your mother as you made it a point to tell everyone. What was its name? Star?"

Shannon flashed an eerie smile. "You think you have it all figured out, don't you?"

Maggie took a step forward. "It's true I took my father's life, and for what he took from me, most would say he deserved it. Nevertheless, it was you who orchestrated the cover-up and you've been blackmailing me ever since. Just between you and me, Shannon, tell me, out of all the diabolical deeds you've ever done, do you feel any remorse for slitting your own mother's wrists?"

Shannon took a step back and let out a loud, hysterical laugh. "Oh Maggie, you never cease to amaze me! You know nothing of my life, the loneliness, and heartache I've endured. Katrina drove my father to his death with all her whorish escapades. I did everything I could to make him leave her and take me with him, but it wasn't enough. I took her out of that asylum and into my home. I was willing to give her another chance, and what did she do? She tried to turn James against me, not unlike you, I might add. No one else could see through your schemes but me. You were both always poking around, trying to find something to use against me. She got what she deserved and you will to.

Maggie's blood ran cold. The hair stood up on the back of her neck as she listened to Shannon's atrocious admissions of guilt.

"First, would you like to know where I hid poor Frank's body? I know it's been driving you crazy, although that was my intention. Accidental manslaughter would've never held a long enough sentence. I'd hoped to visit you one day in Hillcrest, but now not even that will be possible."

"It all makes sense now," Maggie replied, staring her down "Those pills you gave to me so sparingly from time to time to help me sleep...they weren't sleeping pills at all, were they? They were some sort of hallucinogen. You knew about the depressed state of mind I'd been in for some time now. You were pushing me to the brink of insanity. But you couldn't have known Frank would—"

"Oh, my dear, that was just pure luck," Shannon said as she laughed in her face, then shook her head.

"Luck? That's what you call luck! That I would finally have a mental meltdown and accidentally kill poor Frank?"

"Actually, I had planned that very morning to take matters into my own hands," Shannon confessed, "but I got there just in time to see you planting poor Frank into the ground. You really should pay more attention to detail; you never know who might be watching your every move."

Maggie's body quivered as she begged for one last request. "Whatever you have planned for me, please spare James's life."

"Oh, I have big plans for James and I, once you're out of the picture."

If Maggie ever had any doubt of the atrocities Shannon was capable of, all had been confirmed. She did not have any false preconceptions why Shannon had lured her there; she knew her fate lay in Shannon's hands. She said a silent prayer, hoping time would be on her side, for now all she could do was to keep her talking.

"Explain something to me, Shannon. How could you put yourself through school, acquire a PhD in psychology, have a successful practice, and a man who truly loved you, and still make such a mess of your life? It's not too late, Shannon. You've saved so many of your patient's lives that had been in chaos, nurturing and counseling them when they had lost all hope. Can't you see you're one of them? You need help, Shannon. Let me help you."

For a moment, it looked as if Maggie had touched on some small degree of emotion.

Shannon slumped her shoulders and looked away, thereby giving Maggie the break she had been looking for. Her optimism in escaping would be short-lived however.

Reaching into her pocket, Shannon quickly unwrapped an object in clear plastic, revealing a revolver. Pointing the weapon at her target, she immediately cocked the trigger.

Directly behind her a firm voice shouted, "It's all over, Shannon! Drop the weapon! Now!"

She didn't have to turn around to see who was speaking. The voice was quite familiar.

Fighting to hold the revolver steady, she tightened her grip. "You don't understand, Sheriff, it's not what it looks like! Maggie lured me here to kill me just like she did Frank. If I hadn't taken control of the gun—"

Another familiar voice rang out. "It's over, Shannon. We heard everything."

Recognizing James's voice, tears streamed down her face as she relaxed her grip on the gun.

For the first time during the ordeal, Maggie let out a sigh of relief.

A deafening bellow of gunfire rumbled throughout the house, leaving behind the stench of gunpowder as a pool of blood formed on the hardwood floor, branching out like veins beneath their feet. Dying gasps for air could scarcely be heard over cries of panic and devastation, an indescribable horror they would have to cope with if they were to survive.

CHAPTER
40

A GLISTENING blanket of snow covered Patton's landscape, cuddling the mountainside high above the valley. The bustling roar of snowplows could be heard on every other avenue. At the downtown café, hot chocolate was in great demand as the children, all bundled from head to toe, rushed in, eager to be the first in line. The new flower shop bustled with business as loved ones rushed to purchase that special bouquet for Valentine's Day, and James was first in line.

Roses in hand, he crossed the street, only stopping for a moment to exchange a wave and a smile with Clair and Nadine. If he hurried, he might just have time to make one pit stop.

Shaking the snow from his boots, he ran up to the counter and grabbed a handful of pretzels. "I figured I'd find you here."

Larry chuckled. "Well, they'll let anybody out in public these days."

"Watch it, old man," James laughed. "I'll tell Edith you haven't got her Valentine's present yet."

Larry licked his fingers and ran them over his bald head. "I'll have you know I'm all the gift she needs! By the way, ain't you supposed to be somewhere?"

Glancing at the clock, James headed for the door and shouted back, "Yeah, and we expect to see you and Edith later!"

Arriving on time, he swung the door open and smiled. His heart was filled with pride, and he felt a sense of peace like none before. Wanting to savor the moment, he closed his eyes and imagined that time could stand still. Laying the bouquet of roses on the foot of her bed, he leaned across it, tenderly placed a kiss on her lips, and whispered, "I love you, Maggie."

As he walked down the corridor, James stopped at the first window and asked the nurse if she would draw the curtains back so he could get a better view.

"Why didn't I think of that?" the sheriff said.

James almost jumped out of his skin. "Oh, Bill, I didn't see you sitting there. How long have you been here?"

"Not long. I didn't want to disturb Maggie so I thought I'd sneak on down here and maybe catch a peek."

James's face lit up with delight. "Isn't she the most beautiful baby you've ever seen?"

"She most certainly is." He put his hand on James's shoulder. "A miracle indeed."

"Bill?"

"Yeah?"

"Do you ever have nightmares? You know…"

Bill nodded solemnly. Yeah, I know. Sometimes." There was an uncomfortable pause, then he smiled. "She's got Maggie's eyes, you know."

James winked and broadened his smile. "Yeah, but she's got my nose."

"Bill."

"Yeah?"

"Do they think it'll ever be a possibility that Shannon may recover?"

Bill shook his head. "No. The bullet has done too much damage to her brain. She just sits in the corner rocking back and forth, occasionally howling like a wild animal, or so they say."

"You know something Bill, I thank God every day Frank's family finally got the chance to lay him to rest."

A lump formed in Bill's throat. Swallowing hard, he looked down at the floor then back up at James. I've witnessed very few things as gruesome as that. We found parts of his body all over that dumpsite."

"Bil, I know you stuck your neck out for Maggie, jeopardizing your job and reputation; we owe our lives to you."

"It was a tragic accident, James. Hell, you wake up in a daze; think an intruder is in your house. No, Maggie's prison will be learning to forgive herself, and that's going to take some time. But miracles happen everyday, don't they?"

James grinned. "Yeah, they sure do."

Bill tapped on the glass as if trying to get the baby's attention. "By the way, I ran into Mattie Thompson the other day down at the café. Remember her?"

"I think I do. Are you talking about old man Thompson's widow? Didn't she move to the big city after he passed away?"

Bill's eyes lit up. "Yeah, guess she figured out the city life wasn't for her, too many high-falutin' people there. I always thought she'd be back."

"You always thought she'd come back someday?," James nudged Bill's arm. "So does this mean what I think it means?"

"Thinking I might ask her if she'd like to go to the drive-in picture show over in Sikeston; heard they have a real nice one over there."

James arched a brow. "Does this mean she could be the one?"

Bill grinned. "Ah hell, James, with everything that's happened I've come to realize that life's too short. There's more to life than work. It's taken me a while to figure that out."

"Sounds like you're on the right track, Bill."

"Look, I think your baby just smiled at me."

James laughed and said, "I think they call that gas."

"I thought I saw her the other day," Bill murmured.

"Thought you saw who?"

"Lola."

James blinked. "Lola?"

"Yeah, a couple of times. Once walking along Old Mill Road and again down by Jackson Creek. Both times I turned the car around and went back to look, but she was gone."

"You don't think that's a sign of anything to come, do ya?" James asked.

"Hey, you have too much to celebrate to worry yourself about anything right now. What's going to be will be. You know what I mean."

"I do believe that, Bill. I surely do."

"By the way, what did you and Maggie name your little angel?"

"I think we've decided on Angelina, after Maggie's great-grandmother."

"Why that's just beautiful, James. Angelina, our little angel, sounds fitting to me."

If anyone was a true believer in miracles, it was James, and he had been a witness to one on that fateful night nine months earlier. He knew that if not for that miracle, his family wouldn't exist.

James often thought of the stranger who had appeared out of nowhere, warning them of an impending doom, trying desperately to make them believe. He, like the others, now realized what Lola truly was: a guardian angel. His dying devotion to Larry would never be broken, for without his unyielding belief in his own spiritual power, and the enduring quest to seek the truth, ultimately more innocent souls would have been lost.

James and Bill, too absorbed in their admiration of the new baby, couldn't possibly have known what was taking place just steps away in hospital room 221.

Maggie awakened to a distinct feeling of someone pressing his or her hand firmly over her mouth. Squinting her eyes, she gasped to find what appeared to be Shannon leaning over her bed. "If you make a sound I'll slit your throat right here. I swear I will."

Maggie, unable to move, rolled her eyes from side to side, looking for a reason as to why she could not raise her arms. She was horrified to find her arms had been strapped down to the side rails of her bed. Her screams for someone to intervene, to save her from this nightmare, were deafening, but only to her own ears. Thoughts of her precious new baby, of James, and the hopes she had for a new beginning, were now being pushed away from her grasp. The more she struggled to break free, the tighter Shannon's grip became.

Shannon had complete control and continued to torment her. "Surely you didn't think you had gotten rid of me that easy, did you?"

Unable to speak, Maggie pleaded for her life with her eyes.

Shannon nodded. "That's right. I'm back to take away from you what you stole from me. James, your life together, that precious baby of yours…all of it should have been mine. The only way you'll be free of me is in death."

Determined to break free of Shannon's grip, Maggie closed her eyes, summoned an unbelievable strength, broke free, and sprang straight up in her bed.

"How did you get in here? Where did Shannon go, I don't understand. Someone's got to stop her before—"

"There, there, my child, you're safe now," Lola said, appearing next to her bed.

Maggie blinked her eyes several times trying to focus as she looked around the room. "If you hadn't come in when you did, she would have surely smothered me. The baby! I must check on her!"

"Maggie, listen to me!" Lola said, reaching out to her. "Shannon's physical body was never here."

"Are you trying to say I had a nightmare? She had my arms strapped down to the bed with—"

"With what, my dear?"

Maggie frantically looked above and below the bed for some kind of evidence to back up her story, but there was none to be found. Exhausted and perplexed by the ordeal, she lay back on the bed, taking a deep breath.

Lola pulled the blanket up over her shoulders and lightly touched her cheek. Maggie felt a sense of comfort in the fact that Lola was there, but at the same time bewildered by her visit.

"I have a beautiful baby girl," she whispered, smiling.

Lola smiled back. "Yes, my dear, she is quite beautiful indeed!"

"We've thought of you often, Lola. All of us have. I'm sorry we didn't believe in you and what you stood for."

"Everything is as it should be, my dear," Lola assured her.

Maggie's whole life it seemed had been one disaster after another, until now. She just wanted a normal life, minus all the drama and turmoil. If it meant living a non-conventional life, then that was what she would do. She would never again question if the belief in supernatural phenomena were plausible, for she had been a witness to its existence.

"Lola," she whispered.

"Yes, my dear?"

"Is everything going to be okay now? I mean…you don't see any major catastrophes in our near future, do you?"

The lines around the corners of her mouth crinkled upwards as Lola flashed her a smile. "I see a new beginning for you, Maggie, for all of you. My time here has ended, my dear, and now I must go. Close your eyes and fill your mind with only tranquility. Oh, and Maggie, you take extra loving care of your precious baby girl, for she is destined for great things." Lola thought for a moment and added, "Yes, I'm sure of it. She is quite special this one, quite special indeed!"

Maggie's eyes widened. "Exactly what kind of great things are we talking about?"

"Close your eyes, Maggie. Look deep within your soul, and find your spirit, for there you will find the knowledge to change your destiny."

Maggie bade her goodbye with a smile, sank back into her bed, exhaled a sigh of relief, and drifted into a peaceful sleep.

CHAPTER
41

"**MARY I** don't think I can help you do this. I'm getting a real bad feeling about us being in here alone with her. Can we ask a couple of the other nurses to step in? I mean it's not like they're understaffed around here."

"Katie, just shut up and roll her on her side. The sooner we get her bathed and fed, the quicker we can get out of here."

"Mary?"

"What?"

"Did you always want to do this line of work? I mean, did you ever think you'd end up in a hellhole like Hillcrest, bathing and feeding lunatics."

Mary shook her head. "I like to think that the work I do is important and that I'm giving back to my community. Unlike you, I take pride in what I do here at Hillcrest.

"You know they say she killed her own mother." Katie shivered as if a burst of cold air had passed right through her. "Just think of that."

"Yeah, well, she ain't going to hurt nobody now, that's for sure." Mary smirked. "Now help me roll her back over this way."

"Well, I think she got what she deserved. I would've put two bullets in her head if it would have been me."

"She shot herself, Katie."

"Doesn't matter," Katie grumbled. "Whichever way it was she deserved it."

"Katie?"

"What?"

"Are you going to help me get this gown on her or what?"

"Get this, Mary: another orderly that works here, she swears she has walked by and caught a glimpse of her standing by the window looking out."

"That's ridiculous! You can see for yourself she's incapable of such a thing. Who told you that, anyway?"

"They also said they heard some old witchcraft woman in Patton tried to warn everyone about her, said she had some sort of demon inside of her."

"Who, the old witchcraft woman?"

"No," Katie said, pointing down at Shannon. "Her!"

Mary drew in a deep breath, then exhaled. "Are you going to believe such a made-up piece of crap?"

"Are you going to tell me it doesn't make you just a little bit jittery being this close to her?"

"If I believed in that supernatural crap it might. Finish tying her gown in the back and roll her on over. If I didn't know better, Katie, I'd think you were just trying to scare me. Well, it's not working."

The tone in Katie's voice raised an octave. "No, it's not like that at all. Every time we've had to come in here, I've gotten an uneasy feeling. Look in her eyes; they don't look like human eyes, more like animal eyes to me."

Mary had never really looked into Shannon's eyes, had no reason to. Truth was, she had experienced the same uneasy feelings being in the same room with Shannon, but she would never admit it. Working in an insane asylum, one such as Hillcrest requires a certain kind of person. It took a person with nerves of steel and a thick backbone, both of which she thought she had. She had heard all the horror stories; she dismissed them as gossip, rubbish. Nevertheless, unlike Katie, she chose to ignore her instincts. It was easier to blame it on an overactive imagination.

"I don't care what you say, Mary, there's something very evil about this woman. I'll help you finish tonight, but it will be my last time."

Mary and Katie were experiencing much of the same feelings about Shannon that James, Larry, and Maggie had shared.

Shannon appeared incapacitated and from a medical aspect, she should have been. Here you had a woman whose brain had been severely damaged, and had lost all ability to communicate; still somehow, her mere presence evoked feelings of terror

"Katie, don't be silly. This is your job you're talking about. Take a quick break and when you come back, bring me a clean bedpan."

Putting out her cigarette, Katie grabbed a fresh bedpan from the cabinet and headed back down the corridor. She stopped just shy of entering Shannon's room when she noticed a red substance trickling out from underneath the door. Her hand shook as she reached for the doorknob. Slowly pushing the door open, her heart raced with panic. Not far from the doorway, Mary's lifeless body lay curled in a fetal position. The sound of the bedpan hitting the concrete floor echoed along with Katie's blood-curdling screams.

Shannon stood straddling Mary's body, head cocked sideways, looking dazed. Katie watched in horror as the attendants cautiously removed the blood-soaked makeshift knife from Shannon's hand. Katie found herself pushed further back as the room quickly filled with security guards, but her eyes never lost contact with Shannon's.

Later, when questioned about the ordeal, she would only say, "I have looked into the eyes of pure evil, stood next to a monster, and by God's graces escaped her wrath."

EPILOGUE

SHANNON'S TEAM of doctors at Hillcrest eventually diagnosed her as being a severe manic-depressive schizophrenic with an antisocial personality disorder. Her mother had been diagnosed at one time with the same disorders. Had her mother's symptoms been brought on because Shannon mentally abused her, repeatedly, or was it the other way around? Sadly, no one can say with certainty. Some people believe the subject of psychiatry is somewhat like religion. Depending on what psychiatrist you consult with, you may be given several different opinions as to what they believe is fact. How is it, then, that a sick-minded human being such as Shannon, with so many severe mental disorders, could have acquired a PhD in psychology in the first place? Shannon's case was unique indeed! Some believed it demonic or supernatural.

The small town of Patton, Missouri wants to forget; forget Shannon White was ever a part of their community, and forget she ever existed.

Sometimes, late at night, while the sleepy little town of Patton is preparing to snuggle in for a safe peaceful rest, they are reminded that hell is closer than they think. Hollowing screams from the asylum echo down through the valley, reminding them of the evil that resides within its walls. An evil they will never forget.

As you look beyond the gate, your eyes focus on a massive structure of concrete and stone that rises high above the valley and winding stream below. Except for the screams that sometimes come from inside and echo down through the valley, the gray fortress sits on the hill silent as death.

Hillcrest should have had a condemned sign posted at the entrance. However, the souls living inside had been condemned long ago, condemned to a life of living hell.

BONUS STORY
AWAKEN
SPIRIT

AWAKEN SPIRIT

DOORS THAT open and shut by themselves…the soft touch on your shoulder as if to get your attention…only to turn around to find no one there…the sound of footsteps on an empty flight of stairs…the quiet whisper in your ear waking you from a deep sleep, only to realize you're alone in the pervading silence. Most of us have encountered at least one of these unexplainable events if we were truthful. Nevertheless, we look toward scientific explanations to explain away our fear. I know I did! The old saying…'Seeing is believing' is not always the case. We all know what you see is not always what it appears to be. Most of us believe in life after death. Most believe the body is a shell that holds the soul and upon death, our souls are released. However, where does the soul take rest? This is where it gets confusing. According to what religion you have been brought up to believe there are various opinions. I had always believed that when you die your soul went to heaven or hell, no in between. The events that would later happen would make me reevaluate what I had come to believe.

The autumn leaves were beginning to fall and cool crisp air replaced the choking grip of a sweltering summer. For several years, my husband and I had looked for just the right house out in the country. Since before Katie was born, my husband and I harbored dreams of leaving the city, but circumstances never allowed us to explore such possibilities. My husband Jim and I grew up in the country, and wanted the same environment of small town living for our children. We wanted to find a house with plenty of land so that I could have the garden I had always wanted, and he could build his own workshop. My husband was a top sales representative for a well-known furniture outlet, but his desire was to create his own line of furniture. We had scrimped and saved enough money to finally make the move, and being pregnant with our second child was just the incentive we needed.

Our realtor showed us various lovely homes, that while beautiful and spacious still missed that special something. While Jim was still at work I decided to load Katie in the car and go look. I drove up and down quite a few roads when I noticed a house in the distance. I could not explain it, but something drew me closer, and sparked my imagination. I followed the road that turned off Hwy Z to road marker 332 for about a mile, and then fate presented me with a sight to lift my flagging spirits. The most beautiful two story Victorian home I had ever seen sat there, as if just waiting for me to stumble across it. It reminded me of a scene from right out of Gone with the Wind. The second floor had a beautiful terrace that overlooked the property. There was not another house as far as the eye could see. It appeared to be vacant, as suggested by its dark, broken windows. Beautiful as it appeared, a fresh coat of paint would do it no harm, and the landscape overgrown with weeds and wiry vegetation. Despite its flaws, it sparked something deep within me. I felt like it was calling my name. I could not wait to get home and tell Jim.

The next day we got in touch with our realtor and I described the location and the house. She knew the property well. The house had been built in 1865 and was formally owned by the Masterson family. It had been kept in the family and passed down for years. George Masterson once farmed the hundred acres that surrounded the house back in the 1800s. One of the last living relatives, a descendent of Mr. and Mrs. Masterson now owned the property. James Masterson lived in New York and by all accounts was desperate to sell. He tired of the burden and expense required to maintain the old house. To my pleasure, Jim took one look at it and fell in love with it, and although we knew it would be a lot of work, we were excited to make it our own. The realtor started the necessary paperwork right away and our dream inched closer to reality, or so we thought.

The movers met us there bright and early and we started the tedious task of deciding what box went in which room. Jim helped the movers bring in the furniture and I began to unpack.

Katie, our daughter, was an average five year old with more energy than she knew what to do with, and could barely control her obvious excitement. The move, an amazing adventure to a child of that age, had her hurtling around the house in explorer mode. After rummaging through a few of our boxes, I found some her favorite toys and focused her attention on them. With four bedrooms to choose from upstairs, I decided to give her the closest room to ours. While Katie played with her dolls, I thought I would start on our bedroom. I tired easily these days, being eight months pregnant, but I did not have much longer to go. My hormones had raged all during this pregnancy, far worse than last time, and I could get overly emotional at the slightest provocation. We had been at it all day and I soon felt ready to call it a night.

I put a nightlight by Katie's bed. After reading her a nighttime story, Jim and I kissed her goodnight. Not long after that, I peeked around the corner into our bedroom and found Jim fast sleep.

Lighting some candles in the bathroom and starting a hot bath I prepared to relax. The bubbles had never felt so good. The hot water relaxed every part of my body. Then I heard Katie scream, "Mommy, where are you? Why did you leave me?" She sounded so frightened and scared. In my own panicked state, getting out of the tub seemed to take forever. She just kept screaming the same words repeatedly. I could not understand why Jim had not calmed her down. Surely, her screams had woken him? Almost breaking my neck, I finally reached her room. There she lay quiet and still. I was sure she must have had a nightmare. Jim must have been sleeping very sound not to hear her screams, I thought.

The next morning I woke up early so I could prepare breakfast in our new home. Jim was running late for work and only had time to grab a bite and run. The smell of maple syrup caught Katie's attention as she came running into the kitchen.

"Mommy...mommy is you fixing pancakes? I love pancakes," she said.

What she asked next gave me cold chills.

"Mommy did you hear that little girl crying last night?"

"Maybe you were just having a nightmare, baby."

"No mommy I seen her out my window. She was looking in at me."

"Katie that's impossible, remember no one lives close for miles." I gave Katie her plate of pancakes and changed the subject. After breakfast, Katie wanted to take her dolls outside and play. It was a beautiful day. The sun shone bright in contrast to the autumn nip in the air, as winter tauntingly revealed how close it lay. I bundled Katie up and told her to stay close to the back door while she played. I fixed myself a cup of coffee, and started sorting through our important papers. I picked up our contract to the house just to look at it one more time. Mr. and Mrs. Jim and Barbara Delarose; it felt so exciting to finally own our first home. While going through the box, I came across some baby pictures of Katie. Looking at her precious pictures I could not help but wonder what he would look like. Would he be born with a head full of dark hair like Katie? I continuously referred to the baby as if I knew what sex it was, but Jim and I opted to wait until the baby was born. I wondered if he would have the same temperament as our daughter Katie. She had always been a somewhat mild-mannered child. She enjoyed just playing alone with her dolls. Jim often voiced his concern. He felt maybe she was a little too shy, but I did not worry too much. I knew things would change when she started school. It was obvious; she had inherited Jim's beautiful blue eyes and dark hair, and my shy disposition. I had many nicknames in school due to my bright auburn hair and full lips. Little did I know later that would be considered sexy.

Just as I was about to pour myself another cup of coffee, I heard Katie talking outside the back door. She often did that when playing with her dolls. As I listened closer, I heard something that sent chills up my spine. Another little voice said, "Your mommy will leave you too!" I turned around and looked out the back door, only to find Katie playing alone. I called to her to come inside.

"Whom were you talking to?"

"The little girl I told you about mama. She said her name was Laura. She's sad. She said her mama and daddy left her alone along time ago. I told her she could play with my dolls whenever she wanted, and that she could live with us. That's okay, isn't it mommy?"

Not knowing what to expect next, I tried to put on a face to cover my fear and said, "Sure, baby. Why don't you ask her to come inside for a snack?"

"She had to go, but she said she would come back later and play with me."

I was sure I must have been mistaken. I could not have possibly heard another voice. All I heard was Katie talking to her dolls. At least, that is what I kept telling myself. Anything else just did not make sense. Katie had never been one to make up such a story. Extremely concerned, I decided to play along with her story for now, and discuss it later with Jim when he returned home from work.

I knew Jim would be out late. He worked hard, trying to make as many contacts as he could. Starting up a furniture business and trying to sell his ideas for a new line of furniture would not be an easy task. However, we were optimistic and I had always believed in my husband's talents. Right before Katie was born, he surprised me by designing and making all of the furniture for the nursery. The day he surprised me with it he said, "Barbara, I wanted to make something special for the baby, something that would last for all time, like the love between us." I knew then I had found my soul mate.

Darkness threatened to close in around the house, as the hour hand on the clock crept upwards; I started preparing a bath for Katie and helped her into the tub. I wanted to surprise her with some hot chocolate, so I went down to the kitchen to pour her a cup. I stopped suddenly as my body shuddered, and gazed at the wide open door out into the cold dark night. *Wide open? How?* My mind worked but could think of no way it could have occurred by chance or accident. I was even more frightened to find the hot chocolate I'd prepared minutes earlier on the stove had already been poured into two of my cups. It appeared as though it had just been poured. I immediately shut and locked the door and continued trying to make sense of it all. *Could I have left the door open earlier? Had I already filled the cups and had just forgot?* I shook my head and hurried back up the stairs to check on Katie. Then to my horror Katie asked, "Mommy you won't be mad if I ruin your surprise...will ya?"

"What surprise, Katie?"

"Laura told me you made me some hot chocolate. Can she have some too?"

"Katie are you talking about your make believe friend?"

"No mommy. Remember, she was here earlier playing with me."

I took a deep breath and tried to look like I was in control.

"Sure she can, baby. Where is she? I'll take her a cup."

"She's waiting for us in my bedroom," Katie said without hesitating.

I wasn't sure what to do next. I kept telling myself this is just an innocent child's game, but everything in my body was telling me it was something more.

I wrapped the towel around Katie and we started slowly towards her room. With each step I took towards Katie's room, my mind took me back to when I was a little girl after watching a scary movie. I remembered the fear; not wanting to go into my room, fearing the unknown. I felt it again, no longer the small bunched up fear of childhood, but the full grown fear that clutched at my shoulders and weighted me down. Nevertheless, as an adult, intelligent woman, the rational side of my mind screamed that did not believe in ghost and goblins. The screams of rationality faded into the distance, as I stepped back in time to my earlier self.

Holding Katie tight I reached for the doorknob and pushed her bedroom door open. With one quick glance around the room, everything appeared normal until…I reached for Katie's pajamas, I always left them folded on her nightstand, next to her favorite baby doll, sat two cups of hot chocolate, one full, and one partially empty. Before I could say a word Katie turned to me and said, "Mama I bet Laura is hiding, let's see if we can find her."

She walked over to the closet and started to open the door. A loud knock clattered on the door downstairs. I felt myself jump at that sharp sound, then felt a peculiar sensation I could not place. *How much more excitement could I take?* Once again, I grabbed Katie's hand tight. I cautiously made my way towards the staircase. Then, in a loud voice I recognized, Jim yelled, "Barbara, honey, I forgot my key. Come and unlock the door."

I felt a rush of relief come over my body. Maybe he could make sense of all this craziness.

"Barbara, honey, you look flushed. Are you feeling all right?"

I told him I was feeling quite tired and would really appreciate it if he would tuck Katie into bed. Once again, I would brave going into the kitchen. I did not know what to expect anymore. On the stove lay the empty pan I had earlier used to prepare the hot chocolate. The cups were no longer there. I did not have to wonder where they were, *but how did they get there? Had I been so tired that I had forgotten filling them and taking them upstairs?* I was tired but not that tired, yet I could find no other explanation. I had to talk to my husband. I needed someone to tell me that I was not going crazy.

I took Jim a cup of hot tea and collected up enough courage to tell him about my strange evening, and all the oddities I had encountered.

"Barbara, who is this little girl, Laura, that Katie is talking about?"

I began to tell him the events. To my surprise, he had a story of his own.

"I couldn't sleep last night so I decided to go downstairs and make myself a cup of tea. I heard the sound of a small child laughing, coming from within the kitchen, and it wasn't Katie's laugh. When I entered the room the sound faded in the distance. If that wasn't bad enough, I noticed the back door was standing wide open, what I saw next made my skin crawl. A little girl in a nightgown with blond hair, about the size of our Katie, was slowly walking back into the field behind the house.

"Oh Jim, you're really scaring me now!"

I tell you Barbara; I don't think I've ever been as frightened as I was that moment. Anyway, I followed behind her for a short distance, and then she just disappeared in front of my eyes. I wanted to tell you about it, but I didn't know how without sounding crazy. After what I experienced and after hearing what happened to you, I'm beginning to think there's something really unnatural going on here!"

We made the decision to go the following day and find out as much as we could about the history of our home.

We settled down and went to sleep for the night. At 3:00 a.m. I awoke, with excruciating pain shooting through my abdomen. I gripped the bed sheets as pain caused me to convulse. Slowly twisting myself off the bed and onto my feet, I tried to stand. My gown clung to my skin, as water gushed down both legs. My water had broken. Time... The feeling of immediacy gripped me. For a moment, I couldn't focus on anything except that. The baby was not due for another three weeks, but now it had decided to make an early appearance. My efforts to leave the bed must have stirred him; Jim rounded the bed and took me in his arms trying his best to comfort me. With no time to pack, I put on my robe and Jim helped me down the hallway. I quickly realized I could not go any further. This baby pressed down on me with a vicious urgency. It would not wait. I felt the fear return.

Laying me on my back gently on the carpet, he placed a pillow under my head and called 911. After the third push, I blacked out for a moment. I woke moments later to the sweet sound of my precious new baby girl. In my weakened state, I barely registered the events as they unfolded, until the cold florescent lights of the hospital foyer lit my baby in different light. I realized I had barely taken my eyes off her.

My doctor worked on call at the hospital and by luck happened to be on duty when we arrived. After examining us, he gave us a clean bill of health. All the other crazy experiences drifted away into the dark recesses of our subconscious, to be forgotten...for a while at least...

Katie could not believe she had a new baby sister. She just kept stroking her tiny hands and kissing her cheek. Our friends from the city came in dribs and drabs bringing gifts for all of us.

It seemed the phone would never stop ringing. One of the calls came as quite a surprise. James Masterson, the prior owner of our new home wanted to come by and congratulate us. We had only spoken a few times during the process of acquiring the house. He insisted he did not want to intrude, but would love to visit. We told him he was more than welcome. After all, this house had been in his family for years.

He arrived, as the winds changed, and the rain clattered down. We supplied him with his choice of beverage, and tried to make him feel as welcome as possible. With black coffee in hand, he told us how he had been compelled to explain a little bit about the history of our home.

"What I'm about to tell you may upset you; I haven't been completely honest with the both of you, regarding the history of this house. My great, great grandfather built this house with his own hands back in the 1800s. He and my great, great grandmother, Elizabeth Masterson met when they were just children. They farmed this land together and raised a rather large family, seven children to be exact. Then, late in life, Elizabeth became unexpectedly pregnant again. Fragile and weak the pregnancy almost took her life." Taking a moment, he wiped away the tears and continued to explain. "On Nov 15th 1892 Laura Elizabeth Masterson came into this world, exactly a hundred year's ago today."

"Would you like to take a moment Mr. Masterson, we can see that you're visibly upset?

"No mam, I just wish I'd been honest with you folks from the beginning."

James and I could not have been prepared for what we were about to learn.

Collecting his thoughts, taking a deep breath, exhaling, he continued, "The records show that when Laura was about five years old, she and her mother were playing hide and seek when fun turned into tragedy. It appeared that Laura, trying to hide from her mother, climbed the old oak tree. Laura, not realizing the tree limb was weak, fell when it cracked, sending her to her death."

Sure, of the answer, fighting back the tears I asked Mr. Masterson, "Where exactly was this precious child buried?"

Nervous, he began tapping one foot against the floor. "Out back, on your farm, mam. However, a year later a great flood washed away and destroyed any sign of her grave. Up until you folks, every renter I had complained of hearing strange noises, seeing apparitions. I myself don't believe in such things, but like I said, I felt compelled to inform you. If you're both uncomfortable with the situation, I will gladly let you out of your contract, refund your money."

After a long period of silence and wiping away the tears, we declined. This is where most people would think we were crazy. Why would anybody want to live in a house they thought to be haunted, especially when they had witnessed strange events themselves? It was all perfectly clear. This precious little girl had lost her life in a terrible untimely accident, only to have her grave desecrated sadly by a flood. Grief stricken, her family had left her behind. For this reason her little soul had been destined to stay with the farm. All she needed was a family to love and accept her presence until her soul could be released. As crazy as it sounded, that is exactly what we intended to do.

For the next five years we would see her from time to time usually playing out in the field or hiding in the old oak tree out back, never showing any malice but always making her presence known. Then one day as quick as she appeared she was gone. We believe her soul finally found peace and was free to move on.

With the most love and affection we watch our girls, as they play freely on our farm. Katie is now ten and Laura five. Yes, we named our youngest after Laura to pay homage to the little soul that had been lost, but never forgotten.

BONUS STORY
MORTAL
ABOMINATION

MORTAL ABOMINATION

THE TRIAL lasted only one month, three days, and nine hours. However, the torture and humiliation Maria Torres experienced because of it, will be remembered far beyond our lifetime, I'm sure of it.

As an investigative reporter, for the Internet Worldly News, I have written several articles acknowledging the most recent outbreak of hysteria in our culture, due largely to ignorance, pertaining to the psychic underworld. Not since seeing a woman elected President of our free world, had I witnessed such disorder among so many. It has been ten years since the law went into effect abolishing any form of display involving psychic readings, literature, or anything of such matter. Maria Torres was the exception to the rule. Her predictions over the years, securely documented as legitimate, had saved the prior President from being assassinated. She was our government's top advisor and confidant on the subject. Her psychic abilities gave her fame, fortune, and power. Some would find it ironic that in the end she could not predict her own demise.

In the following notes, you will find an account of Maria Torres's actions leading up to the fateful judgment that was handed down to her by her peers.

FOR THE fifth night in a row, Maria awoke suddenly with a somewhat nauseating feeling after a dreadful night of disturbing nightmares. Reaching for her journal, hands trembling, she thumbed through to an empty page and began to write. In the last few days, her visions had become more intense and vivid in description. Placing a piece of red ribbon in-between the pages, she closed the journal and placed it in the night drawer under lock and key. Quietly, as not to wake her husband, she rolled out of bed and headed down stairs.

Opening the French doors, she stood looking out onto the rich green hillside that surrounded the property. The light of dawn glistened across the pool as the sound of chimes played softly with the wind. It was times such as this she could once again relax and pretend her life had some sort of normalcy.

Her gift, or curse as she sometimes would refer to, had been handed down to her from generation to generation. Life had been difficult for Maria, as she had become an orphan at the tender age of twelve. Maria's silent premonition of her parent's sudden death in an automobile accident would forever haunt her. However, the horrific incident fueled her desire to perfect her craft.

Maria, a firm believer her life was destined to intertwine with certain individuals, for the soul purpose of saving others, proclaimed her beliefs in a much-unpublicized event.

In college, Maria met and befriended a young woman by the name of Scarlet Whitman. Scarlet introduced Maria to a young upcoming lawyer by the name of Jon Torres, and soon after, their passion ignited. Scarlet stood by Maria as her maid of honor, and

Maria was the first person Scarlet called when she was made a top official in the FBI agency in Washington, DC. When Maria came forward with information of a planned assassination attempt on the life of our former President, through unconventional means, Scarlet was the first and only one to take her seriously. Together they convinced the President's security to take action, thereby sparing the president's life, and ultimately apprehended one of the most dangerous terrorist organizations of our time. Needless to say, Maria gained the utmost respect of the nation and our government. In an ironic twist, due to fake psychics coming out of the woodwork, wanting to claim fortune and fame, making ludicrous and dangerous predictions, an amendment in the law was created. Anyone adhering such actions would be prosecuted to the extent of the law. Thereby Maria became a silent partner, working only for the good of the government, a psychic informant if you will. However, as we know all to well, informants sometimes have a way of mysteriously disappearing.

AS MARIA stood gazing at the beautiful sunrise peaking out above the clouds, she felt a gentle touch of a hand upon her lower back proceeded by a soft kiss on the nap of her neck. Six foot and three inches, Jon towered over Maria's tiny frame. Jon was not just her husband; he was her confidant, her best friend, and her protector.

"I love you too Jon." She said without turning around.

"I'm sorry you're not sleeping well. Was it the same dream?"

"Yes Jon, it was. This time it was more vivid and detailed."

"Do you feel strongly enough about it to discuss it with Scarlet?"

"The images I'm getting are so clear, Jon. It's always the same young woman dressed in a black suit, carrying an object in her right hand that I cannot quite make out, and in her left hand, I can see clearly she's holding a small handgun. There is some kind of commotion going on in the background, and then it happens. I see the President; she falls, clutching her stomach. The same young woman I see pulling the trigger is now kneeling beside the President cupping her head. No one seems to be aware that she is the assassin."

"Look at me, Maria." Jon said, gently turning her toward him. "You know what you have to do."

"I know you're right, Jon. I shouldn't second guess myself, it's better to be safe than sorry."

"We better get a move on." Jon said looking up at the clock. "I have a heavy case load today, and you need to go do what you do best."

Smiling, Maria looked up at him and said, "I see you winning that case today. The case you've been so concerned with. The judge is going to rule in your favor, I'm sure of it!"

Jon smiled and swatted her backside gently as he turned and headed upstairs.

MARIA DECIDED to call Scarlet and invite her to lunch in the city at Antonio's Restaurant. She reserved a nice quiet table in the back so they would not be disturbed. She did not doubt that Scarlet would take what she had to say seriously and act on it. They had worked together for years and were not only friends, but both had mutual respect for one another. Still, it was never easy coming forward with such dire information.

The hostess welcomed Maria as she came through the door and escorted her to a table in the back. Scarlet was not far behind, but she was not alone.

"I hope you haven't been waiting long. I'd like to introduce you to Jackie Stewart. She just transferred here from the Texas bureau, and her credentials as an FBI agent are impressive."

Maria's legs trembled as she stood up from her chair. Stunned and confused, she found herself unable to say anything.

"Maria, are you okay? Scarlet hurried to her side, helping her back into her seat. "You look as if you've seen a ghost!"

What Scarlet could not have known is, Maria suddenly felt as if she had. It was as if the killer had stepped out of her premonition. Not wanting to divulge her findings just yet, Maria pulled herself together, shook her head and said, "You'll have to excuse me I've been on this stupid diet, starving myself actually. Guess I'm feeling a little jittery."

"I know what you mean," Jackie said, turning toward Scarlet. "It's always an uphill battle for us too. The way we eat, if they didn't have us on a rigorous training schedule we'd be in big trouble as well."

Maria could not fool Scarlet. She knew there was more to the story. "Are you sure that's all it is, Maria?"

Maria folded her menu, placing it flat on the table; she stood up to excuse herself. "I do apologize, but I'm really not feeling well."

"I do hope you get to feeling better." Jackie said, curiously as she reached across to shake Maria's hand.

Maria pulled her hand away. "I wouldn't want to spread any germs."

Scarlet, aware that Maria from the time that they had sat down had been overly anxious, pulled her to the side. "I know this is more than just an upset stomach. I'll come by a little later and we can discuss whatever it is bothering you."

Maria nodded, "You're right, it's so much more than a stomachache, but I can't explain myself right now."

Scarlet looked on with concern as she watched Maria exit the restaurant. Why had Maria acted so agitated immediately upon being introduced to her colleague? Why had she felt so uncomfortable that she had to leave so abruptly? Scarlet could only speculate as to the reasons why Maria had acted as such. She would find out soon enough.

MARIA SCURRIED up the steps into the house, hesitating only long enough to balance her footing as she dashed up the stairs towards the bedroom. She could not get to her nightstand quick enough. Retrieving her journal, she paused for a moment and took a deep breath. Looking for the sketch she had drawn the night before, she franticly thumbed through to the last page. As her eyes encountered the drawing, every muscle in her body became tense. The assassin from her dream now had a name. It was all beginning to make sense. What better way to have personal and up-close access to the President of the United States, than to be one of her hired bodyguards? No, if Maria ever had any doubts about her abilities as a psychic or the legitimacy of her premonitions, this was not one of those times. Taking a deep breath, closing her eyes, she said a silent prayer thanking her spirit guides for leading her in the right direction.

Maria, is everything okay? Jon said, "I thought you were meeting Scarlet for lunch?"

Maria turned to see her husband standing in the doorway. "What are you doing home at this time?"

"I've misplaced some of my important papers I need for court this afternoon. I've looked all over the office and…"

Maria smiled, "File cabinet, third drawer, fifth folder back."

Jon turned around and winked. "What would I do without you? Now, what's going on with you?"

"You know those dreams I've been having, my premonitions, well..."

"Was that the front doorbell I heard?" Jon said interrupting. "Are you expecting someone?"

Maria jumped up from the corner of the bed. "It's Scarlet!"

She raced around Jon and down the stairs.

"Come in, come in!" Maria's voice rose with urgency. "I'm so glad you're here!"

"Slow down, Maria," Scarlet replied, "let's just catch our breath, shall we!"

Maria took a couple of deep breaths and exhaled, then motioned Scarlet to follow her into the study.

"Okay Maria, tell me what's going on."

"Scarlet, for the past few nights I've been having nightmares, detailed premonitions of an attempted assassination involving the President."

"Oh my God!" Scarlet moved in closer, "go on."

Maria acts out her premonition for Scarlet like a theatrical play, describing every minute detail, right down to the description of the assumed assassin. Scarlet, speechless for a moment, suddenly stood to her feet with a look of confusion. As Maria started to speak again, Scarlet interrupted her. "Maria, you know I trust your abilities, your psychic abilities, but this makes no sense! Jackie, you're saying the assassin in your dreams is, Jackie!"

"I know how it must sound," Maria proclaimed, "but I'm sure of it!"

"My God, Maria, she works for the FBI, I hired her for Gods' sake! Her credentials are impeccable. What reason on Gods' green earth would she have to gain by assassinating the President?"

"I can show you my journal, the sketch I drew of her, it's identical right down to the beauty mark above her right lip."

"Okay, just let me think for a moment. The President is scheduled to give a televised speech tomorrow night at the Ford's

Theater. One of Jackie's duties, among several hundred others, will be to help secure the place and guard the President."

"We have to do something, Scarlet! Our Lady President has to be warned!"

"Scarlet, silent for a moment, peered out the window and said, "My career is on the line with this one. You know how I feel about you. Nevertheless, I think this is one time your psychic abilities could come into question."

"But Scarlet…"

"No buts," Scarlet shouted, "We're going to stay quiet on this one. I'll be close by watching her every move."

"If they find out I was aware of this horrific scheme and didn't warn them of our Presidents impending danger…Well, not only will her death be on my hands, I hate to think what they will do to me. Have you forgot, it was my premonition that helped save our last President from being assassinated?"

Scarlet's jaw clenched, her almond shape eyes widened, as she scanned Maria up and down. "I, the bureau, and everyone in our government have not forgot. Nevertheless, Maria, you are human and humans make mistakes. This time my ass is on the line as well. I'm not going to be responsible for tarnishing a young woman's career, and ruining her life. I think you're dead wrong this time."

"No," Maria shouted back, "that's what the President will be, dead, if you do not take my premonition seriously and report this."

Jon, quiet in the other room, decided it was time to step in. "Ladies, I think we need to take a breather."

"I'm done reasoning with her, Jon. Scarlet grabbed her purse and keys. "Maybe you can explain to her the gravity of this situation."

Tears formed in Maria's eyes as she watched Scarlet drive away. For the first time in a long time, she felt helpless. Without Scarlet's support, no one would take her seriously.

"You been at this for hours," Jon said, rubbing her shoulders gently. "Let's try and get some rest, maybe things will be clearer in the morning."

Exhausted, Maria agreed. She could only pray Scarlet would reconsider and take heed to her warnings.

AFTER YET another sleepless night, tortured by the same horrific premonition, Maria paced back and forth across the living room floor. She waited anxiously all day hoping for a miracle, but none came. She found herself agitated with Jon. At the last minute, he had been called away on a case. She didn't want to be alone and experience the tragedy that was about to unfold. Her pulse racing, stomach in knots, she sat crouched in her chair awaiting the Presidents televised speech.

Glairing at the screen Maria scanned the crowd. Thousands of people were at the event hoping to get a glimpse of the President. Just minutes into the presentation she spotted Scarlet to the left of the President. A feeling of dread came over her when she caught a glimpse of Jackie standing to the Presidents right side. Her eyes transfixed on Jackie's hands, she earnestly watched her every move. She looked on with pride, as the first woman voted our President of the United States took a step towards the podium. Her heart filled with emotion as the President spoke of past wars, lives lost, involving Iraq and our country. However, with all nations at peace, our Presidents' main concern was towards extinguishing all forms of underworld drug trafficking. For year's it had been thought to be under control, but now it was resurfacing with a vengeance. Our Lady President vowed to use any means and every source available to the extent of the law to unravel the underworld drug cartel.

Two hours the President spoke to the eager crowd and as she wrapped up her speech, Maria began to feel a sense of calm. Everything seemed to be going as planned, no unusual outburst, no attempt on the Presidents life. Could she have been mistaken? Then, the unthinkable happened. From somewhere in the crowd a sound of thunder exploded. Terrified, people scurried about, pushing one another, trying desperately to escape. Every camera angle focused on our lady President. Blood trickled out from underneath her body, staining the beautifully adorned carpet of the Ford's Theater. As the cameras panned out, a wide shot caught a point eye view of the Presidents body being quickly lifted unto a gurney, Jackie close by at her side.

Her eyes fixated on the screen, Maria continued to stare in horror as the screen turned to black. Mourning for the President, she bowed her head in silence. As shock wore off, anger set in. Grabbing a crystal vase, she hurled it toward the screen shattering the glass into a thousand pieces. She cursed Scarlet for not heeding her warning, and blamed herself for not being able to convince her of the ominous attack. Frantic, she dialed Scarlet's line, but received no answer. Desperate to know what was happening, she dialed the classified direct line she had been given to Scarlet's senior officer in charge, Robert White.

"Robert, thank God you answered. Can you tell me anything? Do you have Jackie in custody? It happened, Robert, just like my premonition!"

Robert replied. "Maria, the President is dead—passed away just minutes ago."

Dropping the phone, Maria fell to her knees.

"BABY, I got here as soon as I could," Jon said, dropping his briefcase at the front door. "It's not your fault, you tried to warn Scarlet."

"It doesn't matter, Jon, the President is dead, and I know now that I should have contacted Robert directly. This is what I do. Jon, I work with the government, using my abilities, to stop this kind of tragedy from happening, you know that!"

"It's not your fault!"

"What are they going to do to me? I knew the President's life was in danger and I could have stopped this from happening!"

A knocking on the front door suddenly interrupted Maria's plea for some kind of an answer, but she would learn soon enough.

Upon opening the door, Jon found himself confronted by several FBI agents, among whom Scarlet stood.

"Jon, may we come in?" Mr. White removed his hat and said.

Jon hesitantly welcomed them.

With urgency in her voice Scarlet said, "Jon, we need to speak with Maria."

Jon turned and pointed. "She's in the den, but I don't think she's up to answering any questions."

Mr. White moved forward, "It's official business, Jon. It's imperative we get some answers."

Jon tilted his head to the side, "You speak as if she's done something illegal, Robert!"

Hearing their conversation, Maria stepped forward pleading, "Tell them, Scarlet. Tell them I tried to warn you about the assassination attempt!"

Scarlet swallowed hard and looked away.

"Scarlet has already assured us, under oath, that she had not been informed by you or anyone else regarding the President's safety."

Maria turned towards Scarlet, "How can you do this to me? You know I tried to convince you to detain Jackie! What about my journal? I have proof!"

"She's telling the truth, Robert. I'm a witness," Jon proclaimed, "I was here when Scarlet met with Maria last night. I overheard everything!"

"Scarlet," Mr. White said waiting to hear her reply.

With conviction Scarlet quickly replied, "As I said in my affidavit earlier, Maria did not informed me of any such premonition."

Furious as to her lies, Jon rushed towards Scarlet, "You're just trying to save your own ass!"

Quickly the agents stepped in to control the situation.

"Maria, I need you to hand over your journal."

"What journal? Maria said smugly, "The one Scarlet knows nothing about!"

Handing Jon a search warrant, Mr. White instructed his agent to search for the journal. Within a few minutes, the journal was in the senior officer's hand, and Maria handcuffed.

"You're not in the rights to do this!" Jon protested.

"Jon, you know our position," Mr. White stood firm, "This is a delicate matter, one of which will be handled by our closed court. Scarlet has been made well aware of the consequences of not informing us of such dyer matters."

Thumbing through the journal he stopped at the last page. "It has always been Maria's responsibility as a confidential member of our government's staff to divulge any threatening behavior that she is aware of, by whatever means. This dated Journal is proof she did not, for whatever reason. It will now be up to the courts to decide her fate. Now, please step aside and let us do our job."

Maria's eyes met Jon's as they led her handcuffed out of their home. Both, aware of the seriousness of the situation, tried to put on a brave face for one another. It would be the last time their eyes would ever meet.

Treason in the eyes of the law is due by punishment of imprisonment, exile, and often death. As an investigative reporter, I would like to give my readers a happy ending to this story, but

I cannot. A source working deep inside the government's agency agreed, and only agreed off the record, to disclose to me the results of Maria's case. It is as follows.

"It is in the findings of our court we as a jury find Maria Torres guilty of treason on this date of October 31ˢᵗ 2020, and in accordance to our law shall be imprisoned for the remainder of her life, in an unspecified location as determined by our government."

Knowledge has it; Maria stood before her peers, head held high, and flashed a slight grin as the verdict was read. I suffice to say her actions must have made that jury feel more than a little uncomfortable.

As for the President's executioner, Jackie, it was determined, her sick motivation for killing our President involved the very thing our President fought so hard to eradicate, drugs. Her recent drug addiction and involvement with the underworld drug cartel had put her own family in harms way. She carried out her instructions, as ordered by the cartel, believing the sacrifice of the President's life, as well as her own, would save any imminent danger to her family by the hands of the ruthless killers. Her cold-blooded deed would not be rewarded.

Scarlet's lifeless body would be found naked in her sauna, wrists slashed, just days after Maria's verdict. My guess, she couldn't live with herself knowing she had traded her soul, betrayed her closest friend and colleague, to save face.

I've tried several times to locate Jon, but to no avail.

If you have not guessed by now, I am, and will, continue to investigate and report to you my readers, all stories of atrocities as such. However, for my own safety, I will be doing so in hiding. One can never be too secure in this new age we live in!

Some of you might find it ironic Maria was sentenced on the 31ˢᵗ of October, sometimes thought of as the bewitching day and month of the year. I tend to believe Maria had a hand in picking the day, hour and minute of that unjustified ruling.

When I think of Maria, I think of someone who took and used her spiritual abilities for the better of humankind, only to be victimized in doing so. To have such a responsibility on her shoulders her entire life is unimaginable. Is it lucid to persecute and incarcerate one for having a numinous ability to see the future? Hasn't everyone at one time experienced some sort of unexplained phenomenon? As our world advances in knowledge, so it too retracts. The evidence of our illogical behavior is well documented, the Salem Witch trials of 1692, and the Witch trial of Maria Torres in 2020.

This is your investigative reporter for the Internet Worldly News signing off.

ABOUT THE AUTHOR

At an early age, Barbara Watkins experienced what she refers to as supernatural phenomenon. As a teenager, she kept a diary and documented several disturbing nightmares that were later used as inspiration in her writing.

Barbara loves to evoke a false sense of security and expectation in her writing, leading her readers into a world of the unknown. Her articles on various subjects, short stories, and poetry, have appeared in *The Heartland Writers Guild, 2008 New York Skyline Review*, and several online publications.

Her charitable contributions include supporting the Partner in Hope program through the St. Jude Children's Research Hospital.

She resides in Missouri with her husband of thirty-five years, and her faithful, loving Boxweiler, Hooch. She has three children and ten grandchildren.

www.ingramcontent.com/pod-product-compliance
Lightning Source LLC
Chambersburg PA
CBHW020307200626
46814CB00006BA/2131